FLOWERS
OVER
THE
INFERNO

FLOWERS OVER THE INFERNO

Ilaria Tuti

Translated from the Italian by Ekin Oklap

First published in Italian under the title *Fiori sopra l'inferno*.

Copyright © 2018 by Longanesi & C. S.r.l.—Milano,
Gruppo editoriale Mauri Spagnol.
English translation copyright © 2019 by Ekin Oklap

First published in English in the United Kingdom by
The Orion Publishing Group, Ltd, 2019.

Published by
Soho Press, Inc.
227 W 17th Street
New York, NY 10011

Library of Congress Cataloging-in-Publication Data

Tuti, Ilaria, author. | Oklap, Ekin, translator.
Flowers over the inferno / Ilaria Tuti ; translated from the Italian
by Ekin Oklap.
Other titles: Fiori sopra l'inferno.

ISBN 978-1-64129-271-9
eISBN 978-1-64129-069-2

I. Title

PQ4920.U86 F5613 2019 853'.92—dc23 2018046491

Interior design by Janine Agro, Soho Press, Inc.

Printed in the United States of America

10 9 8 7 6 5 4 3 2 1

FLOWERS
OVER
THE
INFERNO

AUSTRIA, 1978

There was a legend that haunted that place, the kind that clings like a persistent odor. It was rumored that in late autumn every year—before the rain turned to snow—the mountain lake would begin to exhale sinister murmurs.

They came from the water like steam and rose over the banks with the morning mist when the surface of the lake reflected the sky, heaven mirrored in hell. That was when the hissing began, a sound like a protracted howl that enveloped the late nineteenth-century building on the eastern shore of the lake.

The School. That's what they called it, down in the village, though the purpose and the description of the building had shifted through the years, from imperial hunting lodge, to Nazi command center, to a sanatorium for consumptive children.

Now there was only silence along its corridors, only peeling walls, crumbling plaster, and the echoes of solitary footsteps—and in November, the howling that unfurled through the fog, rising to the top floor windows and onto the pitched roof glistening with frost.

But legends were for children, the elderly and nostalgic, and for the faint of heart. This much, Agnes Braun knew. The School had been her home for long enough that she wouldn't let something like nocturnal whispers get to her. She had memorized the creak of each floorboard and every rusty pipe winding through the entrails of those walls—even though most of the building's floors were closed off now, and many rooms boarded shut. Ever since the School had been converted into an orphanage, public funding had dwindled and no private benefactor had come forward with a donation.

Agnes walked across the kitchen, which was situated in the basement between the pantry and the laundry room. Pushing her trolley, she weaved her way through cooking pots that would soon be steaming with greasy vapors. She was alone, at that hour suspended between night and day; her only companions were the shadow of a furtive rat and the shapes of slaughtered animals left to hang inside what used to be an ice box.

She took the service elevator up to the first floor. This part of the building was her responsibility, but recently this task had begun to fill her with a nameless dread, like a latent fever that never quite flared up.

The elevator groaned under the combined weight of her body and the trolley, the chains and the cables began to squeal, and the cage rattled as it rose, coming to a shaky halt a few meters above. Agnes pulled the metal grate open. The damp-stained first floor corridor was a long narrow band of dull blue, with a constellation of large panelled windows on one side.

A windowpane was banging against its frame in a steady rhythm. She left her trolley and went over to close the window. The glass was cold and fogged over; she wiped at it with one hand and made a porthole of sorts. Down in the valley, the light of dawn had begun to illuminate the village. The roofs of the houses looked like tiny lead-colored tiles. Further up, at 1,700 meters above sea level and between the settlement and the School, the motionless expanse of the lake was beginning to turn pink beneath the mist. The sky was clear. But Agnes knew that the sun that day wouldn't bring any warmth to their steep, sloping clearing—by now she had learned to interpret the migraines that plagued her the moment she stepped out of bed.

The fog rose to engulf everything in its path: light, sounds, even smells became imbued with its stagnating presence, that essence of ancient bones. It seemed to come to life as it climbed over the frostbitten grass, and from its tendrils came forth those laments.

The sighs of the dead, thought Agnes.

It was the Buran, a fierce north-easterly wind. From its source in distant steppes, it had journeyed thousands of kilometers and forced its way into this valley, roaring against the river banks below the tree line, whirling across the floodplains, and howling as it emerged on the other side, only to crash against the rock wall of the mountain.

It's just the wind, she kept telling herself.

The pendulum clock in the atrium chimed six times. It was getting late, but Agnes stood still. She was conscious that she was stalling, and she also knew exactly why.

It's all in your head. All in your head.

She gripped the trolley's metal handle, and the bowls on it clattered as she finally willed herself to take a few steps toward the door at the end of the corridor.

The Hive.

Her stomach contracted with the abrupt realization that it really was a hive. That's what it had become over the past few weeks. There was a subtle, mysterious buzz of activity about the place, like a diligent insect preparing for metamorphosis. Agnes was sure of it, though she wouldn't have been able to explain what was happening in there. She hadn't said a word to anyone, not even the principal: he would have thought she was going mad.

She put her hand in the pocket of her uniform and her fingers found the coarse material of her hood. She took it out and pulled it over her head. A thin veil covered her face and eyes, obscuring the outside world. That was the rule.

She walked in.

The room was completely silent. A few embers from inside the large cast-iron stove near the door were emitting a pleasant warmth. There were forty cots in the room, arranged in four rows of ten. No names to mark them: only numbers.

There were no cries nor calls. Agnes knew what she would have seen if only she'd looked: blank, vacant gazes.

With one exception.

Now that she'd become accustomed to the silence, she could hear him kicking at the far end of the room, building his strength. He was preparing for something, although she couldn't say what. Maybe she really was insane.

Her footsteps brought her closer to cot number 39.

Unlike the others, this subject was thriving. His eyes, which were so unusual, were alert and darted about following her movements. Agnes knew that the subject was seeking out her eyes behind the veil of her hood, but she kept looking away, embarrassed. Subject 39 shouldn't have been aware of her presence, and yet . . .

She checked to make sure that no member of staff was looking through the door, and then she extended a finger. The subject bit it, squeezing her flesh tight between its gums. The expression in its eyes was different now, electric. Agnes pulled back, cursing, and it let out a short, anxious moan.

That's its true nature, she thought. *A carnivore.*

What happened next convinced her that she could no longer keep her suspicions private: the cots next to number 39 were no longer quiet. The other subjects' breathing had turned agitated, as if they were responding to a call.

The Hive was buzzing.

1

TODAY

The crow lay by the footpath, its crumpled feathers streaked with purple and its beak wide open. There was blood staining the ground beneath its swollen belly, but even in that damp afternoon it had already dried up. Who knew how long the poor creature had been there, one blank eyeball pointing toward a sky that promised snow, and the other eye lost entirely.

Mathias had been crouching over it for a while. He wondered whether the fleas had abandoned their host the moment its heart had stopped beating; he'd heard a hunter talk about that once, and the thought had tormented him for some time. It was a detail that seemed both fascinating and ominous.

He touched the crow with the tip of his finger. It was an older specimen. He could tell from its beak, which was bald and pale. Its legs had gone stiff, and its sturdy talons gripped thin air.

He quickly wiped his gloves on his trousers. His father would have smacked him if he'd found out. He'd often caught his son observing the carcasses of small animals in the garden or in the pine grove behind their house, and he'd berated him for it, calling him a word Mathias hadn't heard before, but which sounded quite ugly. He'd looked it up in the dictionary. He couldn't remember what it meant, but it had something to do with madness.

Mathias wanted to be a veterinarian when he grew up, and

he'd take any chance to learn something. His grandfather had once told him that observing did half the job of learning. The rest would come so long as you tried and tried again. The boy stood up, his eyes still fixed on the animal. At first he wanted to bury it, but then he thought it might be better this way; nature was carnivorous and would appreciate those remains. They would not go to waste.

He heard the church bells in the town ring twice, followed by a third half-chime. It was getting late; the others were waiting for him in their secret place.

He set out along the frozen path. That morning, the village of Travenì had woken up to a coating of snow. It was only a light dusting and had melted away too fast, but it bode well for the forthcoming skiing season.

He reached the bluff that rose near the village. The memorial to the fallen soldiers of the Napoleonic wars soared through the low woodland of spruce and pine trees: a bronze grenadier scowling as he surveyed the horizon, his long mustache curling upwards. A blue scarf fluttered from the tip of his bayonet, indicating that a member of their group had already gotten there and climbed all the way up the statue to set up their signal.

Mathias sped up. Earlier that day the teacher had taught them the meaning of the English word "leader." It had made a huge impression on him. He liked how definitive it sounded, but most of all he liked the idea of being an example for others to follow.

The teacher had explained that a leader protects his team, which was exactly what Mathias tried to do with his friends. He knew they saw him as the head of their group, and not just because he was the eldest—ten years, two months, and two weeks old, to be precise—but because they knew they could rely on him.

That was why the scarf tied to the statue should have been his, not Diego's. He should have gotten there first and led the way, though they all knew that path well enough by now. Instead, he'd wasted time staring at some dead animal on the side of the road. Maybe his father was right after all.

The grenadier's bluff was surrounded by sheer rocky cliffs that plunged straight onto the bed of a stream. Water purled through fronds of dark reeds a few dozen meters below.

Mathias set out along the path that led down the cliff in sharp turns, bounding along as fast as he could and gripping the fence that flanked the track whenever he felt stones give way beneath the soles of his sneakers. He was out of breath by the time he reached the gravelly riverbed, his knees shaking and his face burning with the effort.

He followed the gully as it unfurled along its winding route, carved out over thousands of years. There were stepping stones over the water and wooden and metal stairways clinging to the rock walls. Beneath the metal grates the river was streaked with ruby-colored light, and smelled of ice. The light and the warmth of the sun rarely reached the depths of the ravine.

Mathias could hear the sounds of his own breathing and of his heart beating in his chest, and became aware of how completely alone he was. Tourists tended to favor the ski slopes at this time of year; it was too cold down here, and there was always the risk of a fall.

He started to walk faster without quite knowing why.

The sliver of sky he could see through the sharp peaks of the pine trees some sixty meters above his head was spanned by an old railway bridge from a line that was no longer operational. His grandfather's grandfather had helped to build it, a century and a half ago.

Mathias was walking with his face upturned when he

slipped on an icy rock and banged his knee. His exclamation was echoed by a sound coming from the forest. A low cry. He spun around, his breathing shallow.

His mother's words leapt to his mind: "The forest is no place for children."

He pulled himself up and didn't bother to check for any damage to his jeans or scrapes on the palms of his hands, though he could feel them chafing inside his wool gloves. He crossed a gangway that led around a protruding boulder. Wet moss on one side, rapids on the other. The path led to a small cave. Mathias ran the length of those few meters in the dark, telling himself it wasn't fear that pushed his legs to go faster, but merely haste.

When he emerged on the other side, he stopped. A ray of sunlight had pierced the green canopy of trees, bathing the undergrowth in gold. The waterfall that powered the stream took a fearsome plunge and sprayed tiny droplets of water as it crashed down; in summer, when there was more light filtering down here, those droplets were traversed by the colors of the rainbow.

His friends were sitting in a circle on the rocky beach, waiting for him. Lucia, Diego, and Oliver. As soon as he saw them, his fears vanished. A smile appeared on his lips. There was no one behind him. No one had followed him there. He looked back defiantly into the dark depths of the cave. He'd won; he was a true leader.

But soon his smile dimmed until it disappeared altogether.

He was sure of it now.

There was someone hiding in the dark, watching him.

2

The body lay on the grass, covered in frost, the pallor of the skin in stark contrast with the black hair on the head and genitals. Beneath it all, the murky green of mountain vegetation. Pockets of snow persisted in shadier spots close to the woods. Some snow had fallen overnight and a few crystals had become trapped in the body's eyelashes.

The dead man lay supine, arms by his sides and hands resting on pillows of moss. There were no scratches on him. The odd winter flower with faded, transparent petals emerged from between his fingers.

It all looked like a painting, with a color palette of blood gone cold, veins emptied out, and stiff limbs. The cold had preserved everything. There was no smell apart from the smell of the forest: wet earth and rotting leaves.

Someone had taken good care of him. The ground around the body had been laid out with rudimental booby traps of string tied into slip knots.

"To keep animals away from the body. To make sure it stayed intact until we found it," spoke a rough voice into the microphone of a mobile phone, lips pushing out words and a cloud of warm breath. All around was a hive of quiet activity, white overalls, flashing cameras and lights.

"No signs of manual labor: the hands are smooth and there are no scratches on the wedding band. The nails are neat. There doesn't seem to be any dirt."

The wedding band on the body's left ring finger gleamed in the bleak December light; despite the layer of flat clouds that shaded that corner of the world.

The man's face had been viciously assaulted, but the rest of the body seemed unharmed. Blood vessels of an intense blue were visible beneath the skin on either side of the neck. The man had shaved on the day he died. The shadow of a beard they could now see was caused by the postmortem tightening of the skin on his face.

"Minimal signs of hemorrhage, not compatible with the severity of the wounds inflicted. There is likely to be more blood on the clothes, which would have been removed after the fact."

A pause.

"The killer stripped and prepared the victim."

Despite the meticulous arrangement of the scene, there were prints everywhere, on the body and on the ground— now a cross between mud and ice—as if the perpetrator had somehow forgotten to take care of the most basic of details. There was only one other set of footprints apart from the victim's own, and judging by their size—a 10—they belonged to a man.

There were no signs of ligature anywhere on the dead man's arms, wrists, or ankles. The victim had been tall and robust, of relatively athletic build, yet the killer had managed to overcome him easily. He had attacked with animalistic fury.

You knew the killer; that's why you didn't immediately try to defend yourself. What went through your mind in that moment, when you realized you were about to die?

It was hard to tell from the expression on the body's face. The lips were sealed shut, and the eyes . . .

The body had been left in a spot between a natural drainage ditch and a walking path that was used by tourists throughout most of the year. A hiker had found it a few hours earlier. It was neither a coincidence nor a mistake; the assassin had deliberately chosen not to hide it.

"I see no signs of sexual activity, yet the killer stripped the victim."

The chief of the local police force had informed them that the body belonged to a family man who had disappeared two days ago after dropping his son off at school. His car had been found about a hundred yards from the body, shielded from view by trees. It had been pushed off a cliff. There were footprints and tire marks on the ground above.

"The killer travelled on foot. The footsteps lead to the forest."

Detective Superintendent Battaglia paused the voice recording and looked up at the sky. A few crows squawked overhead. Dark clouds carried the threat of snowfall.

They were running out of time. They had to move faster, be more efficient.

Battaglia rose to stand, joints aching. Too many days spent kneeling on the ground. Too many years of this work, perhaps. A little extra weight that should have been shed long ago.

"Hurry up with that evidence."

The forensics team were crouched over the ground, silent white shadows trained to catch details that were invisible to others. They took photographs, collected evidence, and filed everything away. This was where the DNA chain of custody began. It would reach completion a few hours later in a lab at the Forensic Medicine Institute back in the city, sixty miles away.

The arrival of the police had attracted a handful of curious bystanders. A gaggle of tourists and locals lingered beneath the wooden sign that pointed the way to Travenì, the nearest settlement. It was only two and a half miles away. It was easy to tell the locals apart; they all had wild, ruddy complexions and none of that neat ski-slope tan. Their skin had been roughened by the extreme temperatures, and hewn raw by the wind.

"We found the clothes," someone shouted from the forest.

Superintendent Battaglia's first thought was that it looked like a scarecrow.

The figure jutting out through the brambles looked incongruous in the undergrowth. It was made of sticks and rope, a few leafy branches, and blood-soaked clothes.

The head had been formed by stuffing the victim's undershirt with leaves and straw, and placing two crimson berries for eyes. His jacket and trousers hung limp over the wooden skeleton, and his watch had been fastened to a branch that served as a wrist. His shirt was stiff with dried blood. It was hard to tell what color it had been before.

An officer approached them.

"The trail ends at some rocks about a hundred meters north of here," he reported.

The killer knew how to get around. He was a local and knew this place well.

Battaglia picked up the microphone once more, eyes roaming over the clearing where the translucent body lay gathering the snowflakes that had just begun to fall. Someone was covering the body up with a tarpaulin.

"The effigy is a representation of the killer. He stood here contemplating his work, and wanted us to know . . ."

A sudden noise interrupted this analysis. The superintendent turned to watch the scene, perplexed. A man was making his way through the clearing, past the police cars and toward the woods, his feet sinking into the marshy ground every few steps. His tailored blazer flapped in the wind, his shirt was stained with mud and sleet, and there was nothing to shield him from the bitter cold. He looked defiant, but also flushed with fatigue. Or perhaps it was discomfort and embarrassment.

When the superintendent realized who it might be, the only word for it was:

"Shit."

3

Massimo was shin-deep in the bog.

A range of emotions lashed his face: anger, discomfort, disbelief, and above all, shame. Deceptive patches of grass kept giving way under his feet as he tried to clamber over them, plunging him into pools of clinging mud.

The eyes of countless strangers were upon him. He had just been transferred to this precinct, and this was his new team. That must be his new boss, watching him from the edge of the woods.

The snow, which had previously seemed unsure whether to fall at all, had thickened now. It brushed over his burning cheeks; its weight lingered on his skin and was gone in the time it took to blink.

Massimo willed himself to look up. Superintendent Battaglia was an olive-skinned man in his forties, slightly shorter than Massimo himself, currently observing him with narrowed eyes and a cigarette between his lips. A fellow officer had pointed Massimo in that direction, and he'd immediately set off, ignoring the officer's shout of warning. He had marched forward in a show of confidence, and only when he'd found himself sinking into the swamp had he realized why the officer had looked so worried.

He would never forget this day for as long as he lived. He'd arrived at the police station a few minutes late that morning, and had sat waiting in a corridor for half an hour until someone had deigned to tell him that his team wasn't there because they'd been called out for a suspected homicide. No one had bothered to wait for him or leave a message. They'd simply forgotten him.

I was only five minutes late.

At first Massimo thought it was a joke, but the officer had been deadly serious; Battaglia does not have a sense of humor, he'd assured him. Neither do you, thought Massimo, looking at the man's face.

There were only two things left for Massimo to do: sit and wait for the squad to return to the headquarters, or go out and join them, wherever they were.

Regrettably, he'd chosen the second option.

He hadn't anticipated having to drive for almost two hours in a torrential downpour that kept dumping sheets of water onto the asphalt, his face pressed to the windshield while the Sat Nav went haywire. And when he'd finally reached the valley, he'd had to deal with the ice. The car kept skidding over sharp, slippery turns, making his heart skip several beats. Once or twice he got stuck on an upward slope because he had the wrong type of tires on, without the kind of grip needed to deal with icy roads. Then, a passing tractor had stopped in front of him. The driver, an old man with wine on his breath and an unsteady parlance, insisted on helping Massimo. This kind of thing always happened with tourists around that time of year; he'd be happy to haul Massimo's car to level ground.

"Timber, manure, or cars, makes no difference to me," he'd said.

Massimo had accepted the offer with a reluctant shiver. With one last worried glance at the car, he'd hooked the tractor chain to the bumper, jumped back inside, and shifted to neutral.

And that was how he'd arrived in Travenì: hauled by a tractor.

The muscles in his back had seized up from the stress, he had a pounding headache, but at least he could concentrate on the view. There was a primitive beauty about that landscape, the kind that made you lose your bearings. Snow-capped peaks towered over a millennial forest, soaring like dull blades over a thick woodland carpet. They stood like mythical titans and compelled you to turn your face upward while a sense of vertigo filled your soul. Clear rivulets swept nimbly around rocks, icicles, and fragrant moss, gushing through the undergrowth of pine trees and bilberry shrubs. Massimo had noticed numerous animal tracks in the snow lining the road.

It was a world far removed from the one he was used to, a world that whispered of human insignificance, and hinted at the senselessness of worldly concerns. It was a natural paradise—but nowhere near pristine. One side of a mountain was almost completely bare; parked on a plateau were bulldozers and other excavation tools next to a group of sheds that served as a construction site. The slope was being cleared of trees.

Massimo had looked away, as if he'd seen a blemish on an otherwise beautiful painting.

Beyond the last few hairpin turns, on an elevated plain suspended over the bottom of the valley, lay the settlement of Travenì. It was a village ensconced in the hollow formed by a surrounding ring of peaks. Its homes, built in the alpine style, were made of stone and wood; the scent of resin emanated from tidy stacks of wood outside every door. The style of the buildings changed near the small area that constituted the town center, where the buildings were taller, pastel-colored, with Nordic-looking attics, ivy for Christmas decorations, and red bows on the balconies. Along the high street were some traditional diners and restaurants, as well as a grocery store and two coffee shops. Teenagers milled about in packs outside the pub, nursing glasses of mulled wine with their snowboards tucked under their arms; the ski slopes weren't far. There was also room for a pharmacy and a couple of high-end clothing stores for tourists.

The owner of the tractor had left Massimo and his car in the town's main square, refusing the money the stranger kept trying to press on him. He'd raised an arm in salutation and honked once as he drove off. Massimo had looked around. The settlement was like a scene from a postcard except for several leaflets pinned to the noticeboard outside the town hall, announcing a meeting at the school gym that night: the valley's residents were invited to assemble in protest against the construction of a new ski resort. Massimo recalled the construction site he'd seen earlier on one of the mountains, and the trees that had been cleared. Even here, far from the city, it seemed there was no peace to be had.

He hadn't had too much trouble finding his squad; the body had been discovered just outside the town, close to the Austrian border. There was a dirt road that led there through screes and groves of low pine trees. The police had already restricted access to the area with roadblocks on either side of the road, an officer meticulously recording the license plates of every passing car and the features of those curious faces that leaned out to try and catch a glimpse of what was going on.

That was the officer Massimo had shown his badge to, and whom he'd asked about Superintendent Battaglia. Shortly thereafter, he'd ended up in the bog he was still struggling through.

At least his boss was no longer paying attention. He was talking to an old woman who was bundled up in a thick coat that almost reached her feet. She was hard to miss: her hair, styled in a bob with bangs, was dyed a synthetic shade of red that clashed with the gentle, harmonious hues of their surroundings. She was pointing at something in a ditch that led into the woods, while Battaglia nodded.

She must have been a witness. Perhaps she'd been the one to find the body.

A few more steps forward and Massimo finally reached them. Someone offered him a hand to help him out of the swamp; he accepted it with an awkward word of thanks that came out like a mumble.

For the first time since he'd graduated from the academy, he felt like he was being tested. He was out of breath and his palms were clammy despite the freezing cold. He could not have made a worse start if he'd tried.

"Inspector Massimo Marini," he said, holding out his hand to Battaglia. "I've been assigned to your squad. Nobody told me about the body, otherwise I would have come earlier."

He had no idea why he'd said that. He could tell how petty he sounded, like a sulking child.

His outstretched hand was ignored. He lowered it in surrender. This day was not going to get any better.

The man looked at him without saying a word. There was a moment when he appeared to shake his head a fraction, as if in secret warning. It was the older woman who finally spoke.

"The victim didn't bother warning us either, *Inspector*."

Her voice was hoarse and her manner suggested she deemed him utterly inconsequential.

Massimo studied her. Her roguish fringe, sticking out from beneath the rim of a sequined woolly hat, seemed out of place on a face that bore the signs of age and was marked by a hardness that presaged an equally difficult personality. Her bright eyes pierced through him like a pair of thrusting hands, scouring his face as if in search of some kind of proof. She was chewing on the temples of a pair of glasses. Massimo saw she had thin lips; she would purse them every now and then as if weighing up a thought—or forming a judgment.

The heavy coat she wore was tight across her thighs and revealed a stocky build.

A police officer approached them, holding a mobile phone. He handed it to the woman.

"It's the district attorney calling for you, Superintendent."

She nodded and stepped away to take the call, scowling at Massimo.

Massimo froze. He barely registered that the man he'd assumed was Battaglia was now shaking his hand and introducing himself as Officer Parisi. His mouth had gone dry and he could feel the first signs of hypothermia. He tried to think of something to say that wouldn't make him sound like a *complete* idiot, but when he saw her hang up the phone, the words he finally managed to utter turned out to be far from appropriate.

"Nobody told me to look for a woman, Superintendent."

She regarded him as if he were a piece of excrement stuck to the sole of someone else's shoe.

"The thought never even crossed your mind, did it, Inspector?"

Inspector. He was little more than a kid, and looked like he'd just stepped out of a fashion magazine. Teresa had smelled his cologne from yards away. He struck an unseemly note in that narrow mountain moor now filling up with snow and with blood washing off the moss and into the soil—the blood of a man who had been killed in a manner even police officers would rarely see in the course of their careers.

Massimo Marini had a handsome face veiled by a thin shadow. He hadn't shaved. Something must have gone wrong for him that morning. Perhaps more than one thing, judging by his appearance. He hadn't gotten off to the best of starts; the young man's attempt to seem determined had backfired rather spectacularly. But everyone deserves to be given the benefit of the doubt, Teresa thought, even when it seems like a lost cause.

She wondered why he had requested a transfer from a big city to this small provincial precinct. What was he so eager to leave three hundred miles behind?

We run away from what scares or hurts us—or from what holds us captive.

Perhaps it was a failed relationship that he hadn't quite gotten over. But his face bore no signs of anguish or sleepless nights—only tension, the cause of which was Teresa, and not some blushing maiden. There must be something else that had driven him away.

He stood still as snowflakes began to gather on his shoulders, more stooped now than when he'd first arrived.

Teresa suppressed a smirk. She delighted in stretching newcomers' nerves to breaking point, and she wasn't about to make an exception now. There had been something almost pitiful in the way he'd looked at her, like a lost puppy. Teresa knew that for a moment, he'd been scared—scared that he would be reprimanded, scared that he'd been rude, scared that he might have come across as an amateur when he'd wanted so much to impress everyone with his confidence.

She took no more notice of him, and turned to address Parisi, resuming the discussion that had been interrupted by the inspector's arrival.

"We should search the canal, too, through the vegetation down there," she said.

The officer nodded.

Teresa glanced at Marini. She wondered where he'd left his coat, or whatever it was that he normally wore to shield himself from the cold. She refrained from asking the question.

"Will you take a look, Inspector?" she said instead.

He looked aghast for a moment. But he didn't ask for help; he lowered himself into the canal, clinging onto the overhanging branches so as not to tumble into the stagnant water.

Teresa shook her head. What was the use of an ego that size, other than for making life harder?

He did go straight in, though. We didn't have to ask twice.

That, at least, was a good sign: he was willing to do anything to make amends.

Parisi made to remove the special footwear he'd donned for the search and pass it on to his bedraggled colleague, but Teresa stopped him.

They watched together as the inspector's shoes were sucked once more into the mud, sinking into the fetid remains of rotting leaves and God knows what else.

Teresa almost felt sorry for him, though it was an amusing sight.

"What am I looking for?" he asked after poking about blindly for several minutes.

So finally he'd managed to ask for help. Progress.

"The eyes," Teresa replied. "We haven't found them yet."

AUSTRIA, 1978

People in town often spoke about the School, though few knew much about it, and even fewer had actually been there. The stories told about the institute tended to be flights of fancy encouraged by the air of mystery around it.

At dawn on certain days the building, constructed in the Mitteleuropean tradition, seemed to emerge from the low clouds like a mirage of flickering lights. Its rectangular base rested on a mount of solid rock that had been quarried nearby, and on top of that rose the first floor, veneered in carved concrete. A series of intertwined beams separated this floor from the upper stories, built out of finely cut stone. The front façade, from which the east and west wings branched out, was enhanced by four columns of the Ionic order, with gabled windows between them. The third and final floor was topped by a semi-dome. Its central arch held a turret clock that had been broken for as long as anyone could remember; it was rumored that the time it displayed—three o'clock on the dot—was the exact moment when the building's designer, a young architect from Lienz, had died, struck by lightning as he stood near the lake admiring his creation. Nearly two hundred years later, the elderly locals still spoke of that moment as the day God made his wrath manifest, punishing man for his pride, for daring to violate a landscape intended solely for silence, for gales, and for mountain flowers.

Now that she stood closer to the School than she had ever

been, Magdalena understood the meaning of this rumor. Everything about the building felt wrong, completely ill-judged, the whim of an aristocratic class that never seemed to know when to stop.

She had walked up the road that led from the town to the plateau; from there, she'd taken a shortcut, climbing along the path that went over the opposite side of the mountain. The bitter smell of lichens and slimy depths rose from the lake. It looked like the earth's own eye.

She was out of breath by the time she reached the front door, and a lock of her curly hair had escaped her chignon; she hurriedly tucked it back with a hairpin while examining the state of her shoes. Before she'd even touched the door knocker, shaped like a wolf's head, the heavy door opened, and a wide, ageless face stared at her through small, stern eyes.

"You must be Magdalena. Come in, follow me."

Nurse Agnes Braun was like the building she lived in: austere and derelict. Her thick grey hair framed a face much younger than Magdalena had expected. A few subtle touches would have been enough to make her look almost beautiful, but perhaps those kinds of concerns were not welcome in the School. Magdalena had been advised not to wear any rouge for her job interview here, to dress plainly, and to gather her hair in a bun.

Nurse Braun was coolly cordial as she showed Magdalena around what she clearly considered her realm—judging by the regal demeanor she adopted as they walked among slabs of marble, gold-plated friezes, and the few valuable furnishings that seemed to be left. But the building appeared otherwise vacant, and so quiet that Magdalena wondered where its residents could be.

The atrium was pristine and decorated with a mosaic representing the Austro-Hungarian Empire's coat of arms: a double-headed black eagle on a golden background. The walls were adorned with *trompe-l'oeil* paintings of hunting scenes. The only blemish on this delicate backdrop of pastel colors was a pendulum clock with two Moors carved on either side of the dial; the expressions on their ebony-carved faces were terrifying, their gaping mouths revealing sets of curiously sharp ivory teeth.

Agnes Braun sensed the newcomer's shock.

"It was made with artifacts from the African continent," she explained smugly. "It belonged to the director's family. He thought it would make a nice gift to the School."

Magdalena thought it was horrifying, but managed to force a polite smile.

Nurse Braun rested her interlaced hands on her stomach and observed Magdalena.

"Do you think it tasteful?" she asked.

The young woman would not meet her eyes.

"I do," she said, but knew immediately how insincere she sounded.

When she looked up again, she saw a smile spreading over the other woman's face. Agnes Braun seemed pleased.

"You mustn't be embarrassed," she heard her say. "Your little lie tells me you might be suited to this place after all. The School expects devotion, and devotion requires that we forego certain personal liberties—like our freedom of thought. Wouldn't you agree?"

Magdalena nodded without even realizing it. There was something about this woman that disturbed her. Just like the School itself, something about her felt wrong.

The grown-ups were upset. Mathias could tell from the way his mother kept shooting nervous glances his way while she talked to his teacher and some of the other kids' mothers. Every look was like a tug on a leash, a way of drawing his attention and keeping him close even as they stood apart. In her arms she held his little brother, Markus, who was only a few months old. He'd fallen asleep a while ago, but she hadn't put him back in his pram.

The school auditorium was alive with anxious whispers. A heap of multi-colored costumes lay abandoned on the stage, illuminated by floodlights. Earlier, two men Mathias had never seen before had interrupted the rehearsals for the school's nativity play. They'd spoken to the teacher first and then gone up to Diego's mother; after a brief conversation, she had followed them out, looking pale and stumbling as she walked, like a zombie. Only when Mathias's mother had called out to her had she remembered her son. She'd told him to stay put and behave himself; the teacher was going to look after him until grandma arrived. Her voice was shaking.

Mathias saw Diego slumped in one of the collapsible chairs in the stalls, staring at the black sky through the row of windows high up on the wall. Every day, night fell a little earlier, and it seemed as if the blackness had begun affecting people, too. Travenì was no longer the same place Mathias had always loved; over the last few hours, the town had been crushed by the weight of suspicion falling on its residents like snow. Ever since Diego's father had disappeared, the air had been poisoned with fear.

Mathias approached his friend, whose face, half-illuminated by a beam of light from the stage, was like a small moon, sad and perhaps a little furious. Mathias felt he should say something, but he also understood words would be useless.

Diego's father was dead. Nobody had said it out loud yet, but they knew—just like you know when you're about to be smacked, or when you feel a fever building even though your forehead still feels cool to the touch.

Mathias scrunched his hat up into a ball and threw it at Diego.

Diego's hand shot up and caught it, though his eyes were still staring out into the darkness.

A flash of a smile escaped Mathias. Diego was still there, even though he was trapped in a morass of confusion and fear. He was Mathias's best friend and his biggest rival—though in that moment Mathias wanted to tell him he didn't care about being the head of their group, Diego could take his place if he wanted; he had all the qualities of a leader anyway. But he said nothing; leadership had to be earned, not gifted. For now they would continue to challenge each other—though never at the expense of the fraternal bond that united them.

Mathias was on the verge of saying all this to Diego, but a sudden thought made him focus on something else entirely.

"Where's Oliver?" he asked.

On hearing the name, Diego seemed to fall back to earth. Oliver was only a year younger than them, but they all regarded him as the baby of the group.

They looked at each other, sharing the same urgent thought. They had to find him. They had to protect him—especially here, within these walls.

. . .

The hallway that led to the students' bathroom was a dim passageway with no visible end. The lights had been switched off already, and the classrooms on either side of the corridor were black holes emitting a faint odor of chalk and paper.

Oliver swallowed and heard his saliva moving down his throat, an unnervingly clear sound in the stillness of the hallway. He looked for the light switch, but he couldn't recall where it was since he'd never had to use it before. He glanced back at the faint, reassuring glow behind him. The doors of the assembly room opened out halfway down a corridor around the corner.

I'm not alone, he reminded himself.

He turned his head once more to the stretch of corridor ahead, that abyss he'd stubbornly wanted to cross on his own, without asking anyone for help.

Oliver knew: *he* was lurking somewhere in the dark—tidying up the equipment in the gym room, or making sure all the windows were shut in the canteen. He never made any noise when he moved and glared sternly at everyone he passed. But only with Oliver did he reveal his true nature: as cruel as a fairy tale ogre, beyond reason or measure. Oliver's stomach cramped at the thought.

He blinked several times in quick succession. It was as if the gloom were a physical mass stuck to his eyelashes, his skin, his clothes, determined to engulf him. He took a step, and then another. In his imagination he'd entered that bubble of darkness now, edging too close to its core and too far from the light.

If a hand were to emerge now from the dark and drag him away . . . He pushed that thought away, but the cramps in his stomach lingered as a reminder. Surely the door to the bathroom wasn't much further away. A few steps more and he would feel it beneath his outstretched hands, and all his fears would be wiped away by the light. Mathias and Diego would be proud of him and finally see him as their equal.

He advanced with greater conviction until he felt the smooth surface of the wall beneath his fingertips. He ran his hands along the wall and found the door, then felt for the handle, and pushed down. A familiar smell of chlorine and bleach told him he'd come to the right place.

He hesitated, trying to work up the courage to slip a hand into the darkness.

Idiot, he thought, feeling embarrassed even though there was nobody there to witness his fear.

He pursed his lips and stuck his arm out, feeling hot and cold at the same time. Finally he managed to feel his way to the switch, and the neon lights on the ceiling flickered to life.

The blue bathroom tiles gleamed under the cold light. A loose tap dripped water into the sink at regular intervals.

Oliver's chest deflated as he let go of the breath he didn't know he'd been holding. There was nobody else there, nobody waiting for him.

He made for the cubicles, a row of three open doors in front of him. He chose the middle one and began to undo his trousers. He stopped at the first button.

He could feel it. He wasn't alone anymore. There was somebody behind him. Someone else was breathing with him in the silent room—a heavy breath that smelled of garlic and tobacco.

"Hello, you little shit."

Oliver slowly turned around, as if those words, uttered in that rough voice, were some kind of order. He was shaking.

Right there in front of him, making him feel even smaller than he already was, stood the imposing figure of his daily nightmare.

Abramo Viesel was the school janitor. He was older than

Oliver's parents but younger than his grandparents; his body was so thick that he moved with difficulty, and when he walked he rocked from side to side like a ship in a storm. But Oliver wouldn't have called him fat. The word that came to his mind whenever he saw him was "powerful." Like a villain in superhero comics. Powerful enough to crush him.

Oliver looked at the janitor's hands: they were as large as Oliver's head. He imagined his skull imprisoned by those rough, hairy fingers.

"I see you've worked up the courage to come all the way here on your own," he said. "That wasn't a good idea."

Oliver didn't reply. He had learned by now that any word he said was bound to be the wrong one. Mr. Viesel had enjoyed torturing him since the day Oliver had first set foot in the school. The torment had only been verbal so far, and Mr. Viesel had yet to lay a finger on him, but Oliver could feel that, too, would come one day soon. He looked at the man's hands again and saw they were wracked by spasms, muscles rippling beneath his skin.

"They're waiting for me," Oliver said.

Mr. Viesel's belly shook as he let out a quick, low laugh.

"You came here for a piss. So do it," he commanded, standing firm, his shoulder blocking the door.

Oliver squeezed his eyes shut. The pressure on his bladder was beginning to hurt.

"I need to get back," he said. "Please."

"No, you're staying right here. Standing to attention, like a little soldier, until you've wet yourself."

Oliver felt something dampening his cheeks.

"Crying like a little girl now, are we?" Mr. Viesel mocked him.

Oliver thought of Lucia, who was a girl, but also brave and strong. He opened his eyes. His attacker's silhouette seemed to tremble when he saw it through his tears.

The man leaned toward him.

"You know what I'll do if you go telling anyone about this, don't you?"

Oliver didn't reply.

"I'll come for you at night when you're asleep, and . . ."

He made as if to grab him. Oliver let out a strangled scream and Viesel burst out laughing. But then something hit him on the head and bounced off onto the floor. Viesel looked at the object and Oliver followed his gaze. It was a blackboard eraser. It had left a chalk mark across the man's cheek.

Mr. Viesel turned around and Oliver took his chance to squeeze through the gap between Viesel's thigh and the cubicle door, pushing through with all his strength to reclaim his freedom.

"Where do you think you're going?" said Viesel, but it was too late. Oliver was safe now.

Mathias and Diego stood between him and his tormentor.

"So you need your little friends to rescue you," Viesel grunted. "When will you stop being such a wimp?"

"Leave him alone!" said Mathias.

"What's your problem, Klavora? Your father forgot to give you a proper beating this week?"

Abramo Viesel wiped the chalk off his face.

"And I see young Valent is here, too," he said, looking at Diego. He picked up the eraser. "Now *your* old man's come to a sticky end."

"Shut up!"

But Mathias's cry went unheeded. Oliver saw him grab Diego's arm and try to drag him away, but Diego seemed to have turned into stone.

"Let's go!" Mathias pleaded.

"I heard the cops talking in the parking lot, before they went in to look for your mother," Viesel whispered, as if sharing a secret. "Do you want to know what they were saying?"

Diego kept his eyes fixed on the janitor and didn't reply. Oliver thought he looked like he'd been hypnotized.

"Do you want to know how he died?"

Now all three boys were listening, transfixed.

Abramo Viesel raised his hands, curled his fingers like talons, and brought them slowly toward Diego's face.

"They took him into the woods and ripped his eyes out. Like this!"

His tale was interrupted by the voice of a teacher calling out for them from the hallway. Oliver felt Mathias pulling him away and saw that he was dragging Diego out, too.

Behind them, Abramo Viesel was now complaining forlornly about how tired he was, with all his aches and pains, of being subjected to the pranks of these spoiled brats while he tried to clean the toilets. Oliver didn't look, but he could picture the janitor standing there, waving the eraser about in one hand and supporting his back with the other.

He did look at Diego, though, and almost didn't recognize him. Diego's face had gone so pale that he looked dead. Just like his father.

6

In the half-lit room, a projector beamed photographs from the crime scene.

There were close-ups of parted, cyanotic lips, and details of capillaries spreading beneath the epidermis like river deltas. A pale sternum. Black craters where the eyes used to be.

These images were the raw materials of their work, lumps of clay they would mold into the face of the killer, a face to which they would then attach a name. It was always a killer's profile—the portrait of his psyche—that led investigators to his identity, never the other way around.

Slouched in her chair, Teresa considered the slides, with Ambrosini, the regional chief of police, and Gardini, the deputy public prosecutor, sitting on either side of her. She regarded them as friends, though their friendship had no bearing on their professional relationship. Behind them sat the rest of her team.

They had just returned to the police station having spent hours examining the crime scene and collecting evidence until the cold had seeped into their bones. But their work had only just begun, and the day was sure to blend seamlessly into night.

Teresa's eyes, though stinging with exhaustion, were fully focused.

More images now, scenes from a natural landscape untamed by man. The vegetation was dotted with the forensics team's markers signalling every piece of evidence they'd found: traces of blood, prints, and branches snapped by the fury of a beast with human features.

And finally, the culmination of that morbid repertoire: an effigy made out of the victim's bloodied clothing.

Teresa heard Gardini's breath hitch in revulsion. He had just realized that this was no "ordinary" homicide; there was an element of psychosis in it, and perhaps something even more dangerous that Teresa hadn't been able to identify. The usual motives weren't going to apply here. The human mind wasn't capable of nursing this kind of horror out of simple jealousy, revenge, or greed. The meaning of that effigy was far more complex. It demanded their attention because it revealed so much.

"In my view, that's the single most disturbing element," murmured the deputy prosecutor.

Teresa felt the same, though looking at it now she thought she could perhaps glimpse something more. She hadn't yet been able to put her finger firmly on it; at the moment it was still just an indistinct trace beneath the surface that showed up intermittently and slipped out of reach every time she tried to give it a name.

"Something wrong?" the deputy prosecutor asked her.

She didn't respond immediately, waiting for her impressions to take a more concrete shape. Finally, she shook her head and stayed silent. She didn't want to muddle everyone else's thoughts with the vague hunch that if it hadn't been for the context in which they had found it, and all that blood on it, she would have said there was something childish—even playful—about the effigy.

Teresa studied the eyes, which were made out of berries.

"We should figure out where the killer got those from," she said. "I didn't see them anywhere else in the area; it might turn out to be an important clue."

The prosecutor nodded his agreement.

"What could it mean?" he asked.

Teresa wasn't sure yet, but she had a theory.

"It was important to him that they should be there," she said. "If the effigy is a representation of the killer, it's showing him looking at something."

But looking at what? The dying victim? The village nearby?

During their inspection of the scene, Teresa had noticed a detail that had unsettled her: from the angle it faced, the effigy seemed to be looking straight at the bell tower of Travenì's church.

"The absence of a mouth makes it look expressionless," Gardini noted.

"That's the killer's way of masking his emotions," she explained. "It's impossible to tell what he might have felt in that moment: rage or fear, anguish or excitement."

The deputy prosecutor let out a worried sigh.

"He left no clues about a possible motive," he said quietly.

"He didn't *want* to leave any," Teresa pointed out. "I doubt it was an accidental omission. He prepared the scene meticulously; he must have fantasized about it at length. He left it exactly as he wanted us to find it. Think of those traps he set up. He's a perfectionist."

"So he led us all the way to a specific point, but then decided to hide his true thoughts from us."

Teresa nodded.

"I wonder if the absence of a nose might be some subconscious obfuscation," she said. "A more sensual organ than the eyes, and closely connected to libido . . ."

"If that were the case, what would you think it means?"

Teresa rubbed at her eyes. They weren't just asking her for an opinion; she was often expected to make daring predictions, to reveal intuitions that could eventually lead to a conviction.

At worst—as in that moment—she was made to choose which path to take at a crossroads.

"Any inference would be premature," she said.

But Gardini wouldn't let it go.

"Just tell me what you're thinking," he insisted, speaking more forcefully now.

"I wouldn't want to rule out any leads at this stage," she replied, her tone unchanged, and her eyes elsewhere.

The deputy prosecutor leaned closer to her ear.

"It won't happen," he assured her. "We'll investigate every possibility until you deem it necessary to narrow the scope."

"I'm not a clairvoyant," Teresa hissed, not wanting the rest of the room to hear her.

"Nobody's suggesting that," the chief of police cut in. "But you always get it right. Almost. That's why we're pushing you."

Teresa sighed. They would never understand the burden their questions placed on her.

"I can only see a rough picture so far," she said. "If it is indeed true that the suppression of the sense organs is not accidental, that would indicate a particularly repressed personality and elements of sexual deviance. But it's too early to say for sure," she reiterated.

The next slides showed details of the victim's wristwatch: it was strapped to the branch that served as the effigy's wrist, but it was the wrong way around, so the display faced the wood. Teresa had no idea whether that had any meaning.

"And the victim's eyes?" the chief of police whispered. His fingers, which he had been wringing restlessly, were now interlocked in front of his greying mustache.

"We couldn't find them," she replied. "Maybe the birds got them. Or perhaps the killer kept them as a trophy. Their symbolic significance is considerable. Our eyes discover, observe, and measure the world," she explained, motioning with her hands. "They look and they lust—perhaps after what's forbidden? They say the eyes are windows to the soul; there must be some truth in that, given how often murderers cover their victims' eyes so that they won't feel judged, so that they won't falter in their intent to kill."

Gardini turned to look at her. Teresa could sense his uncertainty.

"Trophies? Symbols? We're not dealing with a serial killer here," he noted.

Teresa shrugged, her eyes fixed on the slide show.

"There's a pathological element to this murder," she observed. "It suggests to me that the usual motives don't apply."

"Well, we can all agree there is an element of psychosis involved, but—"

"It's not just that."

"Then what?"

Teresa didn't want to say anything just yet, but if psychosis played such a crucial role—as the nature of the attack suggested—it was still difficult to explain the level of methodical organization implied by all the other evidence they had found.

Either you're completely insane, or you're a cold, careful manipulator. "We'll know more after we have the coroner's report," she said out loud. "I'll take the new guy, the inspector."

The chief nodded.

"Are you going to torture him?" he asked her in a low voice, the shadow of a smile quickly suppressed.

Teresa glanced at their new recruit through narrowed eyes. Marini was still standing, leaning against the wall. He'd tried to clean himself up, but he was going to need a lot more than soap and water to look anything close to presentable again.

"Not too much," she answered, looking away. "Just enough."

7

The Institute for Forensic Sciences was the kind of place that made an impression, especially if you entered it at night, when all the lights were dimmed and there was no one inside but a doctor and a couple of orderlies. During the day it looked like an ordinary hospital wing, with the usual hub-bub of crowded hallways and rooms full of medical interns, but at night it showed its bleaker side. The silence revealed the true nature of the place: a final, solitary destination. It exuded a sense of melancholy, as if the families' despair had stuck to the bodies preserved in the morgue, and their tears had been absorbed by the walls.

Death needs soil, not concrete, thought Teresa, walking past rooms immersed in darkness where everything that would have moved in the outside world seemed infected by an eerie stillness: no windows to let light or air in, and the equipment, switched off for the night, had no vital signs to monitor. These rooms were not meant for the living.

The sovereign of that deserted kingdom was Antonio Parri.

Teresa and Marini found him in one of the teaching rooms, preparing the next day's lessons.

The superintendent knocked on the open door, surprised as she always was by the boyishness of that little man with his dishevelled mop of white hair. Gangly and awkward, he watched the world with his blue eyes wide open behind his spectacles. His curiosity was boundless, and his mind razor sharp. He was often the first person to hear Teresa's theories about a new case.

"You have me working overtime, Superintendent," he reproached her, with a mischievous frown that quickly dissolved into a smile. Setting aside the papers he'd been hunched over, he motioned for her to come in. Seeing Marini, he nodded in acknowledgment. Though he'd only had a few seconds to study him, he could have easily described all his features; it was his job after all, and he did it with the living as much as with the dead.

"I wanted you on this," was all Teresa said, and already those few words revealed so much: the complexity of this case, the peculiarities that bothered her, and her need to confer with an analytical mind capable of seeing what she saw.

"Let's go," said the coroner. "He's waiting for us."

The body was laid out on a steel bed and covered with a white sheet that smelled of soap. Parri always treated his guests with respect and consideration. Teresa had once seen him request a fresh sheet to replace a stained one; the corpse wouldn't have minded either way, but Antonio knew the relatives cared. He didn't just know; he *understood*, which was even more important. His presence made the place seem less oppressive, and he dignified it with his humanity.

The victim's widow had identified the body a few hours earlier while it was still inside a body bag deep in the woods. They knew his name now, but not his story or anything about its untimely ending.

"We've done all the usual tests," Parri explained. "Blood tests, swabs, fingernail scrapes . . . Now there's just the autopsy left to conduct while we wait for the results."

He uncovered the body.

Teresa nodded, gazing at the corpse. There were strips of gauze covering the eye sockets. Another act of mercy.

"No signs of sexual activity prior to death. The facial wounds are deep and point to a violent, brutal motion. My view is that there was no weapon involved. He did it with his bare hands, and even left some fingerprints."

Teresa saw Marini shudder. He'd been standing back, craning his neck every now and then to take a closer look at the body.

"It won't bite," she said. "Come here and take a proper look."

Inspector Marini obeyed, but he moved stiffly, and evidently had no idea how to behave—Teresa could tell from the way the young officer seemed suddenly uncomfortable in his own skin. He didn't know where to place his hands, how to move his feet, what to do with himself.

"I'm not familiar with this sort of thing," he confessed. "I won't be of much help."

"You're not familiar with murder? Then you'd better find yourself a new job, or start learning." Teresa shifted her attention back to Parri. "Do you mean to say he carved the eyes out with his fingers?"

"I believe so. Judging by the clotting in the capillaries here, the victim did not die immediately, but after a few hours. We will have to wait for the full autopsy to establish a definitive cause of death. In any event, it happened on the day he disappeared. I would rule out strangulation; the trachea appears undamaged and there are no bruises on the neck."

"Wouldn't wounds like those kill you anyway?"

The question had come from Marini.

"Is he new?" Parri asked Teresa.

"Indeed."

"No, wounds like these wouldn't kill you, young man."

"If it took a few hours, the perpetrator will have stayed behind to watch over the dying victim," Teresa murmured, lost in her conjectures. "Or perhaps he came back later to rearrange the body and set up the scene he'd planned in his head."

"We found a fingernail fragment in one of the eye sockets," the coroner resumed. "I've already sent it off to the lab for DNA testing."

Teresa felt uneasy, and Parri noticed.

"What is it that bothers you?" he asked her.

"Everything. Nothing. I don't know . . ." Teresa removed her glasses and used her sleeve to wipe furiously at the lenses. "It's as if the murder was committed by two different people. One of them is lucid, methodical, and positioned the body carefully to send a message—though what message?—laying out traps to ensure it would remain intact until we found it, but hiding the car so that we wouldn't find it too soon. The other one is completely disorganized, almost animalistic . . . the way he killed so close to a footpath, unconcerned about being seen, without using ropes or weapons, as if the murder were the result of a moment of uncontrollable fury . . . He left prints everywhere, failing to take even the most basic precautions."

They resumed their examination of the corpse.

"No bite marks anywhere," said Teresa.

"I noticed that too."

"When an attack is motivated by sadistic intent, it is not unusual to find bite marks on the body," Superintendent Battaglia explained for Marini's benefit. "The killer loses control and surrenders to his most brutal instincts. But here we have no marks of that kind. Not even a scratch. He left the rest of the body untouched, as if the face were all he cared about."

"That's another thing that bothers you," Parri guessed.

Teresa nodded.

"I can't figure him out, and that's never happened before. I can't work out who it is I'm dealing with."

"Maybe that's not such a bad thing," Marini interrupted. "Having no predetermined idea, I mean. It's a little early to know what kind of guy the killer might be."

Teresa looked at him. He'd had the same expression when he had arrived at the crime scene that morning: at once embattled and defiant. She couldn't quite believe anybody could be *this* naive.

"You really have no idea what you're talking about," she said.

"I believe I do."

"That wasn't a question, Inspector."

"The profile?" asked Parri, interrupting their confrontation. Teresa hesitated.

"Go on," the doctor insisted. "I can tell you have something in mind."

"We only have a single murder, Antonio. Profiles are for something else altogether."

"But that's what you're thinking about, isn't it? There's a ritualistic element, you saw that straight away, and ritualism leads to repetition. That's how it works, that's how serial killers are born."

Teresa chewed on her glasses. She was tired, hungry, and unsettled. Parri knew her too well, and she felt utterly transparent around him.

Finally, she relented. "Twenty-five to thirty years old. Lives alone. An ectomorph by build, but far stronger than his appearance would suggest; the victim was no weakling. Disorganized, but showing flashes of lucid reasoning. There is method behind his vigor. He is intelligent, but his psychosis has held him back. He probably struggled through school, and if he has a job, it isn't one that he finds fulfilling. An introvert. No partner. I suspect he's never known how to approach women. He may suffer from some form of sexual dysfunction."

Marini sighed, an unconscious reflex that, Teresa had noticed, betrayed his frustration.

"Perhaps you disagree?" she said.

He threw up his hands.

"And what if I did?" he said. "Or did you think I was only here to tag along? Obviously I'd like to discuss things and exchange views and maybe even argue about the case if it helps—but over real, tangible facts."

Teresa smiled. She was used to this kind of reaction.

"You're right," she conceded. "Death is real, here in this place. You can smell it, can't you?"

His eyes blazed.

"I can. Can you?" he replied defiantly.

Parri made as if to speak, but Teresa silenced him with a glance. She wasn't troubled by the insubordination. At last the boy was showing there was more to him than an expensive suit and the pout on his pretty face. Perhaps beneath all that he had a backbone after all.

"Do you want to know how I can be so sure?" she said, moving closer. "It's down to experience. But it's also down to statistics. It's down to hundreds of profiles of people like him who've committed certain kinds of murders. *This* kind of murder. It's not magic. It's not guesswork. I do my homework. So should you."

The night air was bitter and cleansing. Teresa breathed deeply, as if to wash off the blight of all the sorrow she'd just inhaled. She felt this way every time she left the Institute no matter how many autopsies she'd witnessed throughout her career. It was like resurfacing from a deep sea dive.

She walked briskly toward the car, and could hear the soles of Marini's shoes treading the ground behind her, in time with her footsteps. She knew he was angry; she would have been angry, too, in his place. It was exactly what she needed from him in that moment: a healthy dose of rage and youthful zeal.

Anything would do, as long as there was energy and fervor behind it.

He drew level with her.

"What have I done to you?" he asked.

Teresa feigned incomprehension.

"Why do you hate me so much? Because I was late? I'm sorry about that, but I don't think I deserve to be humiliated for it."

Teresa burst out laughing.

"Hate you? I wouldn't dream of it. As for the humiliation . . . that was all your doing. You could have kept your mouth shut."

"See what I mean? You're doing it again! Clearly you have a problem with me," he insisted.

Teresa slowed done and finally came to a halt. She raised her chin to study his face. He looked exhausted.

"The only thing that's clear is the extent of your incompetence," she said. "You don't agree? Then prove me wrong. I'll expect your report on everything you saw this morning. And hurry up, you're late as it is."

8

The hour of nocturnal predators had come. They emerged from their dens and took flight from their nests up in the highest, hiddenmost branches. Snow cloaked the scents of the forest, nullifying the predators' olfactory sense, but it also muffled any background noise, so that the sound of small rodents scuttling in the undergrowth travelled clearly to their sensitive ears. The carnivores waited patiently until their prey had ventured into the open, then pounced and slashed at their victims with sharpened claws.

The forest was silent death and unequal contest.

Animals were territorial beings, just like he was. They rarely deviated from their usual routes, so he had been able to learn their ways. He followed their tracks and listened for their calls. When he had to, he hunted. He could turn into a falcon or a fox as needed, and he killed, though he preferred to use traps to limit the suffering he caused when taking a life. The sound of those creatures whimpering in pain triggered a kind of discomfort deep in his core that he could not explain. It made him feel uneasy. He had learned how to bring death: with a sharp twist of his hands, their necks gave way and their breathing stopped.

It was a bright night, an auspicious one for hunting. The clouds had cleared and frost glistened in the moonlight. He'd set up his snares in the morning while the animals still slept in their dens. Now all he had to do was to pick up their trapped, quivering bodies, the fruits of his labor. He made his way upwind toward the traps, his muscular thighs carving a path through the snow. He could distinguish, not too far from where he was, the thrashing form of a large animal caught in a trap—it was lying on its back, its long legs, slender yet powerful, kicking at the air for purchase, but all this achieved was to tighten the grip of the snare. The creature wheezed with exertion as it fought to escape its fate.

He approached cautiously, not wanting to scare the trapped deer. He placed a pacifying hand on its neck to stop it from strangling itself. He was dismayed to see that it was a doe.

He knelt by her side, and for a moment he was not sure what to do.

He knew from the volume of acorns the squirrels had already amassed in their nests that this was going to be a long and punishing winter. When the weather started to turn, he always checked on the squirrels and the hedgehogs to see what the animals expected of the coming months of cold. They were never wrong, and he knew now that in a few moons' time he would need meat to survive the cold.

He ran a hand over the stiff fur of the doe's gray-brown coat. The creature's heart beat vigorously against its broad chest. Its belly was warm and covered in thick fuzz, and its udder was swollen with milk.

He looked up between the trees and saw it: the fawn was staring at him with enormous, liquid eyes. Its nostrils flared on its thin snout, quivering frantically as it tried to work out whether he was something he should run away from. If the fawn was still beside its mother, this must be its first winter. He noticed that its velvet-lined antlers had barely begun to sprout from their base on its forehead. They would grow to their full length by summer, then fall off the following winter only to grow back once more, over and over again for the rest of its life, and longer each time, until they formed a majestic crown.

He told himself it was old enough to survive without its mother.

The doe seemed to understand what he was thinking, and sought his eyes with her own. She had stopped struggling, though her breathing was still labored. Her neck lay slack in his arms. It would require a particularly violent twist to break it. He would have to apply considerable force, but he was capable of it.

But instead of squeezing, his hands loosened the knots. The doe was disoriented by her sudden freedom; he had to nudge her to her feet. He stroked her straight, muscular back and felt all her primordial energy flowing into his own limbs.

He yelled, and the doe sprinted toward the trees in quick, elegant leaps, until she was reunited with her fawn.

He stayed where he was, still kneeling in the snow, his heart convulsing as it did every time life got the better of his predatory instincts.

Looking for dry earth, he found a patch of ground covered in fallen pine needles and sat with his back resting against a tree trunk while his empty stomach growled in protest. He took out two stained paper bags from the pocket of his sheepskin coat, retrieved a few strips of cured meat from one, and began chewing intently.

The other bag contained something entirely different.

Something precious.

9

The victim was called Roberto Valent. He was a civil engineer, born and raised in the valley. He'd left to go to university and lived elsewhere for a few years after graduating, but had returned with his wife and son when hiking enthusiasts and professional climbers began to discover the beauty in this corner of the world, boosting local tourism. Valent had been managing the construction site for a new ski slope.

The Valent family lived in Travenì, in a chalet made of hardwood and limestone. Their house was the size of a villa, and stood on a sloping, south-facing meadow that must have been sunnier than most during the summer months. There was no fence or wall around it, and the borders of the property were only marked by flowerbeds, currently bare because of the cold.

An old lady with a desolate air about her was taking down the Christmas decorations from the windows, as if the house itself should be dressed for mourning. She was thin and wore a black dress. When she saw the police car enter the driveway, she retreated behind the shutters.

Teresa thought she must be Valent's mother, and knew for sure when she rang the doorbell moments later and the same lady opened the door. Her eyes were red, her eyelids swollen. She said her daughter-in-law would be receiving them in the parlor, and showed them the way, dragging her feet in their felt slippers along a parquet that smelled of beeswax. Teresa offered her condolences, to which the woman choked out a brief reply, her silver head sinking between her bony shoulders. She was the embodiment of frailty, yet she must have carried hidden reserves of strength if the loss of her son hadn't completely broken her.

"Please take a seat. Marta will be here soon," she said before slipping away to make coffee.

Teresa picked the couch, Marini the armchair. He'd come to work early that morning, mercifully in a pair of jeans and comfortable shoes. He hadn't relinquished the blazer, though, or his tailored coat. Teresa, faintly amused, had thought that the transformation had already begun. They'd spent the early hours of the day at the crime scene, now cleared of the forensics team's paraphernalia, but still cordoned off. To work out who had killed Roberto Valent, they first had to establish how he'd been killed—step by step, right up until the final act—and find the answer to a single question: *Why?*

Perhaps the family would provide the answer, though Teresa doubted it. She was here for the usual formalities, to allow the police to gain a better sense of the family, and to reassure those closest to the victim that they were doing everything they could to get to the truth.

The room was furnished in the alpine style, probably like the rest of the house. Honey-colored wood creaked underfoot and covered the walls and the coffered ceiling, its panels interleaved with swathes of silk brocade and other rich fabrics, as well as wool and felt. There was a charming and tasteful selection of objects on display: heart-shaped, inlaid boxes containing gingerbread and candied fruits, and old copper and pewter pots that had been repurposed as vases and filled with aromatic herbs and star anise, releasing a lingering scent into the room. The cushions were soft and embellished with handmade lace. A nativity scene whose layout and coloring suggested it was an antique had been set up on a coffee table near the entrance.

The focal point of the parlor was the *stube*, the traditional wall-mounted stove that took up almost an entire side of the room, and emitted a pleasant, welcoming warmth. There were upholstered benches to its left and right; this was the part of the house where families used to gather in the evenings, once they had completed their chores in the woods or in the stables.

But the family that lived in this house now had just been deprived of one of its key members. Their evenings would no longer be the same; the nights that would follow would seem unending and full of misery. Teresa was sure that nights in Travenì would have felt quiet enough to begin with—it was one of those places where the streets became deserted at the first hint of sunset. Now, to make matters worse, the town had awakened to the knowledge that a killer had been roaming its streets in the dark.

The widow appeared. Marta Valent was an attractive woman whose entrance filled the room with a quiet anguish. She shook their hands loosely, as if wanting to slip away, and accepted their stock remarks with downcast eyes. She joined Teresa on the couch but chose to perch on the opposite end, teetering on the edge of the cushion. Teresa noticed that her beauty was somewhat anonymous, a combination of regular features and fading colors; a blemish or a quirk of nature would have made her seem more interesting, but as it was, there was nothing to report. The lines of her unremarkable figure, with its long, slender bones, were traced by clothes worn with a certain weariness, as if they weighed too much. But a photograph on one of the bookshelves showed a woman with more flesh on her bones, and light in her eyes. It wasn't an old photograph either, and Teresa wondered if perhaps she had recently suffered an illness.

Valent's mother arrived carrying a tray, its tinkling

breaking the silence that had followed the initial exchange of pleasantries. The aroma of coffee seeped through the room; the old woman handed a steaming cup each to Teresa and Marini, but her daughter-in-law's remained on the tray, untouched.

"Nobody had anything against Roberto. He didn't have any enemies," their hostess said abruptly.

Teresa drained her coffee before replying.

"Well, he must have had at least the one," she said.

"Whoever did that . . . whoever did that to him is no enemy, but a psychopath."

"Why not both?"

Marta Valent started like a snail recoiling from a foreign touch. Teresa read the sudden movement as an indication that directness was not a welcome trait in this woman's world, and she found herself wishing she'd been a bit more sympathetic. Marta Valent was, at least for now, a victim who'd just suffered the violent loss of her partner, the father of her son.

"What was your husband like that morning, and in the days before?" Teresa asked in a softer tone, returning to routine questions.

"Just as usual: distant."

Teresa was surprised. She noticed a redness on the woman's ring finger, as if she'd been picking at it, twisting her wedding band around and around.

"Distant?" she repeated.

"Sorry, I meant drained. He worked too hard, that's what we all thought."

"Did he usually drop your son off at school?"

The woman lowered her eyes to the fabric of her skirt, which she had been smoothing with tremulous fingers ever since she'd sat down.

"No, I usually do that," she replied. "But I was ill that day. I suffer from terrible migraines. Roberto had left his phone at home, but I knew he'd be back for it; he can't cope without it."

"Because of work?"

Her eyes darted up to look at Teresa. Something inside her had been ignited.

"Yes, for work, of course," she answered. "But he didn't come back. After a couple of hours I began to worry and I decided to go looking for him at the construction site. But he had never made it there."

Teresa now addressed Valent's mother: "Did you notice anything odd in your son's behavior?" she asked.

The old lady's eyes were dry now, and dimmed, like worn glass marbles.

"No, there was nothing out of the ordinary. He was working too hard, that's true, but it wasn't to be for much longer. The project was due to be completed soon, in a few months or within a year at most. That's what he always told me when I fretted over him."

She took the empty coffee cups and disappeared into the kitchen, beating a hasty retreat. The clinking of crockery in the sink filtered through to the sitting room, together with the sound of quiet conversation.

Teresa knew who it might be.

"Is there someone else in there?" she asked the widow.

"The boy."

The boy, thought Teresa. As if he were someone else's son. A little stranger who lived in her house. Marta Valent had just made an unintended confession: that cozy, immaculate home she worked so hard to maintain was only a projection of what everyone expected of her. The truth was perhaps rather different, involving a mother who was emotionally distant from her own child.

"I would like to meet him," said Teresa, in a tone that made clear that this was not a request.

The woman frowned.

"Is that really necessary?"

Teresa smiled, seeking to reassure her, and nodded.

Diego Valent was a dutiful child: his mother had only to call him once, and without any particular inflection in her voice, for him to appear. He emerged from the kitchen with his little face flushed from crying, his eyes carrying a world of confusion.

A meek and wounded creature, Teresa thought.

The boy approached his mother, who put her hand on his shoulder. There was no other physical contact between them.

"Hello, Diego," Teresa said kindly. "I'm Superintendent Battaglia, but you can call me Teresa."

He watched her wordlessly. The tremor of his sobs had passed, replaced by curiosity.

"How old are you?"

"Ten," his mother answered in his stead, without giving him any time to decide whether or not to trust this stranger. "Diego has a stutter."

Those words struck the boy like a curse, and Teresa saw him squirming beneath the force of his humiliation. She felt furious on his behalf and pitied this woman who seemed to live in some kind of emotional vacuum. It wasn't a recent emptiness either; it had nothing to do with the death of her husband.

Pull your son into your arms, she thought, feeling irritated and sad. *Hold him tight and kiss him. Rest his head against your breasts, that's what they're there for.*

The inner workings of the Valent family were gradually emerging. She understood now why Diego looked like a miniature grown-up, dressed like an adult in classic navy blue trousers, a beige V-necked sweater, and a starched blue shirt.

There was a little bowtie around his neck. Teresa was sure it must feel like a noose to him.

Her instinct was to set him free, ruffle his hair, throw him on the sofa and tickle him senseless. Instead, she rooted around in her pocket and offered him a licorice wheel.

Diego looked at his mother.

"He doesn't eat sugar," she said.

"Ah, but this is special candy," Teresa told the boy. "It's sweet without being sweet."

"Sugar substitutes are no less harmful, Superintendent," the mother insisted.

"Superintendent, yes, but you can call me Teresa," she repeated, addressing the boy.

The woman seemed to realize she might have sounded rude.

"Forgive me," she said. "My husband was very strict about this kind of thing." She gestured at the bowls teeming with sweet treats. "Diego knows he mustn't take any."

Teresa wondered at the discipline they must have imposed on him. That's how you raise a rebellious teenager and an emasculated adult, she thought.

The boy's lips parted as she placed the licorice wheel back in her pocket. He was desperate for that piece of candy, so meager compared to the delicacies displayed in that house, yet so much more meaningful.

He was wringing his hands, mimicking his mother, and Teresa noticed that there was some dirt under his fingernails. She allowed herself a hopeful smile at the sight of that small flaw in the midst of so much perfection. There was life in him yet, a salutary trace of subversion. The boy noticed, too, and hid his hands behind his back. Teresa winked at him in whole-hearted approval.

She stood up, and Marini copied her. Though the inspector had kept quiet throughout—was he finally learning?—he hadn't missed any of the drama that had just unfolded. The look on his face spoke volumes: he was rooting for Diego just as much as Teresa was.

On the way out, the two police officers had a last routine exchange with Valent's widow.

"We'll be in touch soon," said Teresa. "If you have any questions or doubts, we are always available. And if you remember anything that you think might be useful, even if it seems trivial, call us immediately."

"Thank you," said the widow. "I know you will do everything you can to find whoever did this."

An emboldened Diego stood close to Teresa with his head tilted upwards, not wanting to miss anything about this policewoman who must have appeared so strange to his eyes.

Before they left, she stroked his head—perhaps for a fraction too long. She noticed Marini looking at her hand, and quickly pulled away.

Let it go, she told herself.

Back in the car, Teresa found it hard to tear her gaze away from the Valent family home; she kept her eyes on the outline of the house until it disappeared from sight. The pointed roof turning opaque in the sunlight, the dark windows, the shadows she pictured moving behind the glass . . . there was a sense of expectation, as if the house were waiting for something to come and repair the lives of its inhabitants.

She thought of the youngest of them all, the little trooper with dirty fingernails. She was sure he was doing the same right now, staring after her as she was leaving. Diego was a curious, spirited boy, with a spark his parents had sought to stifle with senseless prohibitions and empty tests—all those sweets displayed in full view but kept beyond reach.

He was used to being surrounded by the objects of his

desires every day without ever being able to reach out and touch them. Could there be anything more detrimental to a child's psychology than that?

Yes. A mother as cold as marble.

Teresa wondered whether the father had been emotionally reticent toward his son as well. She was inclined to think he must have been, given what Marta Valent had revealed: she'd described her husband as "strict," she'd even unwittingly called him "distant."

Distant enough that he might have been considered pathologically unemotional?

She told herself it was none of her business, but then quickly dismissed her own reservations; as far as she was concerned children were everyone's collective responsibility.

She looked for a sweet in her pocket and was astonished to realize that the licorice had disappeared.

After a moment's bewilderment, she started laughing.

She'd underestimated him. The Valent boy knew how to survive.

10

The days were getting shorter. Lucia noticed it because she spent so many afternoons shut in her room. Once she'd finished singing all the nursery rhymes she knew, the only interesting thing left to do was to look outside her window at the woods beyond the lawn.

She knew every single branch and the shapes of their shadows on the grass. She would watch them grow longer by the hour and inch closer to the house every day.

She knew why it happened: it had to do with the way the earth whirled around the sun. Even though she didn't always understand everything, she paid attention to the teacher's lessons in school and used her imagination to fill in the gaps. Lucia was aware that she wasn't as clever as the other kids, but she knew how those shadows moved and that they were due to get shorter again soon. She had always been entranced by the eternal battle between light and dark, but these days her fascination was mixed with the more pressing need to see the end of the winter (though it had barely begun), and with it the end of these premature evenings.

She stared into the woods. The wind had picked up and the tops of the fir trees were swaying; a few dry leaves that had fallen off the oak trees spun around in frenzied eddies. It was afternoon still, but already the light looked different; in another couple of hours the world would begin to descend into gloom until it finally slipped into total darkness.

That was the moment Lucia feared the most, for it was then that the ghosts appeared at the edge of the woods. Lucia had tried to tell her mother, but her mother refused to believe her. "Telling lies is naughty," she'd rebuked her, before locking her in her room.

But the ghosts weren't made up. Lucia had seen one. It had a face as pale as the snow that had frozen the village in the past few days, as white as the dog skull she had fished out of the river last summer with Mathias and Diego while Oliver stood apart and watched them.

Yes, that's what the ghost looked like when it stared at her from the forest: a white and gleaming skull.

Lucia was certain that Mathias had seen one, too, the day before. He was the head of their group, the bravest of them all, and yet he'd looked scared at their last meeting; he'd been watching the trees just as she was doing now, as if they were alive and could return his gaze.

Lucia had left a bowl of milk beneath her window. It was full now, but she knew she'd find it empty in the morning—just as she had for the past few days, even though the cat hadn't been home in a while.

Something else was slithering out of the forest, all the way up to her house. Something with a skull for a face.

Lucia had told her mother, but her mother hadn't believed her.

11

AUSTRIA, 1978

"Observe, record, forget."

Those were the rules of the School, unwritten commandments perpetuated by its employees, and passed down from veterans to newcomers. Nurse Braun had explained them to Magdalena, her voice barely louder than a whisper as if in deference to some holy vow of secrecy. And there were so many secrets in that place.

Magdalena had been tailing her more experienced colleague through the School's maze of corridors. Nurse Braun had taught her about every nook and cranny of the neglected building and every task that would be assigned to her now that she'd begun working there. Her training had been rather strange; holed up in the same room all day, typing up notes she couldn't really comprehend, Magdalena had seen nothing of the inner workings of the place outside of the refectory and the dormitory she retired to in the evenings.

By now she'd worked out that the School was staffed by only a handful of people: the director (whom she'd only seen once, on the day she was hired), Nurse Braun, two orderlies who performed all kinds of chores, the cook, and the kitchen maid, Marie, Magdalena's roommate. Marie never spoke, and in all the long evenings Magdalena had so far spent reading in her room, Marie had given her nothing more than a couple of shy, vaguely fretful glances. Magdalena had given up on trying to talk to her and now limited herself to greeting her in the morning, and wishing her goodnight when the lights were switched off.

Not many people would have been able to adapt to life in such an isolated place; more importantly, employment at the School depended on a trait that few possessed: discretion. You had to be willing to maintain a certain reserve for the rest of your life.

It had been a particularly difficult time for Magdalena's family, but then her aunt had found her this job.

"The School has high hopes for you. Do not disappoint it," said Nurse Braun as she ascended the worn steps of the main staircase. She was walking ahead of Magdalena, her body stiff, her shoulders straight like the arms of the crucified Christ who watched them from the mezzanine floor. The crimson sunset filtered through a rose window, engraving the Christ's sorrowful face and setting alight the blood that spilled out of his pierced ribcage. The crown of thorns on his head cast a bloated, twisted shadow on the plastered wall.

Like the tentacles of some monstrous beast, thought Magdalena, burrowing into her wool cardigan.

Nurse Braun always spoke of the School as a living, sentient being, as if its walls had eyes and ears: the School listened, and it passed judgment. Magdalena had been alarmed to hear her speak in this manner.

They reached the first floor where the Hive was located. It was so silent that it might as well have been empty. Their bodies carved through the air as if it hadn't been disturbed for centuries and had absorbed in that endless time the lives and stories of all those that had previously passed through it. Magdalena could feel its weight on her breastbone, on her throat. It squeezed around her until there was almost no room left for her to breathe.

"Observe, record, forget."

Those words meant that nothing that happened inside the School must ever be known beyond its confines. Nurse Braun had explained to her that she might occasionally witness practices she might deem bizarre. She must study their effects and meticulously record them in the notebook she'd received with her uniform.

Afterwards, she must forget it all. Every single thing.

Magdalena saw her take a bunch of keys from the pocket of her uniform, insert one into the keyhole, and pause.

"You will be responsible for their hygiene and nutrition," she said, reiterating Magdalena's tasks, "but you must never, ever cuddle them, or even speak a word to them. Physical contact must be kept to a minimum."

Magdalena nodded, wondering whether the residents were affected by some sort of medical condition. She hadn't mustered the courage to ask.

"And be careful with the subject in cot thirty-nine," her supervisor continued.

Magdalena's unease turned to worry.

"Why?" she finally asked.

Nurse Braun looked away, her eyes on the lake that could be seen beyond one of the windows.

"You'll see," was all she said. She gestured at Magdalena to pull over her head the piece of fabric she had been holding. Together, they lowered white veils over their faces.

"Remember," she said just before she pushed the door handle. "Observe, record, forget."

12

There was something distasteful in how quickly one could return to the habits of day-to-day life so soon after having laid eyes on a dead man—a kind of ignominious vitality, a sense of relief for having been spared a similar fate.

It felt aberrant, diving back into an everyday routine while a fellow human being's mutilated corpse lay trapped in a steel box inside a morgue.

People die every day, Teresa reminded herself. It was just another aspect of life. And yet, it was an uncomfortable thing to witness. It had you savoring every breath you took even while somebody else mourned a person who would never breathe again. It was cruel and inexorable. It was human.

She pulled her front door shut behind her, shrugged off her shoulder bag, and kicked off her shoes. The warmth of the wooden floor beneath her feet reminded her that sometimes it was the simple things that could soothe the soul, like those summers when she was a little girl and ran barefoot through the vineyards, stirring up dust and laughter. She could still smell the mineral scent of sun-baked earth and salt-rich stone, the sour odor of the green vines, the sweet flowering acacias. Sweat, the bitterness of dandelion flowers, drops of wine on her lips, stolen from her grandfather's glass. The essence of happiness.

It was a time that she remembered vividly, the memory amplified by the stillness of her home, still immersed in a silence that had remained unbroken since she'd walked out a few hours earlier. Solitude was an unobtrusive housemate; it took up no room and never touched anything. It had no smell or color. It was an absence, an entity defined in contrast to its opposite. Yet it existed; it was the force that made Teresa's cup of chamomile tea shake on its saucer on those nights when sleep refused to come to her rescue. That tinkling would spread through the house without ever encountering the warmth of another living creature. Solitude wrapped itself around Teresa like a dress a size too small, like an old-fashioned corset that makes you stand up straighter when others can see you, but leaves you gasping for breath when you're on your own.

She had learned to treat loneliness by applying the same principle that makes an antidote work on poison: she absorbed a small dose of it every day. She didn't try to elude it, nor did she seek distractions; she stood her ground and let it bite.

The house greeted her with the black and white smiles in the magnified photographs on the walls: cheerful, sometimes brazen, often imbued with a hint of melancholy that added to their effect. These were the friends who kept her company every evening when she picked up a book and settled into her sofa: Louis Armstrong, Ella Fitzgerald, Duke Ellington, Jeff Buckley . . . Her hibernating soul would come awake with a jolt of pleasure at the sound of their voices. She had bought the prints at a flea market, back when she could still bring herself to get in the car on a weekend and drive for miles looking for things to add to her nest. But that nest had never quite lived up to its name, and she'd spent most of her life there alone. It had taken her a long time to shrug off the sadness.

But she had kept moving, one step at a time, and in spite of everything, she was still standing. She hadn't lost her way, and she had forgiven herself. Life could be terrifying when you really looked at it and discovered what it could morph into, but it was still sacred, inviolable, a momentous journey to be faced with a racing heart and a sense of wonder.

She had to believe that, or else she would have lost her mind long ago.

"We're never truly alone," she murmured into the silence.

She wasn't sure whether she really believed that, or if it was merely a pretense designed to keep her going.

Her fingers brushed over the musical box that rested on the ottoman bench in the living room. The box was the only object in the house that had remained unaltered over the years. It was made of turquoise ceramic decorated with small yellow stars and shaped into the form of a sleeping angel, whose wings of fire-forged clay embraced Teresa and all her sorrows.

It smelled of talcum powder and shattered dreams. She wound it up.

The melody flowed out in notes that sounded like the tinkling of a little bell. It had always seemed agonizingly beautiful to Teresa, a lullaby that made her think of stars immersed in an indigo sea, stretching beyond ephemeral, silver-lined clouds: the enigma of the universe, a mystery that had endured through billions of years.

Teresa was not religious, she didn't really know what she believed in, but if she'd ever been asked for a sign, any sign, of some kind of divine presence in her life, she would have pointed at that sleeping angel, who hurt her with painful memories but also suffused her with a tenderness that heralded comfort.

She wondered if all that pain would finally mean something after she died: tiny fingers to hold, a soft cheek to kiss, the warmth of an angel she could finally look in the eye and cradle close to her heart.

No, she was never truly alone.

She allowed her melancholy to guide her steps as she moved from room to room, keeping time with that aching lullaby.

In the bathroom, she undressed, averting her gaze from the shapeless body reflected in the mirror. After a quick shower, she prepared for her nightly ritual, retrieving from the cabinet her glucose meter and blood lancet. She inserted the needle and secured the cap. She set it to the length required to pierce her skin and pricked the edge of a fingertip. A few drops of dark blood onto the glucose test strip. Seconds later, a reassuring figure on the screen. She picked up an insulin pen. Needles again. After years of this daily torture, they had become her very own crown of thorns. She felt her thighs for a spot that wasn't yet sore, and jabbed.

She sat on the edge of the bathtub for a time, looking at the tiles on the wall, then got up to tidy the room, concealing the traces of her illness inside the cabinet. She dressed wearily, as if the weight of the past few hours had made her body heavier than it actually was.

She went to the kitchen to make some dinner, something she could snack on while leafing through a book on the couch. Maybe she'd have a glass of wine with it, something to help her unwind and ease her into sleep.

She opened the fridge, and suddenly she felt as if she were floating in a sea of anonymous objects. Something else had materialized with the light that had switched itself on when she'd opened the door: a void. She couldn't recall what anything was called anymore. She turned her head this way and that in bewilderment, but her brain seemed only to register meaningless images, figures whose purpose and processes she couldn't identify.

She tried to speak, but her tongue felt like it had shrivelled up, and her jaw had stiffened in panic.

This was her world, but she couldn't recognize it.

She noticed that the lullaby had ended. Her angel had gone back to sleep just when she needed him the most. She was alone again. Alone and afraid.

Massimo hadn't slept. He'd spent the few hours of rest that Superintendent Battaglia had conceded her team drafting the report she'd requested from him. He had rewritten entire paragraphs several times before he was satisfied he'd gotten them right, and finally he had convinced himself he'd done a decent enough job. The night had just begun to fade by the time he'd emailed it to her, so he had been surprised to receive confirmation that his email had been read only moments after he'd sent it.

Like him, Teresa Battaglia was still awake, and like him, she was probably thinking about the murder that had taken place in that forest, sixty miles away. Massimo knew from his own experience how difficult it was to shake off the burden that this kind of evil placed on the psyche. He had always thought that the passage of time and the steady supply of dead bodies would eventually alleviate it, but now he knew better. He had seen men killed for spare change, women abused by those who claimed to love them, and children raised in unspeakable squalor, and yet his soul remained exposed, unshielded by the armor of indifference, and still grieved for every fallen creature.

He arrived at the police station very early, making no effort to deceive himself as to why: he had done it for her. Perhaps he was trying to make up for their disastrous first meeting—or, more likely, he wanted to impress that strong-willed woman who seemed determined to regard him as anything but a competent police officer.

He awaited her arrival in the office, armed with a gift and some news. He was sure she'd appreciate the former, but wasn't so confident about the latter.

Superintendent Battaglia walked in with Parisi and De Carli, another officer from her team who was practically her shadow. She was pointing something out on a piece of paper, and her face looked strained. The two men were nodding attentively, occasionally making a comment of their own. Together, they were clearly a triad, three elements that formed a single unit: the superintendent was the pivot and the two officers the arms of a well-oiled mechanism. Teresa spoke in terse sentences that she often left unfinished; it didn't matter, her companions already knew what she meant. They completed her sentences for her, and promptly assured her that whatever she requested, she could consider it done. They were not trying to suck up to her, it was simply a deep-seated respect.

Massimo suddenly felt foolish about his gift. He placed it on the superintendent's desk, pushing it away with a finger as if in a last-ditch attempt to distance himself from it. Even the fact that he had sat down suddenly felt like a rash decision.

The trio's attention was drawn by this slight movement and the rustling of the wrapping paper. Massimo watched as the superintendent's expression shifted from surprise to irritation, like a large cat coming across some unappetizing prey trespassing on its territory.

"What are you doing in my office?" she asked, every syllable marked out like a bite. This was not a good sign.

Massimo didn't quite know how to break the news to her. He would have rather started with the gift.

"It's my office, too, now," he said.

"Come again?"

Massimo had a feeling she'd heard him the first time.

"There's a burst water pipe in my office," he explained, his tone not nearly as confident as he'd intended. "I'll have to work in here for a while. With you. That's what Chief Ambrosini said."

Massimo saw Parisi and De Carli exchange a glance. Judging by the looks on their faces, the superintendent was not going to be pleased by this development.

"What's that?" she asked instead, spotting the gift.

"It's for you," said Massimo, feeling heartened. Perhaps there was a chance things between them could improve after all.

The superintendent sat at her desk. She studied the package. She opened it.

"Shit."

"Superintendent . . ." said Parisi, smoothing his perfectly symmetrical goatee, but she silenced him. She picked up one of the *krapfen* inside the box and sank her teeth into it, closing her eyes. The doughnut oozed its cream obscenely.

"There's some in there with chocolate filling," said Massimo softly, invitingly, and gesturing at the others to help themselves. But they kept watching the superintendent, looking concerned.

Teresa nodded slowly, her eyes still closed. She was in a state of ecstasy.

"I haven't had one of these in forever," she murmured.

Massimo smiled. He had finally glimpsed something human in her—other than her irritation. It had been easy, after all.

"You'd have been better off keeping it that way." It was De Carli who had spoken, and he seemed anxious.

Superintendent Battaglia opened her eyes: they were like slits.

"I am diabetic."

It took Massimo a moment to grasp the implication of her words, and when he did, he tried to take the box back, swearing under his breath. But she placed her hand on it, defiant.

"Are you trying to kill me?" she asked him.

He could feel his face burning.

"You must learn not to blush, Inspector. And when you feel the urge to swear, for God's sake just do it!" she said, letting go of the package. She gestured at Parisi and De Carli to leave and take it with them. They closed the door as they walked out, as if to contain the conflagration likely to be ignited by the superintendent's fury. Massimo could picture it already: words fired like bullets ringing in his ears, the explosion of her rage.

He felt like a piece of string stretched beyond breaking point.

"What do I have to do to get along with you?" he asked. He didn't mean it as a provocation; he just wanted to understand.

The superintendent was no longer even looking at him, concentrating instead on the photographs from the crime scene she was scrolling through on her computer screen.

"You have to do your job—that is if you even know how to," she answered. "I read your report last night."

"And?"

She looked at him again. "I flushed it down the toilet. You'll have to start again."

In that moment, the exhaustion Massimo had accumulated over the past twenty-four hours hit him all at once, as if a solid, shapeless mass had leapt onto his back and were trying to drag him down to the floor and into the ground.

But he realized he wasn't the only one who felt like hell. He'd thought the superintendent looked strained, but now he could see beyond the mask: stirring beneath its surface was something resembling pain, and perhaps, he was surprised to see, something akin to fear, too.

"I stayed up all night to write it," he said. He wanted to probe her, to find out more, but at the same time he felt the urge to take the conversation down a different route. For some reason, what he'd just glimpsed in her had unsettled him.

"Then you made a mistake. You should have rested instead, and worked on it when your mind was clearer."

But her tone was casual now, as if they were talking about the weather.

"I thought I did a good job," he said.

Teresa Battaglia put down the pen she'd been chewing on.

"Good isn't enough," she replied. "I can't go to the victim's family and tell them we're doing a good job. They want us sweating blood. Do you understand? That's what they need."

He nodded. He thought he *did* understand, now.

"What do I have to do?" he asked.

"You have to study. Something they don't teach you at university: the art of killing."

The superintendent didn't wait for him to reply. She stood up and went to the whiteboard in front of her desk.

"Initially I thought he must be quite young, but perhaps we need to revisit our calculations," she muttered. "I think he might be a few years older."

Massimo was intrigued. He walked up to her.

"Why?"

"Because there is a significant sadistic element," she explained, jotting her thoughts down in her unruly handwriting. "He's had plenty of time, years, to refine his fantasies. I expect he's somewhere between forty and forty-five years old. Possesses great physical strength. Either a local, or loves the mountains. He knows them well. His tracks stopped at the boulders, and that's no accident. He's probably a hunter. Judging by the way he killed, the depth of his psychosis is such that I doubt he drives a car."

Massimo's face twisted into a grimace of disbelief he couldn't hide. The superintendent caught it immediately. "You disagree, then?" she asked.

"Who? Me? I wouldn't dare."

"You can speak freely."

"Yeah, right."

She took off her glasses and stared at him.

"Don't waste my time, Marini. If you've got something to say, just say it and don't make me ask again. If not, you can spare me the sarcasm."

Massimo gestured at the board.

"Don't you think you're maybe . . . overdoing it?"

The superintendent followed his gaze, knitting her brow.

"Overdoing it?" he heard her echoing.

Massimo tapped his finger on the points she'd just written down.

"All these details you're reeling off," he said, "without even the shadow of a doubt . . . Isn't that a bit arrogant? How can you possibly tell if he drives a car or not?"

Teresa looked at him askance, a half-smile hovering on her lips.

"Arrogant? Not in the least. As for doubts . . . well, I have plenty of those, but they're part of the game, they're in the nature of things. When I stop having doubts, that's when I'll start to worry. Don't you agree?"

Massimo crossed his arms over his chest and didn't reply.

"Oh, all right then, tough guy!" she teased. But she turned serious again, and came up close to him, close enough that she had to tilt her chin up to look him in the eye. "I'll tell you something else. He doesn't even have a driver's license. He doesn't drive and he doesn't have a license because he's not able to. He's probably tried, but it's been one of his many failures. His unstable mind won't allow it. How can I tell? From what he's done to the victim and the way he's done it. A man who can claw another man's eyes out with his fingernails is bound to be affected by severe psychological disorders that would be impossible to disguise. He is not capable of successfully completing any kind of course of study—not even driving school. He can't hold down a job. He is unable to commit to anything or to concentrate on anything."

Massimo realized he'd been holding his breath. She handed him the marker.

"Go on then, write," she commanded, and went on with her dictation without waiting to see how he would react. "He lives alone, only a few miles from the crime scene. We need to narrow the area down."

Massimo acquiesced, though he remained doubtful.

"How can you be so sure he lives alone?" he asked.

"No one could bear to live with this type of individual; he will exhibit an alarming lack of personal hygiene and be unfamiliar with the concept of tidiness. The key word here is 'psychosis,' and the extent of his tells us a lot about him. What would you deduce from the fact that he killed with his bare hands and without using any means of ligature?"

"That the murder wasn't premeditated."

"Wrong. The murder wasn't *organized*. There's a difference. And yet there are a number of clues that would suggest the opposite. There are some inexplicable singularities. Contradictions. Something's not quite right."

"Such as?"

"Such as the staging. I mean the way he laid out the body—he didn't just toss it away, he made a display of it—and the traps . . . So, Inspector Marini, equipped as you are with your degree in . . . ?"

"Law."

"Christ . . . and with your experience of life in the big city, you tell us, you lift the veil: is our killer organized or disorganized?"

Silence.

The superintendent's expression flattened into a line of commiseration.

"Just as I thought. You'll have to start from zero—which is exactly where you are right now."

14

Lucia woke up to a scrabbling noise above her head, the sound of claws scraping and scratching insistently at the flagstone roof until the tiles shook and clanged against each other.

It was the crows; they liked to fly up there to devour their latest prey or to crack acorns open by gripping them in their powerful beaks and smashing them against the tiles. That was what Mathias and Diego had said when she'd told them about those mysterious, frightening noises she heard in the early hours of the morning—a time when, even during the summer, both air and light were dead cold.

Over the last few months Mathias, Diego and Oliver had become the center of her universe. Lucia knew she could trust them. That was why recent events had upset her so much. Diego's father was dead. They'd found him in the woods, two days after he'd gone missing.

Her father had shared the news while they were having dinner, and Lucia had found herself unable to move, her food sticking in her throat. She hadn't had a chance to speak to her friend yet, but she'd written him a note that she planned to deliver through their usual secret method of communication: by squeezing it through the shutters on his bedroom window, in the gap behind the hawthorn vase. On a page torn out from one of her school notebooks, she had written just two words: blood oath.

Diego would understand. His family—the one he'd chosen—was by his side and ready to share the burden of his grief, just like Jesus had carried the cross. These were the stories Lucia learned from Father Leandro at Sunday school, tales of forgiveness and paradise that pleased her because they made everyday life and its sacrifices seem more bearable. Even hers.

She brought her lips to the skin on the inside of her wrist; the scar was fading, but the memory of their oath remained vivid.

She rubbed at her eyes, still in the throes of sleep. Her room seemed brighter that morning. She pulled the covers over her face until the tip of her frozen nose met the warmth of her breath. The school was closed for a day of mourning, so she knew she could doze in bed for as long as she wanted. All night she'd been tormented by horrific nightmares. She kept seeing Diego's father, his eyes gone, ripped out—just as they had done with Saint Lucia, her holy namesake. She'd found out about that gruesome detail from her father, who had mentioned it at dinner while chewing on a mouthful of rare steak. Lucia had watched its reddish juices dribbling onto the plate and felt sick.

The scrabbling intensified, as if the birds had been gripped by some sort of savage euphoria. Lucia rolled over in bed and saw where the light was coming from: the shutters were wide open, though she was sure she'd closed them before going to bed. She drew the covers aside and put her feet on the cold floor. She quickly pulled on her wool socks and covered herself up as best she could with her flannel undershirt, which always bunched up around her waist while she slept.

The crows were engaged in an aerial dance of twirls and nosedives over the snow-capped lawn, letting out shrill, hoarse squawks as they flew. Lucia moved closer to the window. There were dozens of them, she'd never seen so many, and they seemed to be drawn to the house. One of the birds made straight for her and crashed into the windowpane, making her jump. She watched the bird writhing on the ground, its wings ruffled, until it regained its balance and took flight once more. It had left a smear of blood on the window and a smattering of barbules that swayed in the wind.

Lucia brought her face to the glass to look at the world through that crimson stain; the snow looked like a carpet of pink sugar paste. A dark, uneven smear cut through it. A thin trail of blood. She followed it with her eyes. It stretched all the way to the foot of her window, where the bowl of milk stood empty. Something was dangling from the corner of one of her shutters.

When she realized what it was, Lucia screamed.

15

The archives at the police headquarters were kept in a cellar of reinforced concrete on the lower ground floor, illuminated by neon lights and populated by dust and endless parallel rows of steel shelves.

Even the elevator didn't quite reach all the way down there, as if the basement were a world apart and didn't belong with the rest of the building. You had to go down a flight of stairs where the lights never worked properly; sometimes they flickered like strobe beams, but most of the time they were black fissures that served no purpose whatsoever. The handyman blamed it on humidity; he said it spoiled the light bulbs. But others went as far as to suggest, seemingly without a trace of self-consciousness, that it was all down to some kind of supernatural presence that was evidently averse to the notion of archives.

The place was also known as Purgatory, for it was there that you were usually dispatched to when you'd done something you needed to atone for.

And it was there that Teresa had sent Massimo Marini, instructing him to look through the physical records and the digital archives for comparable murder cases.

The young detective needed to learn the meaning of discipline, but mostly Teresa had wanted to get him out of her sight for a few hours. She'd seen something flash across his face, something that had alarmed her: he had looked at her as if he could sense her fear.

It was just an isolated episode, she kept telling herself. *It didn't mean anything.*

But for a moment the night before she hadn't been able to recall the names of everyday objects, and even though she'd recovered soon enough, she had still felt lost for several hours afterwards, as if she'd just emerged from inside a tornado. It had never happened to her before, and now she worried that it might be the first of many episodes to come.

She hadn't told anyone. Confiding in other people was just not something she did, but now she found herself wondering how much longer she would be able to provide for herself. It was her worst nightmare, the idea that she might become dependent on somebody else.

Banishing those ominous thoughts from her head, she took the last few steps in the dark and found herself in Purgatory. Its sole other occupant was at the opposite end of the room, sitting at a desk worn with use. His face was lit only by the bluish light of a computer screen.

"You'll ruin your eyes," she told him.

Marini didn't look up. On the desk in front of him, Teresa placed the report he'd sent her just before dawn, and which she'd printed out and covered in corrections.

The inspector gave it a brief glance. "I thought you'd flushed it down the toilet?" he said.

Teresa lowered herself into a chair across from him.

"You didn't do a very good job with it. It would have been a lie to tell you otherwise."

He grimaced.

"I'm not looking for empty praise."

"Then what *have* you come looking for, all the way here?"

Marini didn't respond.

Teresa didn't stop.

"At first I thought you must have run away from some kind

of romantic debacle," she said. "But I was wrong, wasn't I? Your perfectionism, and how desperately you seem to crave my approval, make me think there is a parent involved—too interfering, too demanding, even now that you're a grown man. An overbearing presence. Your father, perhaps?"

"I didn't know you had studied psychology."

"No need for any of that to work *you* out."

He finally looked at her. There was a flush of anger on his cheeks, but also a trace of resignation, which mollified her.

"Come on, it's not the end of the world," she said encouragingly.

"Don't tell me it could be worse. That would be so predictable. I'd have to revise my opinion of you."

"Of course it could be worse, but who gives a damn? You did the right thing to seek out your destiny elsewhere."

"Are you expecting me to thank you?"

"You're welcome," she shot back.

Massimo gestured at a stack of files. "Aren't you going to ask me what I've found?"

"Nothing, I presume."

"But you knew that already."

Teresa shrugged.

"I would have remembered if there had been a similar case before."

She had already known he wouldn't find anything. She was as familiar with the contents of the archive as her grandfather had been with the writing in the little notebook where he kept score for all his rounds of Morra, that ancient card game of chance. Hundreds of dates and numbers. When she was a little girl, she used to sit on his lap and test him; Grandpa Pietro had never made a single mistake. Teresa had relied on the archive on a daily basis for almost forty years now. Religiously. There wasn't a page among those thousands from which she hadn't learned something.

One of Marini's eyebrows shot up.

"I wasn't expecting to have to work with a profiler," he said.

She burst out laughing.

"I sense a hint of irony in your tone, though to be honest, I'm the only one who's actually working here," she replied, winking at him. "All you do is sit around and look confused."

Marini turned his face back to the monitor and resumed rolling the wheel of the mouse. Files pertaining to a number of violent deaths scrolled before his eyes. Teresa could see them reflected in his dark irises.

"I still think the best way to solve a murder is to search for clues and evidence, not try and guess what the killer might look like," he said after a time.

Teresa was beginning to find him funny.

"Based on what I've read on your report, you're the one who's been doing all the guesswork," she replied. She leaned closer. "It's true that criminology is not an exact science. Nothing about it is certain, and every case is different. Criminology is an art. The art of learning to observe and to see things someone like you could never even glimpse. It's not magic; it's interpretation. Probability, statistics. Never certainty."

Marini stared at her for several moments.

"You really believe all that," he murmured.

Teresa let out an involuntary sigh.

"Do you think we're playing some kind of game, here? Cops and robbers?" she asked.

"I think . . ."

"No, you don't think. That much is clear. Let me tell you a story."

"Is it really necessary?"

"Yes, yes it is."

He stretched his arms out and let them fall down on either side of his chair.

Teresa didn't allow his lack of enthusiasm to discourage her. She was used to seeing this kind of attitude in new recruits who found themselves facing, for the first time in their lives, a number of unpalatable truths.

"Our hero lives in a small, remote village," she began. "No more than a few hundred souls in all. He begins his life of crime as a grave robber. He is obsessed with the feet of corpses, he collects them. Some people dream of having a walk-in closet full of shoes; his is full of feet. I know it sounds funny now, but that's not what you would think if you'd seen it."

"Superintendent . . ."

"As a child, he was fascinated by women's shoes, but whenever his mother caught him trying on some of hers, she would punish him by dipping his feet in boiling water. As an adult, he wanted to change sex, but instead he settled for buying dozens of pairs of women's shoes. He stopped desecrating graves and began killing young women. He picked his victims during the summer, when he could see their feet. He would cut them off and fit them inside the shoes he kept at home. The police came close to catching him several times, but I guess you could say he was always one step ahead. So, what do you think—good story?"

"It would make a great film."

"Yes, except that it actually happened, and not so far from here. It was in the nineties, the guy was called Igor Rosman, and his victims were real."

Marini's smirk had disappeared.

"How did the story end?" he asked.

"I arrested him."

He didn't reply. Teresa held his puzzled gaze.

"It's only by studying the minds of criminals like Rosman and hundreds of others like him that we have been able to learn what we now know about the way a murderer's psyche works," she told him. "We know how he thinks and what he thinks about, and we even know where to look for him. That's why it's important that we figure out what kind of killer he is. If he's disorganized, we need to look for a clouded mind, a misfit who lives on the fringes of society."

"And if he isn't disorganized?"

"Then we've got a problem, because people like that tend to hide behind seemingly perfect lives. Do you understand what I mean? It could be that teacher who's handsome and a little bit shy, or the prim and proper next door neighbor, a guy just like you." Teresa rose to her feet. "Come on. We've got a two-hour drive ahead of us."

"Where are we going?"

"Back to the crime scene. He's left a message."

Marini looked at her in confusion.

"Who?"

Teresa threw the car keys at him.

"The killer."

16

"Do you think he wanted to mark out the house?"

Marini had spoken in the faintest of whispers, as if the troubling sight of that exposed flesh were too indecent to be discussed out loud. It was the carcass of a hare, dangling from one of the windows of the house. It had been skinned, and its neck broken. Robbed of its fur, it looked fearsome: its skull was wrapped in lean, taut muscle, and its jaws hung wide open.

Teresa didn't reply. She'd had the same thought.

Hugo Knauss, the local police chief, pulled her aside. Stocky and not particularly tall, with light skin and coppery hair, he always looked like he was smiling, even when he was dead serious. It was because of the way he moved his chapped lips, and how he always seemed to be squinting, the cold-ravaged skin around his eyes stretching them sideways.

"It was the little girl, Lucia Kravina, who called us. She was alone at home," he told her.

Teresa nodded, her eyes on the carcass of the wretched creature.

"Has this ever happened before?" she asked.

"No, I've never seen anything like it, and I've been working here almost all my life. You might get a prankster stealing people's washing from the line, but that's about as bad as it gets. We've already had a murder this week, and now this . . ." He spat on the ground. "Do you think it's some kind of professional criminal who did this? Could it be a warning?"

Teresa believed it was something more dangerous than that.

"No," she said. "I don't think this has anything to do with organized crime. What's the Kravina family like?"

The man snorted.

"The father's a loafer who can't hold down a job. The mother's a waitress at a diner in town, and she works the evening shift at the pub to make ends meet. I've seen better, but I suppose they're harmless."

Teresa refrained from noting how the most seemingly unremarkable lives could hide a sinister ferment, a putrid humus of frustration and rage.

"Harmless," she echoed, rolling the word over her tongue as if each of its letters tasted unpleasant. "There is no creature on this earth that is truly harmless, Chief Knauss."

The man stopped chewing the gum he'd been pushing around inside his mouth ever since they'd arrived at the scene. He seemed personally offended, as if he were the one being scrutinized instead of the little girl's parents.

"We're not savages," he told her. "No one from Travenì would ever do something like this."

Teresa understood: he harbored a misplaced sense of loyalty toward this community and felt he had to exculpate its members.

"So it couldn't have been a local because they would be a local. An interesting observation, Chief," she replied, though she wasn't sure whether he could tell she was being ironic.

Knauss took his leave with a silent nod while Teresa continued to examine the wall of the house. It was bleeding. Crimson tracks ran down the plaster all the way to the snow, like tears. The marks were frozen now, but it was clear that the creature had been killed not long before it had been hooked to the shutters.

Teresa could feel Marini's silent presence behind her.

"They're everywhere," she remarked.

The wall was covered in dozens of handprints belonging to the person who had committed this act.

"What do they make you think of?"

He seemed hesitant.

"Come on, Inspector. Out with it."

"Cave paintings," he finally said, and it was obvious from how tightly his lips were pressed together that he was embarrassed.

Teresa nodded.

"Exactly."

She'd thought the same thing, remembering an image she'd seen somewhere—a TV documentary, perhaps?—of caves full of the same kind of pattern. More than ten thousand years of human history, and as many thousands of kilometers, separated that image from the scene before her, yet there was an impalpable connection between the two that Teresa could scarcely bring herself to admit. For a moment, it had looked to her like a ritualistic expression, the work of a childlike personality wanting to leave its mark on the world, and be initiated into adulthood.

But there was nothing childish in the hand that had left those primitive marks. She brought her own hand to hover over one of them, taking care not to touch it: the print was significantly larger than her hand, the palm wide and the fingers robust. Teresa felt a shiver course through her. It had almost felt like brushing against the maker of those signs.

"There are plenty of footprints, too. They come from the woods," said Marini, breaking the spell.

Their eyes followed the tidy line of footprints. Teresa pictured a lone figure crossing the snowy lawn at night, eyes fixed on the house, and holding a little carcass in his hand.

Why?

"There's only one set of footprints, and they end at the window," she noted.

She watched the expression on Marini's face change into one of horror and determination. He looked at the Kravina home.

"He's still here," he said, reaching for the gun sheathed inside his coat.

"Calm down, Inspector. Look closer," Teresa commanded, leaning toward the ground. "Some of the footprints are much deeper than others. He must have retraced his steps."

She straightened up.

"That's clever. I expect these footprints will also come to a stop somewhere inside the woods."

Marini seemed overwhelmed by all the detail. Teresa could sympathize.

"You can't figure him out, can you?" she asked. "Well, neither can I."

"Are you sure it's Valent's killer who put on this show? Surely any sadist could have done it."

"Any sadist? No. But you're right: it is a show. An exhibition, just like the presentation of Valent's body. There is a deeper meaning to it all that I'm sure we'll figure out eventually."

"What do you think about the dead animal? A threat?"

Teresa shook her head.

"That's not how it works. The urge to harm animals is a trait commonly found in inveterate killers, but they usually act upon it in private. It's like a first step toward fulfilling the fantasies that torment them, clamoring to be put into practice."

Marini looked around.

"Now what do we do?" he asked.

"Now I want to talk to the girl."

• • •

Lucia Kravina was like a grown-up already. She was only eight years old, but she'd been the one to bring coffee to the police officers, and she seemed much less disoriented than her mother, who'd only just come home, and hadn't even given her daughter a hug for comfort. Judging by her appearance, Teresa surmised she must have been very young when she had Lucia, probably before she was ready to stop being a little girl herself. With chipped, black nail varnish, bitten nails, a streak of pink and fading highlights in her hair, and wearing leggings that were too tight for her with a leather jacket cropped just below her breasts, she looked like an overgrown teenager. Parisi had already begun taking her statement, but soon gestured at Teresa to signal they wouldn't glean much from her.

The real child, then, was this woman with absent eyes, which meant that Lucia must have been used to looking after herself. Teresa was sure she was the one who kept the house in her mother's stead. It was a humble home, but it was tidy and clean.

Teresa hadn't approached the little girl yet, but had been watching her from a distance. She had been trying to figure out how to avoid scaring her, how to earn her trust without causing her too much suffering. The child had witnessed enough violence for a day—not only the sight of the wretched carcass hanging from her window, but now the arrival of these strangers barging into her home. And one of those strangers was Teresa.

"Lucia is a strong girl. She's had to grow up fast, but she's as sweet as any child her age."

Teresa turned around.

The man who had spoken was smiling at her now. He was wrapped in a green wool coat, face half hidden behind a thick scarf with a checked pattern, and he wore a felt hat with a thin band and a bow of small, silky feathers. He wasn't much taller than Teresa.

"I'm sorry," said the stranger. "I saw the way you were looking at her."

"You're a good observer," said Teresa.

He smiled and held out his hand. His irises were a remarkably light blue.

"Carlo Ian," he said, introducing himself. "I'm the village doctor. I know the Kravina family well. I was concerned when I saw the police cars."

The man must have been long past retirement age—a whole decade, perhaps. Teresa shook his hand.

"Superintendent Battaglia," she said. "I'm handling the Valent case."

Ian's expression darkened. His eyes shot to the window, toward the form that still hung outside. A forensic photographer was capturing it from various angles.

"Do you think it was the same man who did this and killed Roberto?" he asked.

Teresa didn't get a chance to respond.

"Doctor!"

Lucia Kravina ran into the doctor's arms, and he crouched down to let the child bury her face in the curve of his neck. They stood very close, speaking in whispers, like a pair of best friends trading secrets. Teresa felt relieved. She was glad to know there was someone in that little grown-up's life with whom she could still act like a child. She heard her sob, and watched him dry her tears and make her smile by pulling a lollipop out of thin air.

Teresa almost felt like she was intruding. But the doctor came to her aid.

"Lucia, this lady is here to find out who did this terrible thing," he said to the little girl.

The girl studied Teresa, but her arms remained wrapped around the doctor's neck.

Teresa smiled at her.

"Hello, Lucia. My name is Teresa," she said.

The girl bit her lip. She seemed unsure whether to answer or flee.

"She's here to help you," Ian told her. "Do you trust me?"

The girl nodded.

"Then you can trust her, too. I'll vouch for her." He winked.

Lucia allowed herself a smile. She was a pretty little thing, perhaps a bit too thin, but with eyes so black and brilliant that you could almost see stars reflected in them.

The child told them about the bowl of milk she had been finding empty every morning, and about the ghosts that lived in the forest. Doctor Ian began to look concerned. Marini, on the other hand, looked vaguely amused, as if he thought they were wasting their time listening to a little girl's fantasies.

But as far as Teresa was concerned, she knew exactly what her next question would be.

"Where do you usually see these ghosts, Lucia?"

Without a trace of hesitation, the girl pointed at a spot on the edge of the woods.

"Over there. He hides in the trees and watches me."

17

AUSTRIA, 1978

A new day was dawning over the School. It was the light of a feeble sun; it brought neither warmth nor comfort. It crept over the stone walls of the little chapel, displacing the shadows. Yet it was shadow itself in all but name.

Magdalena sat on a pew across from the unadorned altar and observed the advancing light, feeling a growing sense of revulsion. There was something wrong with the School, and whatever it was, it infected everyone who set foot in it and the nature that surrounded it; every living creature, every pebble, every frigid breath of wind was imbued with a piercing hardness. Even that little church in front of the refectory was devoid of the warmth you would expect to find in a place of prayer and penitence. Only the figure of the crucified Christ that hung in the apse exhibited any signs of human longing. Everything else was built along grey and rigid lines.

Magdalena looked at the crucifix, but couldn't bring herself to pray. Never in her life had she felt so distressed. She was waking up in tears every night, tormented in her dreams by the things she saw in the School.

There was something wrong with it all. Something so slight as to be formless and impossible to describe—which was why she had failed to understand it at first, and had now ended up an accomplice in what was effectively an affront to life.

She brought her hands closer to her face so that she could see them properly. They looked tainted.

No one at the School seemed to understand her anguish. They regarded her with suspicion and monitored her every move, so that Magdalena had begun to wonder whether she was the one singing off-key in an otherwise pitch-perfect choir.

She raised her gaze once more, and in that moment, a shaft of light broke through one of the stained glass windows. The light took on a reddish hue and pierced the crucifix at rib height. The blood seemed to come alive and gush from the wound. This was the second time she had seen this sign. The first had been when Agnes Braun was explaining the rules of the School to her: "Observe, record, forget."

Magdalena shuddered in awe.

That figure before her showed neither hope nor any notion of salvation. It was a representation of torture. The Christ returned her gaze with the disconsolate look of those who know that nobody will help them. There could be no accusation fiercer than the despair contained in those eyes.

Magdalena rose to her feet. She had finally understood what she needed to do: she had to bring change.

She walked briskly through the deserted corridors of the ground floor, as if she couldn't wait a moment longer to start making amends, until she reached the entrance hall. She took a few steps up the main staircase, then stopped.

Agnes Braun was watching her from the mezzanine floor, her interlaced hands resting over her sunken abdomen. Something about the way she was smiling disturbed Magdalena. It was as if she could read her mind, probing and widening the cracks in her soul until the very core of Magdalena's being seemed to shake with fear.

"I need to go to them," said Magdalena, steeling herself.

Agnes shook her head slowly.

"The first floor patients no longer fall within your remit," she said, not unkindly. "From now on I will assign you different duties, more suitable for someone with your temperament."

Magdalena's hand gripped the marble banister. She was sure that her fingers were even colder than the dead stone beneath them.

"*Patients?*" she exclaimed. "I need to go to them," she repeated, more forcefully this time.

Agnes's smile vanished.

"This School has treated you like family, Magdalena. It won't do to bite the hand that feeds you."

"I don't want to bite anything, I just want to help them."

Agnes raised her face to the sky, and the curve of her chin in the air was like a crescent moon.

"Is that not why we are all here?" she asked.

Magdalena took a deep breath.

"The things we do to them don't help. They're . . . *weird*," she said. "This is not what they need. We should—"

Agnes Braun listened impassively to Magdalena's misgivings.

"What we do here is to apply certain medical principles," she replied calmly. "Who are you to question a scientific procedure?"

Magdalena didn't reply. She realized they were no longer alone in the room. The rest of the School's staff was now gathered in the entrance hall, watching with stern looks her attempt to defy the Rules.

"Do any of the subjects display the signs of physical abuse?" said Agnes.

Magdalena looked at her.

"No, Mrs. Braun."

"Do we not provide them with generous meals and perfectly hygienic conditions?"

Magdalena concealed her bitterness.

"Yes, Mrs. Braun."

"Then, for the love of God, what are we even talking about?"

It sounded like she had given this speech before. Magdalena could see, now, that she must have grown used to manipulating people's minds.

"There is one thing missing, Nurse Braun. Love," she said.

For the first time since Magdalena had met her, Agnes looked genuinely surprised.

"Seclusion can have unexpected effects on those who aren't used to it," she replied. "I worry about the strain on your nerves. Go to your room and rest. We won't need you today."

Magdalena's gaze sought out the cook and one of the orderlies, but there wasn't the faintest trace of sympathy in their eyes. Marie was watching from behind the kitchen door, her apron soaked with dishwater.

"Magdalena," said Agnes again, with chilling composure. "Go."

The walls of the School seemed to close in on her, the cold was suddenly more biting, and Magdalena felt her determination slipping away like the water from Marie's wet hands. She retreated. Not out of fear, but from the knowledge that she was alone and unarmed, facing a fortress that could outlast any siege.

She thought not for the first time that the School was a living organism that was now rejecting her as a potentially dangerous foreign body.

She walked out, away from all those hostile gazes. Back in her room, she pulled down her suitcase from the top of the wardrobe and filled it haphazardly with her few possessions. She was certainly going to miss the substantial salary paid by the School. It had felt like a blessing. But now she knew what the money was really for: to buy her silence.

She stopped as she was about to put on her coat.

She suddenly realized that saying nothing at all only ever helps the executioner, never the victim. What would her escape be if not the latest contribution to the conspiracy of silence that reigned within those walls?

She let go of her coat and sat on the bed. The springs creaked under her weight.

She was not going to run away. She was not going to abandon them. She was only going to leave if she could take them with her. All she needed was time. Time and proof.

18

The millennial forest of Travenì echoed with the steady dripping of water and the muffled rustle of snow slipping from overburdened tree branches. All else was silence. The freezing cold seemed to have placed life on hold and stilled its songs for a few months.

Teresa carefully picked her way along the path marked out by the forensics team to make sure she didn't accidentally compromise any evidence. Walking behind her, Marini did the same. He had tried to help her once or twice when she'd seemed about to slip on some treacherous patch of ice, but Teresa had batted his hand away.

"Maybe it's not the same guy. It could just be some pervert, not the killer," she heard him say.

She didn't bother to reply. She was convinced that wasn't the case, and surely the fingerprint tests would soon show a match with the prints found on Valent's body, proving her right. The fact that he'd been observing potential prey—spying on them, even—did not necessarily imply a sexual motive. It simply suggested that his homicidal instincts had awakened once more. There was always a voyeuristic element to these kinds of cases: the killer, patrolling his hunting grounds, might enter people's homes when there was nobody there, perhaps steal some of their belongings—totems with which to fuel his fantasies. Hugo Knauss had said that someone had been stealing people's washing. Teresa had found it an interesting detail. But what was most alarming was that there were no more than a thousand people living in Travenì, tourists excluded, so it was very likely that the killer was known to the victim, and perhaps even to the Kravina family. The thought of little Lucia alone at home worried Teresa. She would arrange for the house to be placed under police protection, like the Valent residence.

It was still afternoon, but already twilight was descending onto the forest. The shortest days of the year were approaching. It was the worst possible time to be hunting a killer who prowled the mountain trails.

"We must alert the municipal authorities, but without causing panic," she told Marini. "And let's be careful with the press; if we stroke the killer's ego, we'll only end up encouraging him."

"Are you worried they'll make front page news of him?"

She wasn't worried, she was certain. It had happened before, and the literature was full of examples of killers who'd ended up in a twisted dance with the press, a game both parties relished.

"It will happen. It's inevitable," she said. "People are alarmed by this kind of news, but also secretly fascinated. It's the lure of evil. It's the same reason your heart's beating so fast right now—it is, isn't it? You're wondering what it would be like to run into him at this very moment, hiding behind that tree over there. You're wondering what kind of face someone like that might have, how he would look at you."

"I'm not afraid."

Teresa stopped to look at him.

"And yet I'm sure I felt your hand shaking earlier, Inspector."

He ignored her and pointed at the stream bubbling through clumps of ivy.

"The forensics team say that's where his trail vanishes," he said.

Once again, the killer had protected himself. Teresa had never seen anything like this before: the perpetrator had no qualms taking risks, spreading traces of his DNA around, walking on the snow and leaving his footprints everywhere, showing them, in dozens of identical prints, the shape of the hand that had ripped the victim's eyes out. But the moment he'd had enough, he was also capable of disappearing inside the forest, like an animal.

"Rational and deranged at the same time. Rational and deranged," she murmured, watching the water flowing in limpid jets.

"If what you say is true, then there's a monster walking around in the village."

Teresa blew hot air onto her stiff fingers. Flecks of ice had caught in the wool of her gloves.

"Someone's going to have to explain to me some day what constitutes a monster," she said. "That's what we like to call them, yet we can't look away, we won't change the channel, and that's because we know they're just like the rest of us: human. That's what captivates us, the realization that a small part of them exists in every one of us."

Marini stood perfectly still and stared into the forest. Perhaps he was trying to work out what secrets it held, what fresh horrors it might soon witness.

"You think a monster lives inside us all?" he asked. He sounded doubtful.

"I'm sure of it. If you're lucky enough that fate has been generous and bequeathed you with a half-decent life, the monster will lie dormant until your last breath. But the monster inside these people has been fed by trauma and abuse."

Marini's eyes searched her face.

"You see them as victims?" he asked with a mixture of shock and revulsion. But Teresa was used to her opinions causing vehement reactions. It wasn't easy to admit there was something human in that kind of horror—it was far more reassuring to regard it as entirely alien.

"They always are," she replied firmly. "Condemned to live off the only thing that can placate their gnawing hunger."

"Hunger for what?"

"Power. Absolute power over another human being."

Marini took a step forward and a twig snapped beneath the sole of his shoe. An identical sound echoed from among the trees further up the slope. They turned their heads toward the noise. The fog seemed to be rolling down from the peak.

"An animal," said Marini.

Teresa motioned at him to stop talking. She could have sworn someone had been watching her from the moment she'd stepped into the forest. She'd told herself it was an illusion, but she didn't think it could be causing auditory hallucinations. She picked up a branch and snapped it in half. From up the slope, about twenty meters to the east, came the same sound.

"It's not an animal," she said, her breath hitching. "It's mimicry."

Someone was hiding up there in the mist and the lengthening shadows. Someone who'd just begun playing a game with them, and who knew he was perfectly safe. Hunting for him now among the mountain's gorges and deep crevasses, just as night was about to fall, would be impossible.

And so, protected by the mountain and the darkness, he watched them both.

19

Snow had transformed the Sliva river valley. The gully through which the river flowed had become a kingdom of ice, its verdant fronds supplanted by a white expanse of shimmering crystal, and the lance-like forms of the fir trees transformed into downy pillows. The voice of the water had changed: the sound that rose from the riverbed was no longer a thunderous rumble, but a subdued murmur. The cold had put a brake on the rapids, while the shallower chutes and the stagnant pools had frozen over.

Even the waterfall beyond the cave, where the Sliva plunged into a deep ravine among boulders carved out by time, had been stilled; only the finest of trickles slid down its gleaming, transparent stalactites.

To Diego the frozen waterfall looked like a stairway to the sky. He wondered if his father had climbed up steps as pretty as those when he'd died. His grandmother kept saying that his father was watching over him from heaven now, but to Diego, this was hardly a reassuring prospect. His father's eyes had never looked at him with anything other than unadulterated sternness. He had never hit Diego, and he had never raised his voice either, as far as Diego could recall. But there was no need for any of that; all his father had to do was to look at him for Diego to know what a disappointment he was. Diego knew that his father's body currently lay in a morgue, without his eyes. But when Diego had dreamt of him the night before, his father had been whole: he had appeared dressed in nothing but a white sheet, and had simply scowled. Even now that he was dead he was displeased with Diego. And now that he was up in the sky, he was going to find out all the secrets and lies that Diego used in order to survive.

Diego reached his friends with a last leap over an old, fallen tree trunk. Mathias and Oliver were throwing stones at the frozen riverbank. When they saw him, they stiffened. Diego had witnessed the same reaction in everyone he'd come across in those last few hours, except for the police lady with the red hair. Instead of being drawn closer, people seemed to be repelled by you when you were in mourning. They recognized the smell of death, and they feared it, just as animals fear the scent of hunters.

He looked pleadingly at his friends while trying to catch his breath.

"It's s-still m-me," he said, tripping over the words. It could be a struggle to get them out, whereas his thoughts always ran so smoothly. He hated words sometimes.

Mathias's hand clasped the back of Diego's neck and pulled him close.

"I was scared you wouldn't come," he said, hugging him tight. Oliver, who was not only a year younger than they were, but smaller, too, soon joined their embrace.

"I r-ran away," he said. His mother didn't want him going out.

Inside the circle of their arms, Diego felt like he was in a nest of familiar smells and shared breaths. But someone was missing.

"L-Lucia?" he asked.

Mathias shrugged.

"She might not come today," he said.

Diego noticed a mark on Mathias's neck. He stretched his finger out to push down the collar of Mathias's coat, but

Mathias wouldn't let Diego touch him; he knew what question he'd be asked next.

"Mom can't do anything about it," he said. "Otherwise there'd be hell to pay for her, too."

Diego and Oliver exchanged a sad look.

"Does it hurt?" asked the younger boy.

Mathias rolled his shoulders as if to shake off the pain he was not willing to acknowledge.

"It's not me I'm worried about, it's my little brother, Markus," he said, breaking the embrace. He picked up a rock and flung it at the river. It shattered the ice and sprayed frozen shards onto his flushed cheeks. He picked up another rock, larger than the first, but this time his hand froze mid-air.

Diego saw him staring at the trees across the stream, squinting as if he were trying to focus on some distant object.

"W-w-what are you l-looking at?" he asked.

"Someone's watching us from the forest," Mathias replied.

Diego followed his gaze but couldn't see anything.

"It must be a deer," said Oliver. "My dad says the cold drives them down into the valley and closer to the village."

"If it's an animal," said Mathias, "then this will scare it off."

He pulled his arm back and threw the rock. It whistled in a taut arc through the air and vanished into the vegetation, swallowed by the snow.

They stood staring at the spot where the stone had disappeared.

"I g-guess it was n-nothing," said Diego. He wasn't sure why, but he was breathing a little easier now.

Mathias started laughing.

"You should have seen your faces!" he said. "You fell for it!"

"Idiot!" Oliver protested.

"J-Jerk."

It landed not too far from their feet, its dull rattling cloaked by their laughter, which quickly died down. The thing rolled onto the flat rock they used as a diving platform during the summer, then came to a stop and stared at them.

They turned toward it in unison. Whoever had thrown it had taken good aim.

It was white and not much larger than a fist.

A squirrel's skull.

20

The police station in Travenì looked like a mountain hotel. Until twenty years ago, the border crossing nearby had bustled with activity, and there had been almost fifty officers stationed there. The station's decline had begun with the lifting of customs controls, and now most of its rooms lay empty, its cafeteria dismantled. Hugo Knauss and his team made do by cooking their own food or bringing in meals prepared at home by their wives. Some officers still spent nights there, returning to the bottom of the valley at the end of the week—unless it was their turn to take the weekend shift.

That was where Teresa had decided to base the investigation. She'd had a sizeable room set up for meetings between her team and the local police, the first of which had just begun. They hadn't got off to a good start.

Teresa looked at Knauss over the frame of her reading glasses.

"Are you telling me we already have names and surnames for a pool of potential suspects?" she asked him, enunciating every word. Those who knew her well knew this was never a good sign.

Knauss held her gaze with his customary lopsided smile, which Teresa had begun to find exasperating.

"We have the situation under control, Superintendent," he assured her.

She rubbed her eyes beneath her spectacles.

"I'm glad to hear that, Chief Knauss. What a relief," she replied.

"Now let's not get personal about this."

"I'm not, but I might if you keep at it."

Knauss did not respond.

"So," Teresa pressed, "do we or do we not have a list of suspects?"

He surrendered—at least for the time being.

"We do," he confirmed.

Teresa took off her glasses, and placed them folded onto the table in front of her.

"Then why the hell didn't you say so before?" she asked.

His smile was genuine now.

"They're good kids. I can vouch for them," he said.

Teresa looked at Parisi, who was standing next to her, then at De Carli, and finally at Marini. It was like she was talking to them; that sequence of glances was the equivalent of a lengthy sequence of imprecations. She felt like screaming, but only allowed herself a sigh, holding her head in her hands. She felt tired in a way she wasn't used to. Her body was alert; it was her mind that was lagging behind. She was finding it difficult to follow conversations, to pluck out the words in her head and put them into the right order.

She kept telling herself she'd just been working too hard, and willed herself to ignore how unsteady she felt. She tried to gather her thoughts, moistening her lips to make the words come out more easily. Taking a deep breath, she focused once more on the case.

"They have a motive, and there is a precedent for vandalism and damage to the victim's property," she said.

Knauss squirmed in his chair, his bulk suddenly diminished, as if he were shrivelling up in his own skin.

Teresa didn't wait for him to respond.

"I want the details for each and every one," she commanded. Knauss tried once more to explain his position.

"They're from the village . . . we've known them forever."

"I don't give a damn if you have your morning coffee with them every day," Teresa snapped.

She regretted it immediately. From the moment she'd woken up that morning, she'd felt unmoored. All day her emotions had seesawed, and that unpredictability was a destabilizing force.

"They are idealists, Superintendent, they're young. They just don't want another ski slope defacing the valley."

"Idealists are dreamers who organize peace marches, Chief Knauss, they don't roam about armed with petrol cans and fire bombs," she said. "What are the charges?"

Knauss signalled to one of his men, and the files were pushed toward Teresa. Within minutes she'd figured out what had happened. The ski resort currently under construction required the deforestation of a vast expanse of mountain slope. She could easily imagine how a certain portion of the valley's inhabitants might be displeased with these plans. The zone of interest had been divided into lots. A number of soil samples from the lots on the ridge toward the north had already been analyzed; the results from the hydrological tests had been positive, and the work was set to begin in the spring, once the ice had thawed. As for the lots further south, near the village, those had already been fenced off and construction had commenced. These were the sites that the environmental activists had targeted; the worst offence had taken place two weeks before Valent's disappearance, an episode of arson for which three locals from the protest movement had already been arrested and charged.

"Parisi, look into it tomorrow morning," said Teresa as she pointed at the suspects' names on the files. She was breathing with difficulty. "Just an informal chat to start with."

"Why wouldn't his wife mention any of this?" asked Marini.

Teresa lifted her head to look at him, but couldn't seem to respond. Her mouth felt sticky. She felt everyone's eyes on her.

"Superintendent?"

Faces. Nameless faces everywhere.

Her confusion mingled with embarrassment. Someone offered her a glass of water. He kept calling her Superintendent, and he seemed concerned. Teresa's instincts told her she knew him, but his name just wouldn't come to her.

She stuck the temples of her glasses in her mouth and began to chew on them. It was a habit she often turned to, but it had suddenly acquired a new purpose: to buy her some time and conceal her distress in the hope that the words would soon start flowing again.

What the hell is his name?

It didn't work.

"Excuse me," she said, getting to her feet. Her words sounded like a disjointed murmur.

She took refuge in the bathroom, closing the door behind her and locking it shut. She'd found it without having to ask for directions; that must mean she knew the place.

She calmed her breathing and looked at her reflection in the mirror: all she saw was a scared old lady.

It's just a moment of confusion, she told herself.

But it was a lie. She knew exactly what was happening to her.

21

At that time of year the valley looked like a termite mound battered by torrential rains: everything churned with frantic activity, and there was an orderly back and forth of movement across the slopes. But unlike insects—burrowing deep into their nests during winter—these creatures were not hampered by the cold. From his vantage point, they resembled colorful dots scurrying over the snow.

They looked like him, but they were different, too. He often wondered what use they were. Termites were equipped with powerful jaws they used to process organic waste, clearing the way for new shoots; if not for their hard work, the forest would suffocate and die.

But these creatures devoured their own kind; they fed on the vital energy of their weaker peers. They had a parasitic relationship with other members of their own herd, something that fell outside the laws of nature, and left an unpleasant taste in the mouth—like grass that is meant for sunny flatlands but ends up growing in the shade.

He studied them. He listened to how they associated certain sounds to particular objects and he imitated them. He learned through experience. He entered their homes.

The woman moved from room to room, attending to her chores. She hadn't noticed his presence. He followed her, ducking behind a corner every time she turned around, breathing in her scent, observing her body.

When he lost interest in her, he climbed up the stairs to the floor above. There was a baby playing in his cot. Their eyes met, and the child smiled. He looked healthy and well fed; he smelled of milk.

He walked past the baby, finding himself drawn to the bed-covers: they were thick, soft, and warm, like the fleece of a sheep. He pulled them toward himself, and in doing so woke up the cat that had been curled up on the bed. It hissed and bolted from the room.

The child shrieked in delight. The mother called its name from the stairs. When she walked into the room, she picked up her son and sat on the bed, cooing at the baby in soft, tender tones. He heard a rustle of fabric, followed by the sound of enthusiastic suckling. The mother had a mellifluous voice, like birdsong in spring.

He could hear her moving above him. The bed creaked beneath her weight and the weight of the baby she held in her arms.

Something fell to the floor, and she called it by its name. "Toy," he mimicked, but she had begun singing again, and her voice drowned out his whisper. He had learned a new word.

While he waited, he looked at the naked sliver of skin visible through the gap between the fabric that covered her legs and her feet. It was pink and smooth. He could sense its warmth and felt a strong urge to touch it.

He brought his finger close but stopped himself.

From the door, standing completely still on the threshold, the cat stared at him with yellow, frightened eyes.

22

A fist between her teeth.

Teresa had spent years biting her fists to muffle her crying. She had found it an effective technique for silencing her despair when it wouldn't do for it to be heard. It used to happen quite often—in a past life that she could never quite leave behind. She had set fire to that version of herself in a pyre of old photographs, but she was not deluded enough to think she could ever be truly free of it. All she had ever hoped for was that she would never again have to suffer so intensely, and it seemed that life had granted her wish: the pain was no longer her enemy, simply a part of who she was. Almost like an old friend. A burden she had to bear in exchange for those select memories she wanted to hold on to.

A fist between her teeth now, and she was biting hard. She had turned the tap on so that the water pouring into the sink would cloak the sound of a panic she couldn't control. She studied her reflection in the mirror, desperate to record every single detail of what she was going through—as if by facing the moment head-on she could somehow force it to end sooner. She had hoped the wave of fear and misery would soon pass, leaving her spent but free, just with another bruise on her heart. Instead it seemed to last forever.

She looked into her own eyes in the mirror, trying to feel less alone, to witness her own disorientation and confront it. She suddenly felt a profound compassion for herself; nobody else could feel that for her. The person in the mirror had lost her bearings, and though she loved herself with a tenderness granted by age and experience, she could not be saved, not this time. It was no longer her choice.

Though she refused to put a name to what was happening to her, she did wonder what the future would hold for her, how resilient she would need to be to face it, and how much more time she might be allowed.

Teresa finally removed her hand from her mouth. Her face was a mess. She splashed it with cold water and dabbed at it with wet paper towels. She couldn't allow anyone to know about the terror that had gripped her; she couldn't stand pity. She had to mask her confusion and pray that a merciful god would ensure there wouldn't be another episode anytime soon.

There was an investigation to attend to, and a team to lead. There were victims clamoring for justice, and there was a killer to catch. The moment of weakness she had allowed herself was over.

23

"I wouldn't, if I were you."

Simone De Carli was eyeing him with his arms crossed over his chest. He was thirty, but with his sparse beard and neat, regular features, he looked a great deal younger. He was short, he looked too thin in his skinny jeans, and he had tattoos on his forearms; one could be forgiven for mistaking him for a teenager.

"What if she's ill? She's been in there for ages," Massimo said.

De Carli seemed dubious.

"All the more reason to steer clear," he replied. His voice had dropped to a whisper now. "She would have asked for our help if she wanted it. Don't—"

Massimo knocked on the door. They could hear the sound of tap water and of paper towels being extracted from the dispenser. Perhaps Teresa Battaglia wasn't dead after all.

"Everything okay, Superintendent?" he asked.

The door swung open and Massimo found himself staring into a pair of furious eyes.

"Do you ever mind your own fucking business, Marini?"

Teresa Battaglia was very much alive and as intractable as ever. Massimo turned toward De Carli, only to discover that his colleague had beaten a hasty retreat.

"I was worried," he said, facing Teresa once more, "but I regret it already."

She looked awful, like someone who'd been weeping uncontrollably. A few translucent drops were caught in the strands of hair near her ears. Massimo remembered how long the water had seemed to run as he stood listening at the bathroom door; she must have tried to hide her tears by wiping at her face with wet towels. But it hadn't worked. He wondered what could possibly have happened to break her like that, without any warning.

"I told Chief Knauss and his men that the meeting was over," he reported.

She glared at him.

"What made you think you could start giving orders around here?"

She pushed past him and headed down the hallway. Massimo could do little else but follow her. He was worryingly close to shouting at her, telling her to go to hell, but he was also concerned for her, though he didn't know exactly why.

"What have I done wrong now?" he asked.

"What? Were you expecting a medal?"

"Just being ignored instead of actively humiliated would be a start."

"Jesus Christ, Marini! I'll tell you what, I'll write you a little apology note so you can go home and show it to Mommy."

"You know what? Fuck you!"

They both froze.

"I'm sorry," Massimo quickly added, mortified.

Teresa pursed her lips in disappointment.

"What a shame, you were doing so well until you came out with that pathetic apology. You know, it doesn't hurt to be told to fuck off, every now and then," she said.

He didn't quite know what to say. She seemed to have gone back to her usual self: insufferable and determined. And admittedly, she did have at least one good quality: she didn't use her position to put herself beyond reproach—or even insults, it seemed.

"Tell Chief Knauss to put a surveillance team outside the Valent and Kravina homes," she ordered. "Tomorrow we'll speak to the widow again."

"Where are you going?"

"To the city."

"I'll drop you."

"No. I still know how to drive a car, in case you've forgotten."

Massimo fell silent. Teresa flung open the door that led out to the parking lot. Snow had begun to fall again in fat flakes that shone in the lamplight.

"So, is it true that the killer always returns to the scene of the crime?" he asked her before she left, with a hint of irony in his voice.

It was only five o'clock, but it looked like nighttime already. Teresa Battaglia stared into the darkness before she answered him.

"If he lacks self-control, then yes. He returns to the scene of the crime. He attends the victim's funeral, visits their grave. He phones the relatives. He even makes up excuses to meet them. Sometimes he does this to keep a tab on things, but more often, it's his way of keeping his fantasies alive. Of savoring the death he has wrought for as long as possible, and basking in the pleasure he's derived from it."

24

AUSTRIA, 1978

The sound of the sirens was drowned out by the roar of the storm, which seemed to shake the building from its foundations all the way up to the topmost garret. In all her years of service at the School, Agnes had never seen a storm like the one that was ripping through the sky that night.

Tripping over the hem of her long skirt, she ran across the empty kitchen to the lobby to check that the main door had been bolted shut as she'd been instructed to do. A flash of lightning lit up the main staircase, and all at once the lights went out. She climbed to the first floor. The wind had shattered one of the windows to pieces, and rain was falling sideways into the corridor. Another fierce gust slammed into the window frame, and Agnes screamed as it exploded in front of her. She felt she was losing control of herself, of her life, of the school itself. The ground that had felt so solid beneath her feet was crumbling now, exposing an ever-growing chasm that could not be filled. The School was sinking, and it was taking Agnes with it.

She crept forward along the wall and craned her neck to look down at the courtyard. The wall behind her was bathed in the blue of flashing police lights. Someone was shouting through a megaphone to open the door. Among the unfamiliar faces dripping with rainwater, Agnes recognized Magdalena.

There's the traitor, she thought bitterly. She should have known that the submissiveness the girl had recently displayed was nothing but a ruse; she must have been waiting for the right moment to turn on those who had trusted her. Agnes wanted to scream and rail at the girl's ingratitude, but the storm would have smothered the sound anyway.

They exchanged a long, hate-filled look, until Agnes pulled herself together.

There was one last command to follow.

Now thoroughly drenched, she opened the door of the Hive only to realize that someone else had got there first. She ran her hand across her eyes to wipe away the drops of water that were blurring her vision. In the darkness, lit intermittently by frightful bolts of lightning, a familiar figure crouched over one of the subjects. As the man lifted the child into the air high above his head, she saw something in his bearing reminiscent of a pagan ritual. Another flash of fearsome lightning illuminated the whole room, exposing for a split second the rapturous expression on the man's face. The windows shook with the thunder that followed.

Agnes shuddered and crossed herself. For the first time since she had been entrusted with the secrets of the School, she was scared.

She closed the door behind her, her soul shaken to the core. The banging on the front door grew louder. They were trying to knock it down. She could feel now that all was lost, but perhaps there was still hope for her. She gripped the set of keys in her pocket and hurried down the steps. She would try to get to the basement and from there, take the tunnel that led to the old stables.

She knew this meant abandoning the child to its fate, but she was also aware that the child the man had taken—the one in cot 39—was no ordinary creature.

25

"There isn't a specific test for this yet, unfortunately. We'll have to reach a diagnosis through a process of elimination and a careful evaluation of physical and psychological symptoms."

Teresa listened as she sat in a chair that was so small it compressed her thighs. The clinic was stifling and aggressively bright; her throat burned with the instinct to flee, but she wasn't afraid. She felt neither pain nor sorrow—only emptiness. She just wanted to go home.

"Of course there are some tests we can conduct. In any event, you should know that the rate of progression varies between individuals: it could be a few years, or it could be thirty."

Carmen Mura had been her doctor for twenty years now, but Teresa still hadn't figured out why she always reverted to a collective "we" in times of crisis.

The doctor pushed a piece of paper toward Teresa, giving her patient's hand a quick squeeze.

"We'll have to ask you to sign this consent form to allow other hospitals to access your clinical history. This is especially important if we establish you are indeed affected. In an emergency, your mental state might prevent you from explaining your situation. And we must not forget about your diabetes."

Teresa nodded. As she took the pen Carmen gave her, she noticed that her own hand was shaking. Perhaps she wasn't as calm as she thought. She scrawled a signature that bore only a passing resemblance to her usual one: it looked like the cardio-gram of her tormented soul.

Carmen continued: "We should start with blood and urine tests, followed by an MRI scan. This will provide us with an extremely detailed image of the brain. We'll run another scan a few months down the line to see if there have been any changes. A CAT scan might also be helpful in determining whether there is any cerebral atrophy. Are you happy with that?"

Teresa nodded. She knew that in the long run, none of it was of any use, but she couldn't bring herself to resist.

"I do want to make one thing clear, though, and I hope you won't mind my being direct: there is, at present, no cure for this."

Teresa sank her fingernails into the handbag on her lap.

The doctor had finally said it. It must have required some courage, and it had taken them almost an hour of empty chit-chat to get to this point.

"Thank you for seeing me so late in the day," said Teresa, rising to her feet.

"Do you have any questions?"

The only question she cared about had no answer. It had to do with life and death and everything in between, all the things that, within a week or a few months or a year, she was going to lose. Forever.

26

Lucia was already awake when the ring of the doorbell pierced the night. She was waiting in the corridor, her eyes fixed on the door. Earlier, was woken up by a nightmare and hadn't been able to go back to sleep; she had gone to the window to look at the snow falling. That was when she'd seen the man.

She heard something tumbling to the floor and her father swearing as he threw his bedroom door open. He staggered toward Lucia with a befuddled look on his face and that smell on him she had learned to recognize; it was the scent of that smoke that made him feel good and made him burst into laughter for no reason until he would eventually pass out.

"What are you doing here?" he barked. "Go back to your room."

"There's a man outside, Dad . . ." she tried to tell him, but he paid her no heed, and ushered her back into her room.

"Your mother must have forgotten her keys again."

Lucia saw him leaning on the wall as he made for the door, his arms flailing as he searched for something to hold on to and help him keep his balance. She hid behind her bedroom door and watched him. He thought she was odd because she believed in ghosts, and recently he'd begun spending even less time with her than usual. But the ghost who wanted to come into their home was real.

The doorbell went off again with a short, imperious ring.

Her father turned the doorknob just as the neighbor's rooster crowed. The animal was like a living clock: every day, no matter what, it crowed at exactly four in the morning. But if it was four o'clock, Lucia thought, surely her mother should have been back by now.

The door opened, and she saw the stranger's bulk filling up the doorframe. Covered in a coat that reached all the way to his feet, he looked like some kind of giant. His hood hung low over his face, and all they could see was a long beard.

"What is it? Do you need help?" said Lucia's father.

The ghost lifted his head. His face was white, like that of a dead person.

Lucia closed the door to her room and ran to hide under her bedcovers, but quickly changed her mind and tiptoed back to the door to stick her head out and watch.

She was scared, but she was also intrigued by the stranger. Gathering her courage, she took a few tentative steps down the corridor. The ghost raised his hand, and she saw there was something hanging from his fingers. He said something, but it sounded like gibberish.

"I don't understand. Do you need help?" her father repeated. He could barely stand upright.

The stranger observed him, his head cocked to one side.

"*Do-you-need-help?*" he mimicked, as if he were playing a game.

Lucia's father swore and tried to shut the door, but the ghost blocked it. The sound of his fist slamming into the wood startled Lucia. Time seemed to freeze for a moment as her father focused on the thing in the ghost's hand. Lucia squinted; it looked like a necklace.

Then the spectre retreated, returning to the fog from which it had emerged. Lucia's father could finally close the door.

When he turned around, she saw that he was trembling.

27

Teresa was studying the light in her room. Not the way it fell on a specific object or reflected off a surface, but the light itself. In the past few hours, she had come to understand its true nature: it was a pulsating force that filled the air, changed color, spread over walls and objects, lapping at their edges, then receding. Darkness was nothing but black light, a rippling of waves, a tide.

There was darkness inside her now.

She hadn't slept. She'd spent the night thinking, clutching at her memories with an urgency that was new to her.

"May twentieth, 1958," she said to herself.

The day it had all begun. Her first day on earth. Had she known then what she knew now, would she still have smiled as she came into the world? It was a story her mother had told her over and over again. Teresa hadn't wailed in the midwife's arms; she had merely opened her eyes and smiled, a toothless grin in a tiny, wrinkled face. It was probably nothing more than a reflex, a reaction to the entirely novel sensation of air on her skin.

But Teresa's mother liked to think that her daughter had been blessed at birth with innate joy. She had named her Teresa thinking that the name meant "treasure." What it actually meant was "huntress," though Teresa had never told her that—and in the end, Teresa had become a huntress of a kind.

Oh Mother, if you could see me today . . .

Laying down her weapons, she had taken refuge in her den that night, nursing wounds that would never really heal. They were deeper than anyone could imagine.

She was used to feeling betrayed by her body and to betraying it herself. She had learned to come to terms with its changing shape, its increasing weight, its downward stretch; with her lined face which no longer caught men's eyes; with her diabetes and the swings in her blood pressure, the hunger and tiredness that sometimes besieged her from the moment she woke up; with how her legs would start to ache in the middle of a shift, and how her eyesight was growing more blurry every year; and even with the scar that marked her abdomen, reminding her every day of what had been taken away from her.

All of that, she could endure—but this was the ultimate betrayal, and she didn't have the strength to shoulder its burden on her own.

She had spent the night curled up in the fetal position, yearning for somebody to comfort her, and wishing she could be a daughter once again and summon her mother back. She longed for a hand to caress her swollen face and her hair damp with tears. She asked herself how long it had been since anyone had given her a kiss. She couldn't even remember.

It was almost dawn now.

The light was changing. Darkness was taking its leave and once again, Teresa had to muster the strength to banish it from inside herself, too. It would have been easier if she'd had a companion beside her. She had never been a romantic, but after a few dozen years spent coping on her own, she was beginning to find the idea of a savior quite appealing.

Her mobile phone vibrated on the bedside table. She had to look at the name on the screen repeatedly before her eyes could focus properly. She lifted herself into a sitting position and cleared her throat to speak.

"You're not quite the person I had in mind," she said.

"That's what you ladies always say, but then you inevitably change your minds."

At least Marini was quick with a joke.

"What is it?" she asked.

"It's about the Valent case. I'll come and pick you up."

28

The police station in Travenì was bustling with activity; a suspect had been taken into custody and was waiting to be charged. They had caught him trying to open the front door of the Valent home. He hadn't known he was being followed. His name was Cristian Lusar and he was one of the three people who had been accused of setting fire to the construction site that Valent used to run.

Teresa realized that of the three suspects, he was also the likeliest match for the killer. The others were a diminutive woman who would never have been able to overpower Valent, and a middle-aged man who suffered from multiple sclerosis.

Once again, Hugo Knauss had withheld information that would have been crucial to the investigation. When Teresa had first inquired about the three suspects, he had failed to mention that it was physically impossible for two of the three to be the killer; what she couldn't figure out was whether his behavior was down to pure carelessness or if it was a worrying symptom of the obstructionism she could expect from that small mountain community. Either way, Teresa was no longer prepared to tolerate it.

Thirty-five-year-old Lusar's physique had been honed by years of rock climbing and off-piste skiing. His body was wiry, chiselled by exertion, sweat, and mountain air. His curly, cinnamon-colored hair framed a squared face with blue eyes and a guarded expression. He did not seem scared.

The door to the room where he had been told to wait was ajar, and Teresa was watching him through the gap. No one had told him yet why he'd been detained, but she was sure he could guess.

He was an arsonist who had been spotted loitering outside the victim's home. He had the hands of a climber, broad and lined with veins that hinted at their extraordinary strength. He seemed like the perfect suspect, yet Teresa was sure that his fingerprints would not match those they had found on Valent's body—which had indeed turned out to be the same as those left on the walls of the Kravina home. That didn't mean that he was innocent, only that he hadn't been the one to physically kill the victim.

"Lead him out," she told Marini.

He looked at her in surprise.

"Why?" he asked.

"Lead him out and take him into the room where Marta Valent is waiting. Then bring her to me, but make sure they see each other first."

"I suppose an explanation would be too much to ask for?"

"If you still don't get it, I'll tell you a third time: lead him out."

Marini finally obeyed while Teresa went into Hugo Knauss's office with De Carli and Parisi. There was a monitor connected to a camera filming Valent's widow as she paced back and forth, biting her fingernails. She must be worried that somebody—a man who had previously threatened her husband—had been trying to break into her home. Or perhaps she wasn't worried about that at all.

The monitor showed the door being opened. Marini walked in, followed closely by Cristian Lusar. The woman's face immediately became even more tense, almost frightened. She averted her gaze and lowered her eyes when Marini invited her to leave the room. She walked past Lusar without looking at him, her hands crossed over her chest as if guarding herself against something. Lusar stuffed his hands in his pockets and seemed rather nervous.

He doesn't know where else to put them without giving himself away.

Lusar looked at Marta Valent, then turned to face the wall. Parisi leaned on the back of Teresa's chair.

"Did you see that, Superintendent?" he whispered.

Teresa lifted her hand to invoke his silence. She had indeed noticed that gesture, but the answer to her question lay elsewhere.

"Proxemics," she told the two agents, pointing at the screen. "The science that allows us to interpret the distance people put between themselves and others. There is always a significance to the length of that distance, and this is certainly no exception."

She continued to observe them.

"Though they maintain otherwise, Marta Valent and Cristian Lusar are no strangers to each other."

That was what the distance between them had revealed. Their bodies had been separated by no more than a few inches, and even that space had been reduced briefly to nothing when they had brushed against each other in a seemingly involuntary gesture. It wasn't a proximity imposed by the circumstances they found themselves in, but a consequence of the trajectory they had unconsciously chosen as they switched positions inside the room. It was a distance that could be considered intimate, reserved to people we know and trust—not to nighttime intruders, or potential killers. It was the distance of embraces and shared breaths.

When Teresa had first met Valent's widow in her home, the woman had been fidgeting obsessively with the wedding band on her ring finger. Teresa could see now how that wedding band represented a union that existed in name only.

Marini led Marta Valent into the room where Teresa was waiting. He walked back out with Parisi and De Carli and shut the door.

"The two of you are lovers, aren't you?" Teresa asked point blank.

The woman opened her mouth as if to protest, then closed it again.

"Don't make things worse," Teresa warned her. "I already know."

Teresa finally understood why the photograph she had seen in Marta Valent's house depicted a glowing, cheerful young woman, and why that same woman now looked like a shadow of her former self. At first Teresa had ascribed the change to sickness. But now she understood: it was guilt.

The woman's eyes shone with tears.

"Cristian didn't do it," she said, crying. "And neither did I."

"And why should I trust you? You've lied to me before."

"What did you expect me to say, with my son and my mother-in-law in the house?"

"You had plenty of other chances to speak; you only had to make your mind up. You could have called me at any point over the past few days."

The woman's hands were fussing with a tissue that she'd reduced to shreds. Teresa handed her a fresh one and waited for the tears to subside. When they finally did, the woman looked at Teresa with resignation.

"Will everyone find out now?" she asked. "I'm worried about the child."

Teresa hoped it wouldn't come to that.

"I'm the only one who knows, for now," she said, though she wasn't sure why she was even bothering to reassure this woman.

"Will you keep me in here?"

"I'm going to need your full statement, and I'll have to ask you to tell me *everything* about your affair. I mean anything that might be relevant to the case, of course."

"We didn't kill him!"

"I'm not suggesting that you did, Marta, but I must also rule out the possibility that you got someone else to do it for you."

"Oh God!"

"One of my colleagues will be with you shortly to ask you a few questions."

"What about Diego? My son will need picking up from school soon."

"I thought they'd closed it for a few days."

"The teachers and students organized a memorial service for Diego's father. He'll expect me to be waiting for him when he comes out."

Teresa remembered the little licorice thief.

"I'll go," she said. "And I'll be discreet."

29

The traffic jam outside the primary school in Travenì was like rush hour in a big city. Cars jostled for the parking spaces closest to the main gates, spraying dirty slush all over those particularly apprehensive parents who had gotten out of their vehicles to wait, umbrellas aloft, for their children.

Teresa couldn't tell whether it was fear triggering all this enhanced attentiveness, or the terrible weather. The temperature had risen by a few degrees, and a mixture of rain and tentative snow had begun to fall from the grey sky.

Teresa was among those milling about by the gate. Marini was with her, holding an umbrella as black as his mood. Teresa kept her hands in her pockets, bringing them out every now and then to unwrap a sweet and pop it into her mouth with great deliberation, while Marini looked on in disapproval. Clearly the young man was a health fanatic, as well as a total bore. He was quieter than usual that day, which meant Teresa couldn't even enjoy picking on him.

"It looks like you have lost your primary function," she told him.

"I beg your pardon?"

"Forget it."

The children emerged like a herd of wild animals bursting with vital energy. They chased after each other, skipping and shouting, oblivious to the rain and the greyish slop that covered the road. Already they'd forgotten why they had even gone to school that morning: the mass they had just attended for their classmate's late father was nothing but a distant memory.

Children could be ruthless—it was all down to their remarkable urge to live. It sounded like a paradox, but to Teresa it made perfect sense; they savored each moment as if it were an exhilarating adventure and couldn't afford to waste time adhering to meaningless formalities they didn't even understand. They were alive, so what else could they do but live?

Diego Valent was one of the last to come out of the school, walking alongside a younger boy who looked emaciated. They were whispering to each other as they walked, and when it was time to say goodbye, Teresa saw Diego stroke the other boy's cheek. It was unusual to see this kind of gesture between friends at that age; it suggested that young Valent harbored a strong protective instinct toward his friend. When he spotted Teresa, Diego hesitated, then finally came to a stop.

Teresa walked toward him, followed by Marini who was trying to keep her dry under the umbrella.

"Hello, Diego," she said in greeting. "Do you remember me?"

The boy didn't reply, but his fretful eyes looked silently at them. He seemed scared, and he began to shiver. Teresa squatted beside him so that they would be the same height.

"Don't worry, nothing bad has happened," she told him. "We've come to pick you up and take you home. Your mom had to run an errand and she asked us if we could help. Is that all right with you?"

Diego looked at her in astonishment.

"Y-you're n-not h-here about the s-s-sweet?" he asked. The stammer was exacerbated by his nervousness. Teresa wanted to hug him.

"That licorice was meant for you," she said. "I'm glad you took it."

Diego smiled—only the slightest of smiles, but more than what Teresa had hoped for.

She held out her hand and he took it.

"What was wrong with your friend?" she asked as they headed toward the car. "He seemed sad."

"O-Oliver often c-cries in s-s-school."

"He doesn't like it?"

"The j-j-j-janitor is m-m-mean to him."

Teresa stopped. Glancing over at Marini, she saw that he, too, had been surprised by this unexpected declaration. It looked like Diego was used to seeing his friend in that state—which, in turn, suggested it was something that happened frequently.

"Mean how?" she asked, but instantly wished she hadn't. It was the kind of cold, cynical question only a grown-up would ask. If the boy was unhappy, did it really matter *how* the janitor was being mean to him?

Diego slowly loosened his grip on her hand, his trust in her slipping away. He didn't answer Teresa's question, and she knew he wouldn't tell her anything else either, at least not that day.

A black SUV careened toward them and stopped just short of knocking over a little girl and her mother on the zebra crossing. From the vehicle came the sounds of loud music and wild cackling: it was a group of boys who looked not much older than eighteen. They had decorated the hood of the car and each of its doors with the picture of a white skull.

Suddenly, a man materialized out of nowhere and threw himself at the SUV with a guttural roar. He looked like the archetypal highland dweller. All they could see of his face was a long beard that emerged from beneath the hood of his cloak. He was tall and stocky, but he seemed weighed down by his clothes. His hands, protected by fingerless gloves, hammered at the metal frame of the car. Two youths stuck their heads out of the vehicle and started yelling insults at the man.

"What the hell is he doing?" said Marini.

The man threw one last, fierce punch at the car, then turned around and walked away, clearing a path through the curious crowd that had gathered to watch the scene.

Teresa tried to follow him with her eyes.

"I want to check him out," she said. "You stay here with the kid."

She set off at a brisk pace to try and keep up with the man. Even from a distance, the black smudge of the stranger's silhouette through the sleet looked imposing. He moved nimbly despite his bulk, and he was not slowed down by the ice that covered the road. Teresa, on the other hand, felt as if she were skating.

They passed the town center and continued down the road that led to the old train station. Beyond that was the forest.

The man didn't show signs of stopping, and Teresa wondered where he could be heading. She walked faster. The icy rain had thickened and the occasional solid flake had begun to fall onto the watery surface. Once they had gone past the railway, too, Teresa finally made up her mind and decided to call out to him.

"Stop!" she shouted over the whistling of the wind.

She was surprised when the stranger obeyed straight away. Until then, she had thought he mustn't even have noticed her presence behind him, but now she realized he had known from the start.

She stopped, too, her eyes boring into the man's back, her heart beating inexplicably faster.

He didn't turn around but stood completely still a few meters ahead of her, his arms by his sides. He was waiting. There was something disturbing about the whole scene, and about him—something feral.

Teresa unbuttoned her coat.

"Turn around, please," she told him. "Did you hear me?"

The man made a sideways dash and began to run.

"Hey!"

Teresa chased after him, battling the urge to reach for her gun. She saw him jump over a stockade and move forward at a swift pace. He wasn't too far ahead, and again she had the feeling he was playing games with her; he could have easily shaken her off, but instead he seemed almost to be waiting for her. Teresa crawled beneath the fence and hurried after him.

They were following the old railway now. The tracks ran parallel to sleeper beams that had been cleaved by time and the inclement weather. Abandoned buildings dating back to the Habsburg era and immersed in a profusion of ivy lined either side of the railroad. Nature was taking back that human space, inching forward with its roots and shrubs. The forest wasn't very far behind; it was only a matter of time before it reclaimed the ground that had been taken from it centuries before.

The stranger veered off the gravel path and leapt over a ditch back onto the path that led to town.

Teresa swore, feeling exhausted. She had to stop to catch her breath, bending over with her hands on her knees. She couldn't give up or he would soon get away, and yet every joint in her body was begging her to stop.

You're too old, her body was telling her.

"Fuck off!" she replied.

She straightened up and started running toward the ditch.

"Hey, I'm talking to you! Stop!" she shouted again. But right then the bed of ferns beneath her feet gave way, exposing a steep drop.

She didn't even have time to scream. Her voice was silenced by the feeling of free fall, and though her arms flailed, trying to get hold of the shrubbery, everything seemed to be sliding down with her. She felt a pang of pain in her right hand, and pictured its flesh cut open.

But then the momentum of her fall was reversed by a sudden jerk that left her gasping for breath. Someone started yanking her up until she found herself back on the train tracks, lying on her back on the sharp-edged gravel.

When she opened her eyes, the stranger was there, towering over her, his face covered by a hood. His long beard tapered all the way down past his chest. It could have been white or blond, and there were pine needles entangled in it.

Teresa tried to get up, but the pain in her back forced her to curl up on her side. By the time she had finally managed to sit up, she was alone. The stranger had disappeared. She couldn't tell whether he'd gone back to the village or sought refuge in the forest. She brushed her hair out of her eyes and looked around, feeling disoriented. Perhaps she'd banged her head. She ran a quick inventory of her bones and concluded that everything was in its right place. Only then did she remember the pain in her hand and looked at it to find that she was bleeding profusely from a cut on her palm. She swore, feeling old and foolish. She took off her scarf and wrapped it around the wound.

"That's what happens when you try to play the hero: you end up on your ass," she muttered.

She rested her elbows on her knees, still feeling unsure about standing up. Why couldn't she have sent Marini instead? He was younger, quicker, stronger.

And better suited to this job than she was?

But the thought of being stuck at a desk, far from the frontline, issuing orders and drawing up profiles without the chance to test them in the field, was more than Teresa could bear. She refused to believe she could no longer rely on her body as she had done all these years up until now.

And that was exactly why she hadn't sent Marini after that man. It was a last-ditch attempt to banish the idea that she might no longer be fit to be a policewoman.

"Superintendent!"

Marini was by her side before she'd even heard him coming. He knelt down and put his arm around her shoulders.

"What happened? Are you okay?" he asked.

Teresa shrugged him off with a sneer.

"What a fucking stupid question," she said. "Do I look okay?"

She saw him hesitate.

"Do you want to sit down for a little longer or shall I help you to your feet?"

"How about you stop talking? That would help me."

Teresa tried to brush the dirt off her clothes and pick out the leaves stuck in her hair.

"Where's Diego?" she asked. She realized with a shiver that she'd almost forgotten about the boy. "I told you to stay with him."

"I left him with a teacher."

Teresa swore.

"So you disobeyed an order. Do that again and I'll send you back to the archive room."

Marini let it go.

"Was it that man? Did he push you? I saw the two of you running," he said.

Teresa hesitated.

"No, it wasn't his fault. I think he helped me," she finally said.

"You *think* he helped you?"

She glared at him.

"It wasn't exactly easy to see what was happening, what with my head bouncing against the ground."

Marini got up again and peered into the forest.

"Why did he run away? Could he be the man we're after?" he asked.

Teresa also rose to her feet, though a lot more slowly than he had, and much less gracefully, too. At least the pain in her back had receded.

"Then why would he save me from crashing down into that?" she said, leaning over to look down at the precipice. "The killer we're looking for has no sense of empathy. He would have stood and watched, and enjoyed it, too."

"So I guess he was just a mountain man who was particularly reluctant to answer your questions."

"Well, a person's spirit is shaped by the environment they inhabit, and as my tailbone can now attest, these mountains are a hard place to live."

Marini took a few steps forward, his eyes fixed on the ground.

"No sign of footsteps," he remarked. "He must have walked along the ballast. I'll run some tests, but . . ."

Teresa stared at him.

"*You*'ll run some tests?" she noted.

He realized his slip and closed his eyes for a moment.

"I didn't mean . . ."

"Leave it, Marini."

"You're the one giving orders, obviously."

"Yes, obviously."

"So what now?"

Teresa brushed her trousers.

"So now you run some tests," she told him, heading toward the road. "Do I have to tell you everything?"

When they arrived back at the school, Diego bid his teacher farewell and walked toward them.

"Shall we go?" Teresa said, smiling at him and offering him her uninjured hand. He looked inquisitively at the dirt on her clothes, but didn't ask any questions. He did take her hand, though. Teresa noticed a white stain on her sleeve. She swiped a finger through the smudge.

"What's this?" she asked Marini.

He shrugged.

"I've no idea."

"P-Poo."

They both turned to look at the boy.

"He's right," said Marini, sniffing at the stain. "It looks like bird poo."

Teresa looked at Diego and gave him a wink.

"The perfect conclusion to a perfect chase," she said, laughing.

30

Lucia was used to being alone and silence didn't scare her. It was something else that was making her sad that morning: she hadn't been able to meet up with her friends. Her father had left just before dawn, instructing her to clean the house and tidy up, and telling her that whatever happened, she mustn't go outside. He would be gone for a while, perhaps a couple of days.

"Where's Mommy?" she'd asked.

He'd told her she'd left. Lucia had accepted that simple explanation; after all, her mother had left them before, though she always came back.

She knew he would only get angry if she kept asking questions, so she desisted. She could always tell when it was better for her to keep quiet. So she would put on a brave face, turn into a strong little woman who knew how to fend for herself, and make their home into her own private castle.

But it had been an odd night. First, that stranger had rung their doorbell, and afterwards Lucia had heard her father rifling through every drawer and closet in the house. In the morning, Lucia had found all the cupboards still open, their contents spilling out onto the floor. It had taken her hours to put everything back where it belonged.

That was how she'd found the gift, underneath a pillow her father had flung into the corridor.

She had stared at it for a long time before she'd worked up the courage to touch it. She knew it was meant for her; she could tell the stranger had left it by her bedroom door intentionally. He must have snuck in while her crazed father was busy ransacking the rest of the house.

As Lucia swept the porch, the ragdoll sat there staring at her. It was a strange little thing, and that was what Lucia liked about it: it was like no other doll in the world. It had been sewn with twine, in coarse stitches that stood out on the jute fabric. Its hair was made out of horsehair and had the same lingering scent that the stranger's visit had left in the house: a pungent but not unpleasant animal odor, the smell of nature and its cycles of life and death. Wild, warm. Lucia had breathed it all in and wondered why she'd been given that gift. She had run her hands over the doll's dress, which was made from bits of fabric and dried cornflowers—papery, deep blue petals that a large, gentle hand, that's how she pictured it, had stitched onto the dress, all for Lucia to enjoy. It was the same shade of blue she had seen in the stranger's eyes when she had cracked her bedroom door open and looked out the previous night.

On the doll's face there was nothing else but two purplish berries that served as eyes; the man who'd made it hadn't bothered to give it a mouth. And like its maker, the doll was expressionless. Lucia thought it might have something to do with the way he spoke—she'd heard him while she'd been eavesdropping.

Lucia had picked up a felt tip pen and drawn a mouth on the doll's heart-shaped face, wishing its maker would also smile, just like the doll was doing now.

The wind changed direction, making the doll's dress billow, and carrying its scent to Lucia. It was almost like a summons.

"I'll be quick," said the girl. "Then we can play."

She scrubbed even harder at the floorboards on the porch. The blood had seeped into the wood, and not even the rain and the roar of the storm had managed to wash it away.

Massimo had begun to find it strangely alienating to return to the city every night after spending his days immersed in the wild, solemn landscapes of Travenì. The evening traffic was disorienting, and the cars' headlights made him feel like an animal caught in the middle of a busy road.

At first, he tried to blame it on tiredness, on endless shifts merging into one another, leaving only a few hours for rest.

But he wasn't convinced. It was as if his body had found a new equilibrium on those mountains and was having trouble readjusting to day-to-day life at a lower altitude. He had become accustomed to vertiginous heights and open spaces, to gales that tore the skin off your face, and the sudden warmth of crackling bonfires. There was a savage beauty in that world that awakened the senses from the hibernation of domesticated life.

Massimo entered the apartment he struggled to call home for a quick shower and a sandwich made out of the few provisions he had left in the fridge. He changed into something more comfortable, put his sneakers on, and went out. The public library wouldn't close until later in the evening, so there was still time to go for a walk and explore the town center. That small provincial town had all the features—both good and bad—of a proper city. But everything was on a smaller scale, shrunken down to a more bearable size, small doses that couldn't kill you.

Massimo felt lonely, but also somewhat liberated. The landscape of that wintry evening, with the skeletal silhouettes of trees outlined against the sky, resembled his life in that moment, stripped of all that was superfluous, like a bare tree trunk, a vessel for the vital sap that would nourish fresh shoots when the time was right. Massimo had turned into the skeleton of his former self. He had left everything behind, abandoning his comfort zone of routines, control, and certainties.

And Teresa Battaglia had figured it out. She had seen through him like nobody else had ever done before. He'd found it unpleasant, and slightly depressing, to realize that he wasn't so complicated after all.

He didn't know why he kept thinking about her, but she had recently become the focus of his every thought and action. She was an affliction, but also a formidable motivation. He had seen how her entire squad gravitated toward her, and now he understood what caused it: her vital energy. People could feel it in her, and they were attracted to it. Teresa Battaglia had the rare gift of making those who stood by her feel stronger. Except that in his case, she also made him feel terribly inadequate.

Teresa Battaglia and the feeling of inadequacy she awakened in him were the reason for the walk he was taking in the freezing cold. Massimo was determined to close the gap that he knew separated him from her, and he was going to do it exactly as she had suggested.

The library was situated in a seventeenth-century building overflowing with marble and chalky stuccos. It was warm inside, and a scent of wood emanated from the boiserie and the desks lined up in the center of the reading room. The smell of paper, the gentle rustle of pages being turned, and the soft light were like anaesthetics against the stirrings of the human soul.

He browsed several sections of bookshelves, glancing every now and then at a piece of paper in his hand.

"Can I help?"

Massimo turned around and came face to face with a pretty young woman wearing a badge on her shirt that identified her as a library employee.

"Thank you, I didn't expect it to be so difficult to find my way around," he told her.

"That's what I'm here for," she replied. "We hold over a million texts in this library, including books, journals, and media."

She sounded like someone in an ad, but Massimo thought she was cute anyway. He noticed she wasn't wearing a wedding band or an engagement ring.

He smiled at her.

"Then you must have come to my rescue," he replied, making an effort to turn up the charm as he spoke.

He had no trouble interpreting the girl's response: she was definitely interested. Perhaps he was interested, too. He didn't know anyone in town. He'd spotted a charming bar just around the corner; maybe he'd ask her out for a drink after work, one of these days.

"You're not from around here, are you?" she said, smiling at his look of surprise. "It's the accent," she explained.

Massimo made a face, deciding to play along.

"Is it really that obvious?" he asked.

She shook her head and her fair curls bobbed against the delicate planes of her temples.

"Not too much," she told him.

The girl gestured at the list in his hand.

"That looks long," she said. "Please tell me you're not one of these college students who constantly fails to graduate," she teased.

Massimo laughed.

"I'm not."

"So it's for work?"

He hesitated. Did he really want to talk to this girl about murders and eyes that couldn't be found?

"Let's just say I'm doing some research," he answered.

She blinked, and her long, golden eyelashes fluttered.

"So it must be something you're passionate about," she murmured. "Let me see."

Massimo didn't even have time to speak before she'd grabbed the piece of paper from him and started reading through it.

Her smile began to fade. It occurred to Massimo that they hadn't even introduced themselves.

"Do you stock these?" he asked her. "I found most of them online and . . ."

She didn't wait for him to finish. Her manner became abrupt.

"Take a seat over there, I'll find these for you and bring them over," she said.

"I'll come with you, there's loads on there," Massimo offered.

The girl looked at him, her face even more serious than before.

"You can't have them all, anyway. There's a limit to how many you're allowed to borrow. Now, if you'll please take a seat . . . I'll be quicker doing it alone."

Massimo could easily guess the cause of the sudden change in her behavior. The list of books he was looking for included, among others, such titles as *I Kill with My Bare Hands*, *Totems of Flesh*, and *The Taste of Blood* . . .

"I'm not planning on killing anyone," he joked, trying to reassure her, but she'd already disappeared behind a bookshelf.

Massimo felt strange and uncomfortable. This girl didn't mean anything to him, and yet her undisguised revulsion had caught him by surprise. One look at the titles of a few volumes of criminal psychology and forensic psychiatry had been enough for her to decide that he wasn't to be trusted. She might even think he was dangerous.

He thought of Superintendent Battaglia again. She didn't have anyone waiting for her to come home either. He wondered if the loneliness bothered her, and if, like him, she searched the crowds daily, frantically looking for a friendly face.

Massimo looked down the corridor. There was no sign of the librarian. He imagined her with a peeved expression on her face as she searched the shelves for the titles he'd requested.

Perhaps he'd been looking for the wrong kind of company. There already was a woman in that town who'd caught his attention, and she wasn't the kind to be put off by his interests. But he couldn't go to her empty-handed. He needed to make a small offering to the goddess of destruction—for that was what she was—to calm her ire and propitiate her favor.

The thought made him smile. He checked his watch; perhaps the botanic gardens might still be open.

32

The thread was shiny and tough, made of material he had never seen in the forest. The people who lived in the village used it to catch animals from the lake and the river. The first few times he had seen them doing it, he'd thought there must be some kind of sorcery involved in how the fish had leapt out of the water and thrashed about, suspended in air. But then he had noticed the thread glinting in the sun, and he had understood: it was just that it had no color, like the sky on an overcast day.

He moistened the thread with his lips to slip it more easily into the tiny hole, and pulled it through. Thus stitched together, the bones rattled against each other. They looked like bits of dried wood, blackened by time. He had washed the dirt off them and smoothed the bite marks left by the rats. He had neglected them for too long, but the hush of winter had once again awakened in him the feeling that he no longer wanted to be alone.

Sometimes he felt like a fox and thought he needed a pack. He thought he had a lot in common with that tawny, fleet-footed creature: it too could adapt to the most extreme environments, surviving winter upon winter. It wasn't fearful, but cautious. It approached humans and often followed their tracks in search of food when there wasn't enough of it in the woods.

But other times he felt like a lynx, solitary and free, a feline with claws so sharp that they left gashes on the trunks of the trees it so effortlessly climbed. He looked at his hands, his skin as thick as wood bark. His fingernails were long and hard. Every day he sharpened them with whetstone, like farmers did with the blades of their scythes when the fields turned gold in the summer sun.

His hands hadn't held another human hand since time immemorial.

He stroked the bones that he had threaded back into their original positions. They felt velvety beneath his fingertips and smelled of dried earth. He held them in his palm and felt as if he were caressing again what had once been a hand.

33

"**A**re you trying to bribe me again?"

Teresa Battaglia was eyeing the coffee Massimo had just placed on her desk. But he wouldn't let her intimidate him. He knew by now that the superintendent liked to bark, but he had never seen her bite.

"Would it work?" he asked.

She flung her bag to the floor and kicked it under her desk. To say she lacked elegance would have been an understatement.

"Definitely not," she told him. "Did you put sugar in it?"

"You can't have sugar."

"Whatever. What the fuck do you want?"

Massimo found her manner of speaking appalling.

"Why can't you just ask a question without . . ."

"Shit! I've stained my shirt. Anyway, what do you want?" she said before he could finish. She rummaged for a tissue, and he promptly offered her one. She stared at him for a moment before taking it.

"Don't you have a life?" she asked.

"Why do you ask?"

"Just the fact that you're here, attending to an old lady like some sort of houseboy. Just so you know, I'm not the one who decides who gets promoted around here."

Massimo didn't even bother replying. He had figured out by now that this was what she needed; some tense, snappy repartee to help release tension. He let her finish the coffee.

"I was wondering why you've been drawing up a profile for a serial killer when all we have is a single homicide," he said. "It didn't occur to me the other day."

Teresa Battaglia was impressed. For once, she didn't look at him as if she thought he was an idiot but seemed genuinely intrigued. She eased herself against the back of her chair.

"I see you've been studying," she muttered, picking out a sweet from her desk drawer. She threw it at him.

"Isn't that what you wanted?" Massimo replied, catching it.

She started laughing.

"I don't want anything. I can solve the case myself. I was just giving you some advice on how you could get better at this."

"Yes, and I took your advice. Now, can you please answer my question?" he insisted.

She made a vague motion with her hand.

"Ritualism. Mutilation. Staging. Need I continue? It looks . . . it looks like the start of something."

"The start of what?"

She looked at him as if it were obvious.

"A trail of death," she said.

Massimo sat down in front of her.

"Do you think he'll kill again?"

She seemed to hesitate.

"I do," she finally answered. "That's why I haven't been sleeping and I jump every time I hear the phone ring. It will happen."

Massimo had expected that reply, but there was still something sinister in hearing her say it out loud.

"Then what are we still doing here?" he said.

"What would you have us do? Comb through twenty thousand hectares of woodland? Search hundreds of homes and question thousands of people? Because that's what we'd have to do, you know."

"So there's no way to prevent it," he said.

"There might be, if he makes a mistake."

"Will he?"

"Now you're asking me to look into a crystal ball and take a guess."

"I'm asking you how good he is."

She shook her head.

"He isn't good, he's savage. But is there really much of a difference between the two? I don't know. Would you call a wolf that catches its prey good, or would you say it was just being itself?"

Massimo remembered the conversation they'd begun in the woods behind the Kravina home.

"You're saying that's the way he is, and he can't do anything about it," he said. "You realize how wrong that sounds, don't you?"

She smiled. She looked tired, or perhaps she was just bored of listening to someone she regarded as a novice, and not even a particularly talented one at that.

"Maybe the truth is they see the world more clearly than we do," she said in a low whisper. "They see the inferno beneath our feet while we stop to look at the flowers. We are lucky that we have a veil between us and the world, but their past has robbed them of that filter. That doesn't mean they're right to kill, of course, or that I'm justifying what they do."

"So what *does* it mean?"

"That in some distant past, they suffered, and their suffering has made them what they are. If there's anyone who should know what that means, it's me."

It was the first time this woman had told him anything remotely personal, the first time she had offered a glimpse—however hazy—into the history of her own life. Massimo grabbed the lead she'd thrown him, knowing that she would soon regret doing so, and pull it right back in.

"What do you mean, you should know?" he questioned, unable to stop himself.

But she seemed lost in altogether different thoughts.

"Because I can see beyond the flowers, just like they do. I can see the inferno," she murmured.

Her words faded into silence. The ticking of the clock on the wall behind them seemed to say that the time for confessions was drawing to a close.

This was the moment Massimo had been waiting for. He pulled the gift he had bought her out of his pocket and put it on her desk.

He saw her frown. Teresa Battaglia slipped on her glasses and brought her face close to the little sprig with pointed, leathery leaves, heavy with red berries.

"In Japan they call it *Nan-ten*, or sacred bamboo. It has ceremonial functions in Buddhist temples. Here we call it nandina. It's evergreen and it grows in gardens."

The superintendent raised her eyes to his.

"It's not a woodland plant," she said.

He nodded, satisfied.

"The eyes for the effigy came from a garden in Travenì," Massimo confirmed. "If we can figure out which one, maybe we can trace the killer's footsteps."

"And find out whom he's been watching," Teresa went on. "Whom he's yearned for."

Lucia didn't like disobeying her father, but one thing that bothered her even more was to be separated from her friends in a time of need.

She had received the secret signal to gather at the creek: two rings of the telephone, followed by a pause, and then another ring. It was reserved for emergencies.

She had dressed and gone out without giving much thought to the possibility that her father might come home while she was gone. Opening the front door, she had been greeted by a fairy tale landscape with a touch of eeriness about it: the fog was so dense that it had altered the features of the world beyond recognition. It got into her mouth, made it feel sticky with the taste of something damp, rotten. Lucia realized that if there was someone hiding in that whiteness, she wouldn't be able to see them until they were close enough for her to feel their breath on her face.

She walked quickly to the center of Travenì. The streets were deserted, and she could barely make out the lights inside the homes and restaurants. It was no time for tourists, and as for the locals, they were all staying indoors where it was warm. Lucia followed the main road that cut the town in half until she reached the square with the small church and the medieval clock tower. This was the spot where brave knights had repelled the invading Turks. When the teacher had told them that story, Mathias had asked whether there were any bones buried in the ground there.

The whole class had laughed at that, and the teacher had told him off for asking such a morbid question. Lucia didn't know what "morbid" meant; she'd had to ask Diego. Mathias had told her that his obsession with bodies—living or dead—disgusted his father, too, and that one day his father had called him a "psychopath." It meant that your mind didn't work right. But Lucia didn't think there was anything wrong with Mathias.

Still, the thought that there might be the remains of an ancient battle beneath her feet scared her that day. She sped up, taking the road that led from the city center to the twin lakes of Flais and through to the border. She didn't go that far, though, and stopped at the fork in the road near the railway station. Somewhere in that mist was the path that led to the statue of the Austro-Hungarian grenadier.

Lucia used the sound of her footsteps to guide her. When she heard the crunch of gravel beneath her feet, she followed that noise all the way to the slope. The higher she climbed, the thinner the fog became. The outline of the bronze statue emerged from the heavy air like a gargantuan shadow. Over on the other side of the promontory were the woods and the trail that led down into the gorge.

Through the haze of fog, Lucia spotted a scarf wrapped around the statue's neck. As if by magic, her fear dissipated. She took the last few meters to the statue at a sprint and reached the top of the hill with her breath singeing her throat. The world at her feet looked like a low-lying cloud.

The shadows became sharper. Some of them were moving, flying onto the grenadier's shoulder; others waited on the edge of that realm of grey and evanescent shapes, standing still around her like a circle of guardians.

That was when she first heard the ticking, vibrating through the air like a volley of pebbles thrown onto the gravel, then falling quiet.

Lucia wasn't alone. She turned around and peered into the mist, its shape and consistency shifting endlessly. The noise picked up again, then quickly died down. It was coming from the statue, just a few steps from where Lucia stood.

It was the sound of teeth. Chattering teeth.

Lucia looked closer at the outline of the monument and noticed the figure crouching at its base. She had never seen that familiar form so hunched, filthy, and thin, as if it had been missing from the world not just for a day, but for weeks.

"Mom!" she shouted, running to her. She huddled against her and hugged her. But she was cold, and she smelled different.

"Mom?" Lucia called again but received no response. Her mother's teeth kept chattering.

Lucia swept her mother's hair away from her face, and as she did so, her own mouth fell open in a silent scream. Her voice, sucked back inside her body, failed her.

Down in the gorge a few meters below, Lucia's friends were shouting, too, but she didn't even have time to wonder why.

There were police cars keeping watch outside the local hospital in Travenì. Teresa and Marini had just arrived in town when they received the call from Hugo Knauss, informing them that a woman had been found severely disfigured and in a state of shock.

The victim was Lucia Kravina's mother. The little girl's father could not be reached; Lucia herself had been the one to find her.

An ambulance had been sent from a village at the foot of the valley, but when the on-call doctor saw the severity of the woman's injuries, he had called for an air ambulance to take her to the hospital in the nearest city. They were waiting for the helicopter now.

"She hadn't been home since the day before, but her disappearance wasn't reported," Knauss told Teresa. "The family had been on the social services' radar in the past because of the parents' addiction problem. But it looked like they'd recovered from it. At least the mother had."

"And the girl?" asked Teresa.

"Doctor Ian is looking after her."

Teresa remembered the elderly village doctor. It was a relief to know that the child was with him.

"Has the mother said anything?"

"No. She was catatonic when I saw her, and I can understand why. She must have been through hell and looked the devil himself in the eye. Jesus Christ."

Teresa agreed.

"Yes, Melania Kravina has seen the face of the devil," she said. "That's why it's so important that we talk to her. She's the only one who can describe him to us."

Knauss scratched at his head beneath the rim of his hat. He seemed reluctant to encourage that line of thinking, in case Teresa really did mean to pester the seriously injured woman.

"She's been heavily sedated," he muttered. "The doctor who saw her first said they'll put her in an induced coma as soon as she gets to the city hospital. It might last for days, possibly even weeks. Do we have that kind of time?"

They didn't.

The noise of the approaching helicopter's rotor blades was becoming deafening. A dazzling light illuminated the landing pad, and the snow began to swirl in the air. Teresa watched the stretcher being wheeled out; there was a respirator attached to Melania Kravina's mouth, her face covered by a sterile mask for facial injuries. Teresa saw her vanish into the helicopter, which took off before its door had even closed.

She became conscious of Marini observing her.

"You knew he was going to do it again," he said.

It wasn't a question. Yes, Teresa had known and now felt responsible for what had happened.

"There are so many inconsistencies," she said. "He's been acting like a serial killer right from the start, and yet he let her live. Why?"

"Maybe she ran away."

She glanced at him.

"He bit her nose and her ears off," she said, whispering so that the curious onlookers who had begun to gather at the hospital wouldn't hear her. "You can't run away from that kind of savagery. He's lucid, but he leaves traces behind.

He behaves like an animal when he attacks, but there was something graceful in the meticulous way he positioned the first victim's body. This time, he didn't do anything like that. Roberto Valent was a forty-three-year-old male. Lucia's mother is a twenty-three-year-old woman. Serial killers choose their prey in keeping with very particular fantasies, which is why their victims always have certain shared traits. But I see nothing like that here. He appears to be acting randomly, but that's not true. It can't be."

"Why not? Because of the statistics?"

Teresa heard the sarcasm in his tone, but she was so tired that when she replied, there was no inflection in her voice. "Because the subconscious travels along predetermined paths, Marini."

"What if it didn't this time? What if we're dealing with a mind that is somehow different?"

Teresa was barely listening to him.

"Then it wouldn't be a human mind, Inspector. Now if there was some common element here, an identifiable pattern . . ."

"He steals their senses."

"What?"

"Sight. Smell. Hearing. That's what he's stolen from the victims."

Teresa was taken aback. She hadn't spotted that connection. She asked herself if Marini's theory could really explain what was happening in Travenì, whether the monster—as the newspapers and the locals had begun to call him—could really be looking for something he didn't have: the ability to *feel*.

If it was true, it was a frightening prospect: it would mean that there was a creature roaming among them capable of formulating a complex homicidal scheme with a specific objective in mind. And it would mean that he wouldn't stop until he had achieved it.

Sight. Smell. Hearing. He rips them out and takes them away. What does he want to do with them? Why does he need the senses?

She looked at Marini.

"You might actually have stumbled on a half-decent idea there," she said.

His eyes widened.

"Stumbled on it? What if it's the result of some very complex logical reasoning?"

Teresa didn't even hear him. Her mind was racing to put together a coherent picture using the latest fragments they had gathered.

"The senses. Parts of the face. Identification?" she mused— more to herself than to Marini.

"I still think 'robber of senses' is much more apt a description," he replied peevishly.

"According to psychoanalytic theory, identification is the most primitive form of attachment. It's the primordial form of love," said Teresa.

Marini let out a bitter laugh.

"Makes sense. He loves his victims and that's why he devours them," he said.

"He doesn't *love* his victims. That's not how it works. He *wants* something. There are always two sides to identification: tenderness and the urge to obliterate."

"I don't follow."

"Think of the oral stage in the development of infant libido: according to Freud, infants incorporate the object of their desire by eating it."

Her explanation was interrupted by the return of Chief Knauss.

"Doctor Ian says the girl can talk now."

• • •

Lucia was finding it difficult to trust them. It would take time for her to get to that point—but Teresa would make all the time that was needed. She didn't want to ambush the little girl with questions that would scare her and cause her to retreat even further into her shell.

She sat Lucia on her lap and waited until the little girl's body had stopped shaking. Then, she turned her around so they were face to face.

"Don't worry. You can talk to me. It will be our secret," she said reassuringly. She could tell that Lucia was worried about betraying her father.

"Swear it!"

Teresa didn't hesitate.

"I swear," she said, her hand on her heart.

So Lucia told her about the stranger who had rung their doorbell the night before, the blood that had appeared on the porch the next morning, and how her father had turned the house inside out in a frenzy.

Teresa hoped the child would never discover that the blood on the porch had belonged to her mother. It was likely that her father had instructed her to scrub the house clean to remove the traces of something he was concerned about.

"Who do you think hurt your mommy?" she finally asked.

Lucia had no doubt.

"The ghost who lives in the woods," she said.

"Oh, yes, the ghost. Have you ever spoken to him?"

The girl shook her head.

"He watches me, but he never comes near. Maybe he doesn't want to talk because he doesn't know how to. Except for last night. He was the one who rang the doorbell."

Teresa felt something surging inside her.

"So the ghost who watches you from the woods is the same

one who came to your house yesterday?" she asked, wanting to be sure.

The girl nodded.

"What does he look like?" she asked. "Can you describe him to me?"

"He has a skull instead of a head."

There was a new predator in the forest, charging through the trees with a fierce roar. Its coat was black and lustrous, with a skull and crossbones on each flank. It ripped off branches and shrubs and plucked rocks from the earth. Bird nests fell to the ground in its wake, breaking with the sound of frightened, flailing wings. From the belly of the beast came a shrieking, howling cacophony.

The SUV advanced in a mad dash along barely distinguishable paths. It carved its way through gaps that were too narrow, leaving petrol fumes in its wake. It forded a stream, raising waves of water and volleys of ice. In its progress through the woodland, it encountered occasional signs of human expansion: man-made clearings where the trees had been cut down and the undergrowth uprooted, and where excavator vehicles now stood, resting, like sleeping metal pachyderms. The new ski resort was beginning to take shape and that shape was deforestation.

Inside the vehicle, four boys were shouting and drinking beer, high on alcohol and a savage elation.

"Faster!" one of them yelled, raising his fist toward the sky through the open window.

He felt like a wrathful, destructive god, emboldened by his youth to abhor restraint and despise beauty.

The vehicle scrabbled furiously over a slope, slipping and hissing as it went. Its tires peeled the moss away and gripped at the soil beneath, but then it skidded, landing back on the dirt road with a thud.

The boys laughed, throwing squashed, empty cans outside the window. The driver scaled through the gears and the engine revved up. They drove at breakneck speed through the hairpin turns on the road that led up the mountain.

But just as they came out of a turn, they were forced to swerve to avoid an obstacle on the road. The car slammed against the side of the mountain. The boys screamed. The car bounced back onto the path, spun around by ninety degrees, and came to a standstill, the engine stopping.

Silence reigned once more, broken only by their heavy breathing.

"What the fuck was that?" said one of the boys as he tried to get out. The metal door panel had buckled, and he had to shove it free with his shoulder. He rolled out onto the road, drunk, but managing with some trouble to get back to his feet. He was bleeding from a tear in his jeans.

The others all laughed, with one exception.

"My dad's going to kill me," he slurred, reaching for another can of beer.

"I need to pee," said another.

There was someone standing in the middle of the road, watching them. It had taken them a while to notice the dark, motionless figure on the edge of their field of vision. Somehow it looked imposing even in the middle of that majestic natural landscape. They remembered now what they'd seen in the moment before the crash: a man standing with his arms stretched out in front of him, as if to stop the advance of a runaway train.

He was wearing a kind of coat they had only ever seen in old photographs. His face, covered by a rag that was also wrapped around his head, was a dark smudge where the spark of human expression would normally reside.

The boys who were still inside the SUV managed to get the engine running again, and began honking the car horn, yelling at the man to get out of the way. The stranger covered his ears, as if startled by the sudden commotion.

The boy who was out on the road started to laugh.

"Who the fuck are you?" he asked, spitting in the man's direction. "Hey, I'm talking to you!" He walked up to the man and tried to kick him.

The man grabbed him by the neck and squeezed. The boy gasped for air, his fingers curling around the man's large, rough, ruthless hand. He could barely hear his friends' screams. The arm that was holding him captive was strong, and so was the hand that was crushing his throat. It pressed unhesitatingly against his skin, blocking the passage of air.

The rag that concealed the stranger's features slipped by an inch down the skin of his face and the boy came face to face with a skull.

The eyelids were painted black, and the skin white. They looked like the eyes of a warrior—hostile and hypnotic. He felt his will to resist slipping away. He raised his hand to touch that face, and he knew then that it was real. The man's mouth fell open, exposing a set of wide, sturdy teeth the color of ivory, like the jaws of a beast—a beast that now roared with fury.

The boy felt tears running down his cheeks. He knew that he was going to die, that this man who was holding him still, as if he were no heavier than a sprig, wanted to kill him.

Instead, the stranger loosened his grip on the boy's throat and finally freed him. He shook the boy around as if he were a rag doll, but he didn't hurt him.

The boy gasped for breath. As he coughed and coughed,

with tears streaming from his eyes and blurring his vision, he dared to look once more at that face. The man was studying him. He seemed to have seen something that had made him change his mind. Something unexpected that had stopped him in his tracks.

37

The car that belonged to Melania Kravina, Lucia's mother, was parked on a lay-by off the road that led from the Flais lakes down to Travenì, a snake-like ribbon of black asphalt in a glacial landscape. The temperatures recorded in that natural hollow between the Alps and the village were among the lowest in the entire country. Every animal and mineral form there was coated in crystals of ice.

The woman had dropped one of her colleagues home before disappearing, and the snow that had fallen overnight had covered her car. The head of the forensics team who were just finishing up on the scene had already told Teresa that they hadn't found a single fingerprint. Which could only mean one thing: someone had wiped the car down.

"The husband?" Marini asked.

Teresa nodded, her eyes looking for the footprints the snow would have erased.

"He turned the house inside out and told his daughter to clean it," she said. "Then he went out and did the same with the car. He knew where to find it because he knew which route his wife would take that night to drop her friend home. He was worried about something."

"A secret."

The snow that had piled up on the side of the carriageway was dotted with a variety of animal footprints. Deer, birds, rodents . . . When nobody was looking, the forest behaved like a single organism. Every form of life left a trace of its passage.

There were skid marks on the asphalt beneath the layer of ice that the forensics team had scraped off.

"This is where the killer grabbed her," Teresa muttered, picturing the scene in her head. "He came out from the dark. She braked to avoid him and ended up in the lay-by. That's how he approaches his victims. There's no wooing."

Marini squatted to check the black marks on the road.

"Wooing?" he inquired.

"There's always a plan, a pattern, in a serial killer's dance with his chosen victim," Teresa explained. "First there is the aura phase: the killer gradually withdraws from reality into a world of increasingly defined and elaborate fantasies that will eventually spur him into action. Then the trolling phase, which marks the beginning of his hunt; he has sighted his prey, and begins to desire it. After this there should be a third so-called wooing phase: the approach to the victim. But in this case, it's missing. He's gone straight to the next phase: the capture. Then the murder phase. And finally the totem phase, the killer seeking to prolong his pleasure for as long as possible."

"How does he do that?" asked the inspector, standing up again and beating his heels against the ground to shake the ice off.

"He photographs the body. Or he dismembers it. He preserves it . . . He needs souvenirs, because when the delusions created by his fantasies begin to fade, he will realize that everything is just as it was before, and that temporary sense of omnipotence will be replaced by frustration. It's an endless cycle. The only way to quell his inner torment is to kill again."

"But he didn't kill Melania Kravina," Marini pointed out. "Technically, he's not a serial killer."

Teresa smiled.

"You're wrong. He is. He's just learning how."

Among the trees, someone called for back-up. Teresa and Marini went up to him. For several moments, nobody spoke. Blood stained the snow where it had become trapped in the frozen pool of water at the mouth of an underground spring. This was where Melania had been devoured.

De Carli walked up to Teresa.

"We've had a call from Travenì, Superintendent. A group of kids showed up at A&E saying they've been attacked. They're in shock."

38

On the way to the village hospital, Teresa couldn't speak. Her mouth was heavy with something that felt a lot like fear. The fear of being too late if the perpetrator decided to kill again. It was bound to happen, though it was difficult to predict when.

There had been an accident from which four boys had emerged virtually unscathed, blaming "some psycho." One of the boys had been assaulted and claimed he'd been on the verge of dying; the stranger had apparently held him by the throat until he'd almost choked him—but then, for whatever reason, he'd let go. This young man's name was David, and he was Hugo Knauss's son.

When she reached the hospital Teresa decided to interview his friends, who were gathered in a waiting room under Knauss's watchful eye.

Teresa went up to the chief.

"I'm sorry about your son," she said. "How is he doing?"

Knauss nodded in acknowledgment.

"Right now it's the shock that's affecting him the most," he said.

Teresa noticed that his customary smile was gone. She wondered if he was embarrassed as well as worried. He was the chief of the local police force, and his son was the village bully.

"If you'd rather be with him . . ." she suggested.

"I'd rather be looking for the culprit, Superintendent."

Teresa nodded, and turned to face the kids. They were not much more than teenagers. She thought they looked terrified—they were used to being bullies, but today they had become victims. An entirely new and disconcerting experience. She looked at their faces, analyzing their expressions. Fear gave them a child-like appearance, dilating their pupils and turning the corners of their mouths downwards, but something else was affecting them, something that at first she couldn't quite identify. Terror tended to paralyze people, but this was something different, something causing a restlessness in the boys, a lack of composure in their gestures, a constant wringing of the hands, an endless exchange of worried glances. The pack was in disarray, and it was trying to rally.

What was so troubling as to overshadow their fear? The answer came to Teresa of its own accord. She might have experienced it herself, in the past.

Guilt.

She recognized them from the incident outside Diego's school when they had almost run over a little girl in their SUV. They had gone from bullies spoiling for a fight to a bunch of frightened little boys.

"I'm Superintendent Battaglia," she told them. "This is my team."

The boys looked at her pleadingly. Teresa knew why they looked so worried: they had been drinking all day, the alcohol levels in their blood way over the legal limit.

Yet they seemed sober now, subdued by fear.

She had already read the statements they had given while still in a state of confusion. She didn't want to waste time with questions she already knew the answers to; the details of the accident were clear, and they were already being verified by a team of investigators on site. There was only one thing she was interested in.

"His face. What did it look like?" she asked.

The boys seemed bewildered. They had given contradictory statements on the matter, and now she was determined to get a conclusive response. She could have split them up and questioned each of them separately, but she suspected that this would be counter-productive. They needed to be surrounded by the rest of the pack; they would not be able to cope with the tension otherwise.

There was an art to interviewing witnesses; it required a degree of self-control to avoid planting ideas into people's heads that would hinder rather than help the search for truth. Teresa waited patiently for someone to work up the courage to speak. She could sense Marini next to her vibrating with anticipation. If it were up to him, he would have gone right up to the boys, lifted them up by their collars, and shaken them like fruit trees until they dropped some nugget of information.

One of the young men finally spoke. "I didn't see him," he said. He sounded like a teenager, and the braces on his teeth clashed with his leather jacket, which was embroidered with the face of a demon.

"His face was covered," said one of the other boys, encouraged by his friend's reply.

"Covered how?" asked Teresa.

The boy mimed the act of wrapping something around his head.

"There was light-colored fabric around his head, like this. It came down to his shoulders, too."

"Like a bandage?"

"No. It looked like . . ."

"A turban," said the boy who had spoken first.

"No way, that was no turban," the third boy chimed in. "It was more like a scarf wrapped around his head and his face.

Only the eyes were showing," he explained, demonstrating with his hands.

His friends nodded.

"Are you sure?" asked Teresa.

"Yes," they chorused.

"But then at one point we saw his mouth," said the kid with the braces. "And it looked like . . . I swear it looked like he wanted to bite David!"

He burst into tears and neither of his friends tried to comfort him. It was Chief Knauss who put his hand on the young man's shoulder and drew him toward his chest.

Teresa puzzled over their description, the emerging portrait of the suspect's physical features, trying to make sense of the rudimentary picture they had obtained. A man with his face covered up and a long coat that came all the way to his calves. His feet wrapped up in thick socks and boots. His age impossible to determine. An enigma.

She thought back to the stranger she had pursued along the old railway tracks. She couldn't say for sure whether his profile matched. She couldn't have described him in any great detail anyway. It had all happened so fast. Or perhaps her mind was no longer sharp enough.

"Does it sound like anyone from Travenì?" she asked Knauss, more out of habit than with any expectation of a positive answer. The chief shook his head.

"No, I've never seen anyone like that."

"Are you sure?"

"My eyesight's still fine, Superintendent."

"It's not your eyesight I'm worried about, Chief."

Knauss exhaled heavily, as if letting go of all the tension he'd accumulated that day.

"My son is lying on a hospital bed right now," he said. "I think you can count on my cooperation."

Teresa wasn't so sure, but she refrained from saying so.

"Fine," she said, beckoning to Marini. "Let's hear what your son has to say."

The boy was sprawled on the bed, his injured leg in a brace. Doctor Ian was by his side, dressing the wound. He smiled when he saw Teresa and Marini.

"How's he doing?"

"Just needed a couple of stitches and some painkillers. He'll be ready to go home in an hour or two."

Ian finished bandaging the wound, secured the gauze with a clip, and took his leave with a nod.

Teresa approached the boy, who'd kept his head turned toward the window. He hadn't looked at her once.

"I'm . . ."

"I know who you are," he interjected. "The whole village knows."

She found a chair and sat down by the bed. Marini stood by the door.

"Does it hurt?" she asked.

"What, my leg? No."

There were bruises on the boy's neck, but Teresa was sure that they weren't the cause of his pain either.

"It's hard to feel whole again when you've had a brush with death," she said. "Something always breaks."

He finally looked at her.

"How would you know?"

Teresa was conscious of Marini's presence behind her and didn't reply. She turned around and signalled at him to leave. He shot her a look halfway between disappointment and irritation, but in that moment, she had neither the time nor the inclination to explain that sometimes, in their line of work, you had to know when to take a step back and disappear. She waited until the door was closed before focusing on David once more.

"So? How would you know?" the boy asked her again. He'd sniffed out a crack in her armor and wasn't about to let it go.

Teresa sat on the bed. The mattress sank under her weight and brought them closer. She could feel the boy's hand against the side of her leg, but she didn't draw back. Neither did he.

"I almost died once, a long time ago," she admitted. "I know how it feels."

David studied her closely.

"An accident?" he asked.

Teresa pursed her lips and shook her head.

"An accident with rather strong arms and legs," she replied. "He hit quite hard."

"Who was it? Someone you were arresting?"

"My husband."

The boy looked at her. He was surprised, and perhaps a little doubtful. Teresa wondered if he would decide to trust her.

"How did it end?" David whispered.

Teresa smiled.

"Very badly, but I'm still alive," she said.

He lowered his eyes.

"The good thing about how you're feeling right now," she told him, "is that it will help you see the true magnitude of things."

"What things?"

"Life. Its joys and its sorrows."

David turned his head once more to look at the snow outside the window.

"Doctor Ian said I was lucky," she heard him say, "but I don't believe that. It wasn't luck."

"Then what was it?"

This time the boy stayed quiet.

"What was it, David?"

"It was *his* decision. It wasn't luck. I'm alive because *he* decided to spare me. I was going to die, I could see it in his face, but then something changed."

"What?"

He shrugged. Teresa could feel the emotion pulsating from him. It was powerful, an energy that pervaded the room.

"I cried," he murmured. "I cried, and he let me live."

Teresa hadn't expected that.

"How do you know for sure that's why he spared you?" she asked.

"Because he looked at my face, he was looking at my tears, and . . . And he changed, something in him changed, and that's why I'm alive now."

Teresa didn't know what to think. She placed the summary of the description his friends had provided onto his lap.

"Does it match?" she asked him. She watched him read it closely before looking away.

"Yes."

"Is there anything you'd like to add to it?"

"He has blue eyes, or maybe green. God, I can't remember!" He put his head in his hands. "I looked at him, I really looked at him, and still I can't remember!"

He seemed distraught. Teresa patted his hand.

"Don't worry," she said. "It's the shock. And you had other things to worry about back there. How old do you think he is?"

"Thirty, maybe forty. His face was painted."

"Do you remember anything else? It's important, David. You're the only one who's really seen him."

"I'm not the only one. You've seen him, too," he said. "Outside the school. He was dressed different, but I'm sure it was him."

So it really had been him. Now she understood where the

stain on her coat sleeve had come from. The man must be using animal excrement to paint his face.

"But that's just the means to an end," she said to herself. "He paints his face because he wants to look like a skull."

39

Light towers illuminated the forest with a premature, unnatural dawn. A few birds had begun to sing already, their cries ringing across the sky through sporadic flakes of snow.

The marks left by the SUV were still visible on the road. Shards of glass from the car's broken headlights showed the exact spot where it had crashed against the rocks.

The sequence of events as the boys had described it was backed up by the footprints on the ground. Early signs suggested that they matched the prints found on the Valent crime scene.

"It's him," said Marini.

Teresa was sure of it. She nodded in greeting at the regional chief of police and deputy public prosecutor Gardini, who were standing across from the police tape that bordered the marks.

"The boys frightened him. Why?" she wondered.

"He attacked in anger, because he was hit," said Marini.

Teresa didn't agree. From the account the boys had given, it sounded like the stranger had stood with his arms outstretched, as if to stop the vehicle. He had wanted to protect something.

"No. He did it to defend himself. He felt threatened," she replied.

"Do you think he lives in the woods?"

"Do you reckon that would be possible?"

"No—at least not in total isolation."

"I want to see the survey maps of all the mountain shelters in this area. He might be using them as bases."

Someone from the team cried out in surprise as a herd of roe deer crossed the path right in front of them in lithe, powerful leaps. It was a spectacle of sinister allure; this was not normal behavior for those animals.

"Something's scared them and driven them down to the valley," said Knauss, voicing what everyone was thinking.

Teresa eyed the gloom among the trees.

"He's here," she muttered. "He's watching us. Again."

The darkness and the forest were protecting him once more and there was no question of going in to look for him.

"And who knows where he will be tomorrow."

40

The Sleeping Bear was Travenì's only pub. It took up the basement of a building that dated back to the Middle Ages and faced out onto the main square. A short flight of stairs carved into stone led down to the bar; its walls were as thick as an outstretched arm, and the vaulted ceiling was coated in dense, uneven plaster. The relics of a rustic, sylvan past were ensconced among the protruding stone slabs of its interior walls. The only windows were tall, narrow rectangles decorated with lead-beamed, vividly polychromatic glass. From the air bubbles in the panes of glass, Teresa deduced that they must either be antiques, or meticulously accurate replicas. She didn't think any natural sunlight could filter all the way down there, even in the middle of the day, if not in the form of a dazzling rainbow of colors. A collection of beer tankards of various shapes and sizes hung over the pinewood bar. A carved devil's head with enormous curving horns and yellow, malevolent eyes observed the patrons from a wall in a corner of the room. It had a mane of black hair and pointed teeth.

Teresa was staring at it as she sat slumped in an uncomfortable chair, cradling a pint of beer she had barely sipped, and half-heartedly nibbling at peanuts from a small bowl. De Carli and Parisi were busy playing pool; Marini watched them from his perch on a bar stool. The whole unit had come down from the city as back-up, and the rest of them—the only ones who'd managed to eat something—were spread over a couple of tables at the back of the room. They'd left it up to Hugo Knauss and his men to patrol the streets that night.

The pub was half-empty. Teresa knew it was partly her fault, and the owner must have been thinking the same, judging by the glares he sent her way every now and again. Teresa responded in kind, and he always emerged defeated from the ensuing staring contest. Yet he persisted; Teresa couldn't understand why.

The sound of animated chatter announced the arrival of new customers, a group of four who made their way toward Teresa. One of them in particular carried himself with a bellicose air that instantly irritated her. She knew who he was, having met him a couple of times before, and she also knew why he looked so upset.

"Good evening, Mayor," she greeted him when he stopped by her table.

"Serial killer?" he barked without even acknowledging her greeting. "Do you know what that means for this village? It's a disaster!"

He was shaking with fury. Teresa didn't let it intimidate her. She could understand his worry, but the press release the regional police chief had issued at her suggestion was a necessary precaution in the interests of public safety.

"We never said anything like that," she told him. "But we can't deny how dangerous the situation is, either."

The man planted his hands on the table and leaned menacingly toward her.

"I'll tell you what's *really* dangerous," he said, his face reddening. "A stranger coming here and telling us what we should be scared of!"

Her eyes darted from her beer to the man's face.

"Am I the stranger you're referring to?" she asked, though she knew the answer already. To the people of the valley the rest of the world was a foreign land full of perils and populated by incompetents and unscrupulous swindlers. Their small world embodied a perfection that ought to be preserved even at the cost of a few lives. But Teresa had seen the cracks beginning to form in that picture, showing a glimpse of a reality that was far from idyllic.

"Travenì has no need for you or your lectures," the man hissed. "We've survived for hundreds of years without any help from city folk. And we will continue to do so."

Teresa fished a peanut from the bowl and placed it in her mouth. It had a rancid taste, though perhaps it was the bile rising in her throat.

"You know how to survive, do you?" she said, echoing his words. "Perhaps you should tell that to Valent's widow; it seems her husband never got the memo."

The mayor hurled an insult at her, and with a furious swipe of his hand knocked everything off her table. Her tankard shattered in a spray of foam and beer as it hit the floor, while the peanuts rolled away underneath the chairs and benches.

Teresa sprung to her feet, shooting one glance at her squad to warn them off from getting involved.

"Don't you fucking dare do anything like that ever again," she said, enunciating every word. "I will not tolerate aggression. Have I made myself clear?"

Something in her tone persuaded the mayor it would be better to desist. Teresa knew she could be much tougher than people imagined when they first saw her. And if there was one thing she was no longer prepared to countenance, it was violence.

The man seemed to calm down, though he was still breathing heavily. His friends put their arms around his chest and quietly encouraged him to leave.

"The ski season has just begun and the Christmas holidays

are around the corner," he gritted out. "Any damage to our reputation now means empty hotels and deserted ski slopes."

He was trying to justify his actions. It was a partial retreat. Teresa allowed him to vent.

"And what are we going to do about the fifth of December, huh? How are we going to celebrate the eve of Saint Nicholas's Day? We'll have worshippers dressed as the devil coming down from the mountains to the village, and we usually expect hundreds of tourists. But what's the point of a parade if there's no one around to watch it?" he continued.

Teresa listened patiently to his arguments. The mayor had good reason to be worried, but the police's priority was to protect the locals and deter curious tourists.

"I am not sure you understand how serious the situation is, Mayor. A man has been killed in broad daylight, along one of the paths favored by hikers," she said. "He was physically strong, yet he wasn't able to defend himself. He didn't even have time to try. The killer clawed the victim's eyes out; we still haven't found them. A woman has been attacked on her way home from work. She's missing part of her face, too."

Silence had fallen over the pub.

"Do you know what that means?" Teresa resumed. "That the attacker ate it or put it in his pocket and took it with him. Either way, I guess this place already has a devil of its own, and I'm afraid it's pretty real. I'll tell you what I've been wondering about, Mayor: Does this village intend to cooperate, or will it take yet another assault before it decides to do so?"

The mayor's eyes and those of his friends shifted to the demonic mask that hung near the beer tap. They saw something else, now, in its predatory snarl.

"Nobody's saying we won't cooperate," said the mayor.

Teresa shook her head.

"You see everyone from outside your community as trespassers—even us, though we're here to help. You huddle together and reject the outside world thinking that will save you, but all you're doing is making things worse."

The mayor didn't react. He left without saying a word, followed by his friends. Perhaps they were still angry, or perhaps they were now also a little scared.

Teresa sat back down among broken glass and scattered peanuts. The barman hurried over to wipe her table clean and mop the floor, his eyes downcast. A young woman brought her a fresh glass filled to the brim with beer, telling her sheepishly that it was on the house.

Slowly the chatter resumed, though it was quieter than before. Teresa sipped her beer. Only then did she notice the man sitting at a table on the opposite side of the pub. Doctor Ian raised his tankard in Teresa's direction, and she did the same. She watched him rise to his feet and walk toward her, bringing his hat and beer with him.

"May I?" he asked.

"Of course."

The doctor sat down.

"You mustn't take it personally," he said. "The mayor is a good man, though his methods are questionable. For many families in Travenì, having fewer tourists would make it impossible to make ends meet. There's not much else to live on around here."

"I don't enjoy frightening people or spreading panic, Doctor, but this time I don't have a choice. Fear is often the difference between survival and death. It can save you."

"Oh, I understand, of course. Fear originates in the most primitive part of our brain, the one we have in common with reptiles. Even after millions of years of evolution, its core is still here," he said, tapping at his head, "in a tiny hub the shape of an almond. God must think it indispensable if He hasn't seen fit to change it in any way."

Teresa smiled. It seemed bizarre that a man of science should bring God into play when discussing human anatomy.

"This village was completely isolated until just a few decades ago, and people were used to struggling to scrape together two meals a day," the doctor told her. "Some of them were farmers, but most of them loggers who survived on hunting and the timber trade. It wasn't uncommon for women to have miscarriages during the harsher winters, or to abandon newborns who looked too weak in the churchyard of the convent further down the valley. Those were different, desperate times. Fortunately, those days are a distant memory now, but I do think that hunger is encoded in the DNA of the people of this valley."

"I didn't know things had been so difficult."

"They were. Modern transport links have helped eradicate poverty, and the development of tourism in recent years has improved many people's lives. But not everyone is willing to accept change."

"Are you referring to the activists who are boycotting the new ski station?"

He nodded. "Transitions are never easy," he added.

Teresa turned her glass around in her hands.

"Speaking of children," she said, "there's something I'd like to ask you."

"Go ahead."

"Was the first victim, Roberto Valent, a little cold, as a father?"

Ian frowned.

"No, not at all," he quickly replied. "Why do you ask? Is there a new lead to . . . ?"

Teresa shook her head. She didn't even know why she had asked him.

"It was only a theory, Doctor, and it isn't even relevant to the case. There's no lead. I just wanted to have a more accurate sense of what kind of person Valent was."

"Roberto was a well-respected professional and a model husband. He spent all his free time with his wife. As for his relationship with his son, I would say it was excellent. Diego is a perfect boy."

Teresa was beginning to understand the criteria by which the doctor made his judgments. They were rather different from hers.

"A perfect boy," she repeated after him, nodding her head. "Just like his dad wanted."

"Roberto even did some volunteering, did you know?"

Teresa didn't reply. She asked him whether anyone in the village had ever shown symptoms of mental instability, increasing in severity over the past few months. He dismissed the question.

"While isolation can cause a mind to falter, murder is something else altogether, Superintendent. I've known almost everyone in this village from the moment they were born, and I'm certain there isn't a single one among them who would be capable of anything like this."

Teresa studied the crucifix around his neck. She refrained from noting that murderers were no less children of his God than saints were, and they could be born anywhere—even Travenì.

41

"**S**tay right where you are."

Parisi hadn't even looked at Marini as he'd spoken, concentrating on his game of pool with De Carli. He was winning fairly easily, but De Carli wasn't about to give up, and every now and then he even made a decent shot.

"She can look after herself," said Parisi with a smile. "If you go to her, you'll only piss her off."

"And it doesn't take much to piss her off," De Carli added while trying to work out the best angle for his next shot. He got it wrong and missed.

Massimo looked at Teresa Battaglia. Her altercation with the mayor had turned every head in the room in her direction. Marini had been about to head over to make sure that awful man knew she had back-up.

"I haven't even moved," he said. "How could you tell?"

Parisi shrugged, pocketing another ball.

"Because you're not the first. We've all been through it, and she's made it clear to each of us that's not what she needs." He looked at Massimo. "If even her own team starts to treat her like she's weak, how can we expect people who don't know her to do any different?"

"It's harder for a woman," De Carli concurred. "She has to prove over and over again that she is not on the verge of collapse, and that she has the authority to keep us all under control."

Massimo drank a sip of his beer.

"I'm not in any danger of underestimating her," he said. "She steamrolls over me every day."

Parisi burst out laughing.

"It's obvious that you're her favorite. She ignored yours truly for almost two years before she learned my name."

"It must be all those sweets he brings her," De Carli teased.

Massimo grimaced.

"She's a woman," he said. "They usually like that sort of thing."

"Ah!" said Parisi. "That's exactly the kind of thing you mustn't say. If you think of her as a woman rather than just a person, that's already a form of discrimination in her eyes."

Marini found that he was rather confused with regards to all that had to do with Superintendent Battaglia.

"I have to say, it's the first time I've ever been made to feel sexist about an act of kindness," he protested.

The two officers looked at each other and laughed.

"She's your superintendent," said De Carli. "Completely asexual. A superior being who could make your life very, very complicated—and, I should add, would be delighted to have a reason to do so."

"So I've noticed. Doesn't she have a family?"

Massimo saw the expression on his colleagues' faces change, as if they'd suddenly been troubled by some dark thought.

"She did," said De Carli, but his colleague silenced him with a glare.

Massimo couldn't understand the secrecy.

"That's it?" he asked.

Parisi pocketed another ball.

"It didn't end well," said De Carli, murmuring again. "Let it go."

"What happened? What did she do?" Marini asked, feeling increasingly baffled.

Parisi placed his cue stick on the pool table.

"Superintendent Battaglia does have a family. *We* are her family."

De Carli copied him.

"We might never say it to her face, but we'll always be there for her."

Massimo was struck by their responses. He looked at the superintendent and wondered how she had managed to earn that kind of devotion. She seemed unaware of the reactions she induced in those around her, or perhaps she simply didn't care. In any case, he thought she seemed terribly lonely. That, more than anything else, was what stuck in his mind, for he could sense that loneliness was not a condition she was involuntarily subjected to, but something that she stubbornly sought out. Parisi and De Carli guarded her secrets. They had made it clear to him that he shouldn't ask too many questions, and that he'd do better to avoid the subject altogether. Massimo wondered again what might have happened to her family. Beyond her caustic wit and difficult personality, he could see there was a profound, sensitive humanity to her. He had noticed it while watching her deal with little Diego Valent, and again every time he saw her lay eyes on a victim. Like that boy they'd just interrogated in the hospital. She was deeply empathetic, and that same quality caused her pain.

Parisi put his hand on Massimo's shoulder.

"Another beer?" he offered, smiling.

Marini nodded.

"One day you'll understand," said De Carli, turning his focus back on the game.

"Understand what?" Massimo asked him.

"Why we care so much about her. It'll happen to you, too."

42

FOREST OF TRAVENÌ-ABERLINZ, 1988

The late afternoon sun warmed the crooked boards of the mountain shelter, releasing the aroma of old timber—a mixture of honey and hay. The forest, swaying in the warm breeze, shone with a bright, iridescent green. Spots of shimmering light floated among the blades of grass—diligent insects and feathery pollen. The birds sang their melodies from dawn to dusk, before the crickets took over with their chirping.

The child learned about the world through a gap in the beams supporting the wall, opened up by time and the alternation of hot summers with harsh winters. His tiny fingers stuck out on the other side where they twirled in the air, free at last. The animals of the forest had learned to recognize them and no longer feared them. Sometimes they would come close enough to lick them or to brush their fur against them. He would seek out those moments of searing contact and feel just beneath their skin the beating of a heart like his own.

The first time he'd felt that, on a night two springs before, he'd been surprised. He had pressed his body right up against the wall so as to push his arm as far out as he could through the gap. He had learned to identify life by placing the palm of one hand against the chest of a deer, and the other against his own. He had felt it pulsating in time with the night, accompanied by the hooting of owls and the rush of water in the stream. He had stayed like that for a while, looking at the sky while the creature grazed on the other side of the wall.

By now he had become familiar with the motion of the stars and the moon, the geography of the world above his head, the dance of time and of the seasons, the alternation of life and death in the forest.

Through that gap he had watched animals being born, but also going to sleep forever, and being consumed until they became one with the soil. He had watched the females choose their mates and wondered where he had come from.

He twisted a piece of string between his fingers, made a knot, and lowered it through the gap. Resting his ear against the wooden boards, he listened to the light hopping steps of the lizards that came to bask in the sun. It took a while to find the right moment, but he had time to spare, and the fox had taught him how to be patient. He jerked at the string and the knot tightened around a lizard. He pulled it toward him and through the gap. The tiny animal writhed almost weightlessly in his hands. Cradling it in his palms, he stretched his arms out toward the darkest corner of the room.

That corner where no light could ever reach was where the creature that had recently been keeping him company always chose to hide. It was scared of the outside world, though there was no reason why it should be. He would protect it, just as he had seen mothers do with their young.

He called out to it with a low sound, but it didn't emerge from its hideout. He tried again, throwing morsels of food at it, but even those weren't enough to lure it out of the darkness.

He placed the lizard on the floor and made it run backwards and forward on its leash of string. Finally, he heard the rustle of something moving.

A little hand appeared from the dark.

43

Teresa had been authorized by the regional chief of police to move her team to the police station in Travenì. Conducting the investigation from within the village would save time and resources. But the truth was that she felt another attack was imminent. Death wasn't done with that place yet. Teresa was sure of it.

She had let some air into the room and made up her bed with the sheets and blankets Chief Knauss had passed around. After a hot shower, she'd injected herself with her dose of insulin and unpacked the few personal belongings she'd brought from the city.

Outside the window, the streetlights in the courtyard illuminated the heaviest snowfall Teresa had seen in years. She stood watching the large flakes fall, looking for a sense of peace she hadn't felt in a long time. She remembered the winters of her childhood, the houses buried almost to the roof in downy banks that the wind sculpted into waves, the toboggan slides down the hills, the tussles on the snow, and the benevolent weight of the crystals coming to rest upon her upturned face.

In the past few hours she had been deliberating whether to stay on this case. She could feel she was no longer able to push her body to the limits of what this investigation required. Of course, it would continue to do her bidding despite everything: her unreasonable demands, the many indicators of her ill-health, exhaustion, fear. The soreness in her muscles, the cold, the heat, the lack of sleep. The problem was that she just didn't want to ask all that of her body any longer.

But at the same time, it wasn't solely Teresa's decision to make. The voices of the victims rang in her ears throughout the day, and only grew louder at night. They would not allow her to rest until the killer was found, the cycle of death broken.

Like a weary fighter, Teresa pulled the curtains shut over her memories, her own private needs. It was her way of picking up her weapons and getting back to her feet. From her bag, she took out a brand-new diary she'd bought that morning. She tore the plastic wrapper off and opened it, running her fingers over its pages.

The time had come to reorganize her daily life, to become even more methodical than before, and learn to be her own guardian. She would write down the salient moments of her life; she would start with that night from her past, until she would arrive, one day, at the future—for she wanted to record the dreams she had yet to realize, her ambitions, her plans, and everything else for which there was still room in her life, no matter how much time fate decided to assign to her. She also wanted to test her memory in the days ahead and see whether she would forget any of the things that happened to her. She was not going to surrender to the idea that she was sick.

On the first page of the diary, she wrote down the word she hadn't yet been brave enough to say aloud: the name of the illness that had maybe—just maybe—begun its attack on her mind.

The price of writing it down was having to admit it into her life. It was officially part of it now, a character in her story; and yet her lips still refused to breathe life into that sound, as if by letting the word lie sleeping silently between the pages of that diary, she might somehow postpone her punishment.

Two raps on the door startled her. She closed the diary, but immediately opened it again to erase the word in a feverish swipe. She wasn't ready to face it just yet.

She opened the door to find Marini leaning against the frame. He smiled at her, holding a bag of cookies. This was becoming a bad habit of his.

"You haven't had anything to eat," he said.

Teresa took the cookies and read the label. Just as expected.

"They're for diabetics," she protested.

"Fine, I'll have them back then . . ."

Teresa held them fast.

"I let you go home for just a few hours and instead of minding your own business, you go and buy me cookies?" she asked.

He didn't reply.

"When will you stop craving my approval so badly? It's pathetic. I'm not your mother," she said, though without animosity. She had begun to find him rather sweet. Irritating, but sweet.

"You're my boss. And you're good," he replied.

"So I've been upgraded! Just yesterday I was still a glorified fortune teller."

"I never thought that."

"Really? Well, maybe you should have. Our investigation is at a dead end."

She would never forget the smile that formed on Marini's face; it wiped out days' worth of fatigue and tension.

"We have a name, Superintendent. And it matches the profile you came up with."

44

Lucas Ebran, thirty-nine. He lived with his mother in a village in the valley, off the road that led to Travenì. At the age of thirteen, he had set the school bathrooms on fire; more recently, he'd had an argument with the neighbors. They were convinced he had killed their cat. Their dog had also disappeared after being seen with him. They suspected Ebran because they thought he was odd, and they'd begun to fear the unhinged looks and the silences with which he responded to their greetings.

"Pyromania and potential animal abuse. Good work, Parisi," said Teresa.

"His father was a hunter," the officer added. "He killed himself with a gunshot in the mouth when his son was a teen-ager. Lucas was the one who found the body in the basement."

Teresa tried to imagine how traumatic that must have been, especially at that delicate time in life when we are on the cusp of maturity, but still carry inside the impulses and insecurities of a child. She pictured him walking down the stairs that led to the basement, smelling the scent of death, opening the door into the darkness, and finding his father's maimed body.

"What does he do?" she asked.

"He's unemployed. He knew the first victim: he worked as a bricklayer on the site for the ski resort. He was fired two weeks before Valent's death for his inability to complete any of the tasks assigned to him, no matter how simple."

Teresa felt her whole body tingle with an excitement she had to keep under control.

"His psychosis wouldn't let him," she said distractedly.

Parisi continued, "He's been spotted lurking on the edge of the woods, spying on people's homes. Someone's been worried about him harassing their teenage daughter. We're looking for him now."

Teresa could feel the whole squad looking at her as they awaited her response. She was about to make a decision that could change a man's life. Ebran was either a savage, blood-thirsty killer, or just a misfit who lived on the fringes of the community, completely harmless.

Maybe someone else poisoned the cat, and the dog had simply run away. Maybe Lucas Ebran had acted out as a teen-ager because he'd suffered from his father's abandonment, and he detested his neighbors because he felt the weight of their judgment. He spied on other families because he envied them and would have liked to know some of that warmth himself, and he liked to stare at beautiful teenage girls because he'd never had a girlfriend in school.

Maybe Ebran was all this, but not a killer. Still, Teresa couldn't leave any room for doubt. She hated her own intran-sigence sometimes, and the only way she could live with it was by constantly reminding herself that someone might be about to die and was currently going through the last few moments of their life completely unaware of how close they were to its end.

"Fine," she said. "Give me five minutes, then call up the deputy public prosecutor. There's something I need to sort out in the meantime."

45

Teresa found Hugo Knauss in the kitchen, where he was making himself a cup of tea. The kettle was sputtering on the stove, and he had a teabag ready on the table, with a slice of lemon on a saucer.

"Put that mug down and turn around," she growled.

He was so surprised that he did as she commanded.

"What's wrong?" he asked. The light accentuated his features. With his darkened skin, roughened by the cold, he looked like a wooden mask carved by a sculptor with a sense of humor: the ears were too big, the nose was too small, the eyes were too close together . . .

Teresa didn't let his affable expression fool her. She was sure there was no emergency grave enough that would wipe that impudent smirk off his face. It was his trademark, a permanent fold in the texture of his face. She had to put him in his place, and she had to do it now. She had already waited too long.

"What's wrong? How about every single thing you've done since we got here," she answered. "Lucas Ebran: does the name ring a bell?"

Knauss lowered his gaze momentarily before replying: he knew he had made a mistake. The only question now was whether he'd intended to actively disrupt the investigation.

"Ebran," said the policeman with a sigh, turning off the stove. "He's not our man."

Teresa could have slapped him. He just didn't get it.

"The problem isn't Ebran. Not really. The problem, Chief Knauss, is that I need to know I can trust my colleagues. I need to know I can count on the eyes and ears of those who work with me as if they are my own, and I can't say I feel that way about you. Can you guess why that might be?"

She cocked her head to one side while she waited for him to respond.

Knauss wet his lips and let his eyes roam over the room, as if he were looking for the right words to say. There weren't any. Teresa hadn't come there looking for an explanation or an apology. She had come to restore a hierarchy, a sense of order. It may not have been pleasant, but it was certainly necessary. Sometimes she felt like an ageing stag rutting with the younger bucks in a bid to protect its leadership of the herd. Except that she'd been born a female, and she wasn't exactly dying to lock horns with the others. It was draining and unnecessarily tiring, but if it was going to help her do her job better, she was ready to hit harder than anybody else.

"So?" she prodded.

Knauss sighed again.

"It won't happen again," he said. "I'll tell you everything."

Teresa nodded.

"David is in the hospital right now, probably because he came face to face with the killer we're looking for, and yet you're still here trying to get the better of me," she said. "Your son is alive by a stroke of luck. Remember that, next time you feel like you ought to lead the investigation in my stead, Chief."

She saw him swallow.

"Ebran is a wretch," said the man, "and his mother is ill."

"And his father died, and he has no friends," Teresa said in a sing-song voice. She took a step closer and lifted her chin to look him in the eye. "I don't give a damn if you think that means he can't be the man we're looking for. I don't give a damn if you're incompetent. But don't try to derail my investigation again."

Knauss seemed to have stopped breathing.

"I never tried to derail it," he said.

Teresa did not move a millimeter from where she stood.

"If you withhold any information ever again, or so much as put a foot wrong, I swear I'll kick you off the case."

46

There was no sound left in the world except for the subdued crackle of fresh snow falling over the old. The night had transformed those early, timid flakes into a silent blizzard. It was a formidable winter. The forest was an expanse of crystal, of creatures curled up in cozy lairs, and tree branches weighed down with a heavy whiteness they would periodically shrug off, bending all the way to the ground as they did so. A few animals were still out in search of food, their eyes gleaming in the darkness, their coats white, shards of ice sticking to their whiskers, and steam blowing from their nostrils.

From his hiding place at the foot of a centennial fir tree, he observed the forest, hugging himself for warmth, biding his time.

He was hunting for a prey he'd been stalking for weeks. He had studied its habits, its routes, its encounters with its own kin. He knew that sooner or later that night, it would pass by that spot, and he had readied his welcome accordingly. His prey was a creature of habit; even the blizzard wouldn't change its plans.

He soon saw it approaching. The lights of the metallic vehicle on which it travelled cut into the depths of the forest, and as they came around the first bend of the road, they briefly illuminated his hideout.

He got up to follow, bending low into the undergrowth as he walked. The vehicle made slow progress. The darkness had caught it out on a particularly insidious stretch where the mountain was at its harshest, and the ice so thick that it wouldn't melt until spring. The vehicle scrambled and lurched forward, spreading pungent fumes into the air.

His prey was nervous. He could tell even from that distance by the tension in its face. Its sunken eyes were narrowed in an attempt to recover their focus. Its lips looked as if they were being pulled into its mouth. It was agitated, and probably also scared. This was his kingdom, and his prey felt out of place in it. It was already trapped.

Just as expected, the metal vehicle stopped at the third bend. For a long moment, it stood still in the middle of the road, and nothing happened. Then, the door opened, and his prey climbed out. He watched as it emerged into the freezing air, huddling into its clothes and fussing with its hat.

In front of it lay a dark shape resting on its flank, lit up by the yellow beams from the vehicle. The snow hadn't buried the figure yet, and its bristly fur glistened in the night.

His prey approached the carcass of the wild boar that he had earlier placed on that spot. It seemed to be deliberating how to load the boar onto its vehicle, to take it away and feast on its flesh.

Watching his prey, he prepared to pounce. He shifted until he was behind it, then walked out of the woods. The snow muffled the sound of his footsteps. It was, he thought, like walking on clouds.

His hands were itching to go. But his heart was calm. There was no rush, no urgency. Only the need to take a life, just like the winter took the life of the flowers and the grass.

He stopped just a few steps away from his foul-smelling prey. Standing in the blizzard, he waited for it to become aware of his presence and turn to face him, revealing the eyes he had recently begun to recognize, and the likes of which he had not seen in any other animal except his own species; they reminded him of dirty river water after a flood. They were murky and treacherous, and slippery, too.

His prey had been hunching over the carcass, but now straightened its back and turned its head to stare through the flurries of snow at the figure that now blocked its way back to its vehicle. It stood up. He could tell from its expression that it still hadn't realized the truth.

It hadn't realized that those who scorn life must forfeit their own someday.

It hadn't realized that those who prey on the weak will sooner or later find someone on their path who is stronger than they are.

It hadn't realized that it was already as good as dead.

47

How far gone am I? I feel lost, even though my mind is still working. What will become of me when the real confusion sets in? (Confusion: that's what I'm going to call it.) I suppose the tiredness of these past few hours can only worsen my condition, instead of keeping my synapses firing, and stimulating the brain cells I've got left, those that aren't already moribund. I don't even want to think about those that have already died.

I didn't mean for this diary to turn into some sort of litany of sorrows, but it looks like I've become a grouchy old lady, as well as a pain in the ass.

Anyway: where was I?

Lucas Ebran: prime suspect.

Following two days of silvery skies and early twilights, the roofs and the streets of the villages in the valley glittered that morning under the light of a radiant sun. It was as if the blizzard had cleansed the world. Gone were all traces of dirty slush at the side of the roads, of the marks the rain left on the windows, and the putrefying flora in the ditches. All was pristine and covered in rounded heaps. The world smelled of ice and of logs burning in fireplaces.

By the time Teresa and Marini reached Lucas Ebran's house, Chief Knauss's car was already parked in the driveway. The chief had insisted on preceding them so as not to upset Ebran's mother, who was elderly and unwell. He was sure he'd do a better job than they could at finding the right words to explain this intrusion. He had just called Teresa's phone to let her know in advance that Ebran wasn't home and his mother didn't know where he was.

When she got out of the car, Teresa glimpsed the shadow of someone looking out of the window of the neighboring house. The figure retreated immediately.

"The neighbors seem nosy," said Marini.

Teresa avoided looking at their house again.

"They want to go back to feeling safe," she said. "They'd be prepared to go on a witch hunt if it meant getting rid of what they fear."

Hugo Knauss himself opened the door to let them into the Ebran home. He could hardly look at Teresa after their argument. And she didn't trust him anymore; his reticence could prove dangerous. It was the same attitude she'd seen in Valent's widow. The people of Travenì were protective of each other, and diffident toward outsiders. Nobody wanted to answer the police's questions. In fact they tried to keep all interactions to a minimum, even avoiding eye contact if possible. They would rather shield a murderer than feel they were being observed and judged by people they considered foreigners. Teresa had only now realized how the community viewed tourists: as a necessary evil that had to be endured. She would never find support and collaboration from within that historic, impregnable village core forged by centuries of isolation.

So she had instructed Parisi to look more closely at the dynamics within the village, though without informing Chief Knauss. They had to find a weak link, someone who would be willing to talk, someone who—just like Teresa and her team—didn't quite fit in, and might, out of resentment or a need for attention, be ready to disclose the sins of the village. Teresa knew what these communities were like, she had dealt with similar cases before; there was always someone who had been ostracized, who was brimming with bitterness and yearning to even the score. She had to find that person. What she wanted was a name, and a profile that matched. The killer knew the town well. Surely the town must know him, too.

Ebran's mother was older than Teresa had expected, or perhaps she had been worn down by a difficult life. Her over-weight form was squeezed into a tattered, stained armchair. Her legs, visible under the rim of her skirt, were swollen. Her uncombed hair fell over her face, and she had a dazed look about her. She seemed frightened and angry and was barely answering Knauss's questions. She kept giving the same reply: she knew nothing, she understood nothing. She started railing at Parisi, who had been watching her.

"You come here looking for my boy, when the whole town is full of secrets! People who'll go to church in the morning and creep into the wrong bed at night! A bunch of hypocrites! Why don't you go and count how many bastard children there are in Travenì. Hundreds!"

Teresa looked away, partly in embarrassment, and partly to hide her morbid fascination with that struggling creature. She felt pity for her, and fear for herself, fear that she might one day turn into someone like her.

"Make her stop," she told Marini. She sounded like she was pleading, and realizing this, she left the room.

The rest of the house was the same as the living room: neglected and stuck in a distant past. Lucas's room was like a teenager's: old posters with frayed corners hanging on the walls, a guitar nestling in a corner, the bed unmade, clothes scattered all over the floor.

Teresa heard Marini behind her. There was no sound coming from the living room anymore.

The inspector put on a pair of gloves and picked up a shoe.

"Size ten," he said. "It matches the profile of the killer."

Under the bed and in the cupboard, they found stacks of porn magazines.

"He certainly enjoys a spot of violence," said Marini as he leafed through them.

Teresa pulled them out of his hands and threw them onto the bed.

"If it were that easy to draw up a psychological profile, even you could manage it," she told him.

She couldn't help but feel sorry for that mother and son who had, at some point in their lives, been cut adrift. She forced herself to remain alert and detached.

"The fact that at his age he's still relying on photographs to satisfy his urges, rather than an actual woman—that says something," she said. "I doubt he's ever had a romantic relationship. He lives with a mother who is the embodiment of physical and mental breakdown. And it's likely he doesn't have any friends."

"It's been years since I last saw this kind of magazine. Doesn't he know it's easier and cheaper to use the internet these days?"

That was when they realized there wasn't a single electronic device in the entire house. No computers, no mobile phones, not even a TV. It was as if they had gone back in time.

Teresa pointed out the date on one of the magazines.

"They probably belonged to his father."

The furniture and fittings revealed a difficult financial situation. There was a shelf filled with books on the local fauna, and more of the same on the bedside table. It seemed Ebran was fascinated with wild animals. A map of the world on the wall was dotted with felt-tip pen marks. Teresa let out a melancholy sigh. "All the trips he could never afford to make," she whispered.

She could feel Marini's eyes on her.

"It's almost like you feel sorry for him."

"It's called empathy."

"He could be the killer."

"Yes, he could be."

"Doesn't that mean anything to you?"

"Of course it does. It means that before crossing the point of no return, every serial killer is a human being in pain. Often abused. Always lonely."

Marini's phone rang. After a quick conversation with the headquarters in Travenì, he hung up.

"A man has been reported missing. His name is Abramo Viesel," he explained. "He didn't show up at his sister's for dinner last night, and his phone's been unreachable for hours. The sister can't go anywhere because of the snow, but she's worried. She says it's never happened before."

Teresa parted the yellowed lace of the curtains and looked out of the window. In the garden, cutting through the snow, was a tuft of pointed leaves and crimson berries.

Abramo Viesel was a janitor at the school in Travenì. He was divorced and had no children. Once a week he went to see his sister, Caterina, for dinner; she lived with her family in a chalet just outside the village, in an isolated stretch of flat land.

Teresa and Marini had been forced to wait for a snowplow before they could drive to her place. They were following it now as it pushed at walking speed through a series of sharp, tricky turns. Marini was focused on his driving and hadn't said a word since they had set off. Teresa observed the landscape. The moment they'd begun to climb, they had been swallowed by low clouds girding the mountain peak like a crown. The world had transformed once again, this time into a limbo of mist, ice, and fading light.

After a few hairpin turns, the snowplow stopped. The driver stuck his arm out of the open window to draw their attention. They stopped the car and got off. The air was saturated with minuscule particles of water. They were breathing clouds.

The man pointed at something in the middle of the road. About a hundred meters from where they stood, two flashing lights cut through the fog.

"Stay inside and don't come out for any reason," Marini told the driver, who needed no convincing.

Marini and Teresa drew their weapons and started walking. They saw a jeep with its engine still running, its exhaust fumes mixing with the mist.

They edged forward, alert to the shadows around them, jumping every time a lump of snow happened to slide off an overburdened branch.

"There's someone inside," said Marini.

Through the back of the vehicle, they could see the head of a man wearing a hat. The license plate matched the one they were looking for.

Marini called out Abramo Viesel's name, but the figure in the car didn't move.

Teresa pointed at the snow beneath the door on the driver's side. It was red. Blood was still dripping down onto it. She closed her eyes for a moment.

Once again, we've come too late, she thought.

Martini opened the door and swore. The body had been placed on the driver's seat, its hands bound to the steering wheel with string.

"The skin's covered in blood, but the clothes are clean," he said.

Teresa was still gripping her gun, and she felt her hand shake as she lowered it.

"That's not his skin. He's peeled the skin off and put the clothes back on."

She had to walk away to regain her composure. When she looked again at the scene she saw a shape on the road lit up by the car's headlights. For a radius of two meters around it, the ground wasn't white: the floury snow there looked like a pool of strawberry ice cream. The involuntary association made Teresa feel sick. It was blood. This was the spot where the killer had celebrated his ritual.

She squatted down and swept the snow aside, exposing the hide of an animal.

"Maybe that's how he makes them stop," she said out loud to ensure Marini heard her.

He went up to her. His face was drawn, and he looked deeply distressed. He wiped away the rest of the snow and managed with difficulty to turn the carcass over. It was a wild boar.

"The legs are tied together with rope," he said. "He must have used a trap to catch it. He didn't shoot it. The neck is broken . . . That would require a huge amount of strength."

Teresa nodded.

"Our killer doesn't like weapons. He kills and hunts with his bare hands."

"But that uses up a great deal more energy."

"And it's risky. Never underestimate the strength people can muster when they're fighting for their lives. But they don't care."

Marini looked at her.

"Who's they?" he asked.

"People like him. They're obsessed with blood. Ed Kemper would dissect the bodies of his victims to play around with their internal organs."

"Do you mind if I throw up?"

"Not all over my evidence, Inspector."

"Is that what you think the killer is doing?"

"What do you mean?"

"The skin is not here. Did he take that with him, too?"

Teresa sighed. She felt tired and defeated. There was no sign of the rage she desperately needed to feel.

"Call headquarters," she commanded. "And get the forensics team here."

She rose wearily to her feet and noticed a bloodied rock on the ground a little way off, far from the tracks around the jeep. It was sheltered by the branches of a fir tree, and the snow hadn't covered it. The killer might have used it to knock the victim unconscious, perhaps with a blow to the back of his head.

She went back to the body and looked more closely at its

head. She tried to look under the fur hat without touching anything: even the scalp had been removed.

She felt a light puff of air stroke her face. It was warm. She looked uncomprehendingly at the body's blank eyes. And when the truth began to dawn on her, she felt like her body might finally fail her.

"He's alive!" she shouted.

49

Bergdorf, 12 November 1978

Day 94

Initial observations indicate that the subjects remain healthy, exhibiting no signs of illness or serious pathology, despite continuing to show symptoms of what our esteemed colleague René Spitz termed "anaclitic depression." I would describe their condition as a waking stupor.

Interestingly, one individual has shown a partially dissimilar reaction. Unlike the others, this subject demonstrates a high level of responsiveness, despite the absence of external stimuli. Though he, too, lacks facial expressions, the attendant has twice described him as appearing to be "aware."

As I had predicted, he has begun to reject physical contact and has responded aggressively to an attempt to approach him. The attendant is convinced that the subject exerts some kind of negative influence upon the others.

Though it has no scientific basis, and rests on mere superstition, her suspicion indirectly supports my own theory: that the subject possesses the traits of a "primitive alpha male." In Freud's definition, he is a "Father," a dominant male, an individual equipped with exceptional authority, capable of ruling over the masses and subjugating the primitive horde—the earliest incarnation of human society.

The "Father" possesses a mysterious power that might be termed animal magnetism. Like a hypnotist, he uses his eyes to exert his influence. There is notably something sinister about hypnosis itself: one takes without asking, one enters uninvited.

We must conclude that the subject in question possesses what Freud described as *mana*.

In light of the attendant's observations, I have studied the behavior of the individuals situated in proximity to the subject.

As of now, I can report that those closest to the alpha male are deteriorating at a slower rate than the others, as if some form of communication were helping them overcome their isolation and draw strength from elsewhere (from the "Father"?).

We must thus concur with Spitz's closing observations: social interaction is crucial to human survival.

To those who might object that the subject is too young to manifest the characteristics of a "Father," I shall reply in Freud's words:

"Just as primitive man virtually survives in every individual, so the primal horde may arise once more out of any random crowd."

That is what is happening here.

50

Superintendent Battaglia had decided to follow the ambulance that was carrying Abramo Viesel to the hospital in the city. Massimo, who had insisted on driving, was spurring the car as fast as it would go in the wake of the ambulance's blaring sirens. Neither of them said a word on the way. He was pretending to concentrate on the road, she on the view outside the window, and on those sweets of hers that so irritated him. He didn't understand how she could be so cavalier with her health. She was popping them into her mouth one after the other, so slowly, he thought, that she had to be doing it on purpose to goad him into voicing his disapproval. But Massimo didn't take the bait. His sense of unease left little room for anything but silence. He could picture Teresa's thoughts and knew she must in turn know his. At long last they had something in common, but it was something horrific: an act of violence so extreme that it numbed the soul. Together, they had witnessed a profound darkness and come away from it with their stomachs cramping and their hearts burdened.

They arrived at the A&E to find a frenzy of activity as the paramedics unloaded the stretcher. Soon, Viesel was swallowed by the sliding doors, and calm reigned once more.

"You should go home," said the superintendent.

Massimo opened his mouth to object, but she didn't give him the chance.

"I'll stay. Go home and rest for a couple of hours. I'll call you when it's time."

It wasn't a suggestion; it was an order, though her voice when she imparted it was so tired that he could barely hear it.

Massimo watched her walk toward the entrance, looking exhausted in mind and body. It was obvious that something inside her was beginning to give; something had cracked and was making her falter. Yet she stayed on her feet and kept going, despite everything.

He returned to his car, turned the engine on, and realized that he didn't really feel like holing up in his apartment—that place he still didn't quite consider a home.

He drove aimlessly around the city center, hoping that it might relax him, but having to deal with the traffic and with reckless pedestrians worsened his mood. He was waiting at a red light when he remembered that he wasn't too far from the public library.

Why not, he thought.

When the light changed to green, he took a turn instead of driving straight through.

He had already devoured the books he'd borrowed earlier, reading well into the night and during the short breaks he took for lunch and dinner, and he'd been surprised to find he was actually interested in the material. He wanted to continue this journey into the psyche of a murderer partly to better understand how Teresa Battaglia worked: what she thought, *why* she thought it.

At that time of night, the library was full of university students. Massimo tried to blend in and made a point of not looking for the girl who'd pegged him for a sociopath the last time he'd come. He made straight for the section he was interested in and started scanning the book spines.

Would Teresa Battaglia also come here, back in the day, and turn her face up to the shelves, a fire inside her urging her to find out more, to look beyond the surface of things?

He could picture her there, the temples of her glasses between her lips, constantly blowing her red fringe out of her eyes.

"I'm sorry."

He turned around. It was her, the librarian girl, and this time she was smiling at him.

"Hi," he said.

"I'm sorry," she repeated, biting her lip.

Massimo shrugged.

"What for?" he asked.

"For thinking you were some kind of murderous psycho."

He laughed.

"What makes you think I'm not?" he teased.

"I saw you on TV, on the news."

"Oh, so psychos can't be on TV?"

She laughed, too.

"You could have told me you were a policeman."

"You didn't exactly give me time to mention it," he replied.

He saw her lower her eyes briefly. She must be feeling guilty. *Shit, now I'm beginning to think like the superintendent, too.* He didn't know whether to be pleased or worried about that.

"My name is Sara."

"Massimo."

"I was hoping you'd come back. I'd like to make amends," she said, and took from his hands the book he'd been leafing through. "This one's not for you."

"It's not?"

"No."

He watched her examining the shelves. She seemed to know what she was looking for, and when at last she found it, she stood on tiptoes to pick it out.

"Here," she said, handing it over.

Massimo studied it dubiously.

"*The Paths of the Mind and its Deviancies*," he read aloud. "*A Manual of Psychology.*"

"Someone returned it just the other day. I thought of you straight away."

"That's strange. I don't see any mention of dismembered corpses or maimed victims."

Sara glared at him, but soon a smile took over.

"To catch the killer, you have to figure out the way he thinks, right?" she asked.

"Huh. I feel like I've heard those words before."

"Here's my number, by the way."

Massimo looked at the piece of paper she'd just given him, and his cheeks turned red. It was, he thought, rather charmingly old-fashioned.

It was in times like these that Teresa found herself wondering how she could love her job when it offered such a disturbing insight into the cruelty humans were capable of. She could not understand why people feared death and not life. Life was savage, a fratricidal battle that always left a trail of blood behind.

Abramo Viesel was battling, too, in a hospital room somewhere on that floor. Teresa had waited until a doctor had emerged and updated her on his conditions, which were critical. It was stuffy inside the waiting room. Teresa opened a window and stood there, facing the garden, looking for fresh air and silence.

"Coffee?"

She turned around. Marini was back. He hadn't done as he'd been told; he was wearing the same clothes as when they'd parted earlier and looked just as exhausted.

"No, thanks," she said.

"Now what do we do?"

Teresa looked out at the garden again.

"Lucia Kravina's mother, the kid with the SUV, and now Viesel . . . I can't figure out why he's let three of the victims live," she mused.

"Four."

They turned around to find Parri in the room. The coroner nodded in greeting, touching Teresa's arm, and peering intently into her face.

"How are you?" he asked.

Teresa smiled. She knew he wasn't one to ask that question casually. He must already be assessing her fatigue levels.

"I hope you're not going to ask me if I've eaten and slept enough in the past twenty-four hours," she said.

Parri studied her over the frame of his glasses.

"This is consuming you," he said gravely.

Teresa saw how surprised Marini seemed at Parri's tone, but his unflinching honesty was something she'd become used to. Parri was her friend, and he'd been worrying about her for what felt like an eternity. Teresa could still remember what he'd said to her one night many years ago as they stood by the corpse of a victim she had been too late to save: one day, this job is going to hurt you one too many times.

Teresa wondered if that moment had finally come. She looked at her reflection in the window.

"How can you tell?" she said, examining the bags under her eyes. "Is it because I look like shit?"

Parri burst out laughing, but his eyes retained a trace of concern.

"I was about to call you," he told her. "The results of the tests on Roberto Valent's body have come in."

Teresa regained her focus.

"And?"

"He died from cardiac arrest, I would say about an hour or two after the attack."

She looked at him in surprise.

"That means the killer must have stayed with him all that time."

"Yes. It's unbelievable."

"He doesn't kill. He never meant to. The death was unintentional," Teresa deduced.

Parri nodded his agreement.

"What do you make of it?" he asked.

"Maybe it's a refusal to accept what he's done? But it can't be, it doesn't make any sense. Nothing does. Serial killers aren't conscious of the seriousness of their actions. They regard their victims as objects. They don't feel empathy; they've never developed it, often because of some kind of trauma in their past. They don't show remorse because for them, killing is a necessity."

"Perhaps this is not your typical serial killer," Marini suggested.

Teresa shook her head.

"Avoidance of a violent act is just not compatible with the profile of a serial killer," she noted. "The ultimate aim of their actions is always to bring death. It's their only relief, the only thing that can temporarily quieten them."

"I guess the only person who could help you make sense of it is the woman, Lucia Kravina's mother," said Parri. "But they've put her in an induced coma, and I think it'll be a while yet before they bring her out of it."

Marini looked at Teresa. "You told me about Igor Rosman and about his collection of feet," he said. "What if our killer's doing the same?"

Teresa tried to look at the facts from a fresh perspective.

"He's not collecting human limbs, it's something else," she said. "He's taken eyes . . ."

"Nose and ears."

"And now skin. What will it be next time?"

Marini picked up her coat and put on his own.

"We still haven't found Lucas Ebran," he said. "And it's the fifth of December today—Saint Nicholas's Day: the perfect night to kill undisturbed."

51

Once again the time had come when the whole appearance of the village was transformed for one winter night—like the moon when it is gradually obscured by encroaching shadows even when the rest of the sky is clear.

He had looked for the source of those shadows but had never been able to find it. He had searched for it on the mountain slopes and down in the valley. He had examined the heavens and the earth beneath his feet. Nothing. He'd understood, then, that the darkness came from somewhere beyond, from the unfathomable.

There was a shiver of that darkness inside him, too. It spread out every time he took a life, and it made him feel cold; it thrashed about like a trapped animal, but vanished as soon as he paused to capture its sound.

He looked at his hands. The smell of blood wafted up to his nostrils. He wondered at his own unease. All around him, life and death were engaged in their daily dance, like a butterfly and a moth at twilight.

That night the people of the village were going to face their fears, disguised as creatures half human and half beast. They would wear long horns the likes of which he had never seen in the wild, drape themselves in animal pelts, and brandish sticks and torches; they would paint their faces until they looked fearsome; that night, they would become like him.

He wore his sheepskin cloak and wrapped it around his waist

with a strip of leather. He put on his headdress. The shadows projected onto the walls by its majestic antlers looked like the branches of a bare tree.

He dipped his fingers into the bowl and rubbed their tips over his skin. He watched his reflection on the pewter turn white.

He stood like that for a moment, staring into his own eyes. Then, he picked up the object that had recently captured his attention: a book he'd found abandoned in the village. He had barely understood the words at first, but now they evoked clear images in his mind. He started leafing through it and stopped at the page he'd marked with a leaf from an oak tree.

He opened and closed his mouth a few times—a hatchling testing its wings before leaping into the void—until the words began to flow.

"Yes, su-such you shall be, you, qu-queen of all graces, after the last s-sacraments, when you go beneath the grass and waxy flowers, to mold among the skeletons."

He looked at the skull beside him. It had eyes now, and it had a face, but it was still missing the warmth of life.

He had captured a lizard for him, so that he wouldn't feel lonely when he left, and so that he wouldn't be scared at night. He'd found the animal inside the deepest of crevasses and had woken it from its winter sleep. Unlike the other creatures that hibernated during winter, this one hadn't curled up in a ball because its body didn't require any warmth; its blood always ran cold, even in the summer. He'd tied it to his companion's hand with a piece of string. He caressed its tiny head as he was about to leave, and in doing so brushed against the skeleton's phalanges. They made a brief clicking sound, and so he waited, hoping this creature, too, might rise from its sleep as the lizard had done.

But nothing happened.

52

Can I still do this job?

It's not physical effort I'm worried about. I'm used to drag-
ging this body—this old grumbling friend—around with me, I'm
used to dealing with its complaints even when they make me grit my
teeth in pain.

It's not my swollen feet I'm ashamed of, or how my hands lose
their grip sometimes, or how my eyes go blurry until I can't distin-
guish the words on a page.

It's the idea of my mind fading away that keeps me up at night:
what am I, if not my thoughts, my memories, my dreams, my hopes
for the future? What am I without these feelings, without my dig-
nity?

Here I go again, spoiling these pages with troubles that aren't
worth the ink they're scribbled in.

Anyway: where was I? (I've been asking myself this question too
often these days . . .)

Item 19 on the agenda: security measures for the feast of Saint
Nicholas in Travenì. It's the night of the Krampus. Who knows
whether our own Devil will show his face. I'm ready. I'm waiting
for him.

Travenì had shed her mourning clothes and spruced herself up
for the occasion: the streets were decorated with silver lamps
shaped like snowflakes, and strings of fairy lights stretched
from building to building along the main road. Windows

and balconies were adorned with Christmas decorations, and a candle burned behind every pane, as tradition dictated. An enormous fir tree that smelled of resin had been put up in the main square; at dusk, it had come to life with thousands of lights, a shining comet at its tip.

The fires were kindled. The stalls began to light up and spread the scent of mulled wine and roasted chestnuts. The chatter became more animated, fuelled by a sip or two of alcohol and the arrival of the first tourists. A loudspeaker intoned Christmas carols. The pub and various small restaurants radiated a smell of hot, fragrant food. The streets soon filled up with a peaceful throng.

Teresa noted that the mayor's fears had been unfounded. What had happened instead was what she had feared: the horrors the village had recently experienced had attracted rather than repelled people. There was something more to the spectacle in Travenì that night, beyond demonic masks and ritual bell-ringing, something even more alluring: the thrill of knowing there was a real demon out there among all of those costumes. Teresa had seen it happen before, but the workings of the human mind still surprised her every time.

She quickly ran through the security measures they'd put in place to close off any possible escape routes for the killer. They worked in theory, but would they hold up in practice? There were officers spread through the crowd, many of them in plainclothes. Teresa herself had decided to coordinate everything from the field. She wanted to be in the thick of things, to breathe in the same air the killer was breathing, and to see his possible victims the way he saw them. She knew he was bound to come; the opportunity was simply too good for his ego to pass up—the chance to witness the impact he was making, the crowds he'd drawn to that place.

Teresa hoped that it would be enough to satisfy his fantasies of omnipotence for one night, before the monster inside him demanded another sacrifice.

"May I have a word, Superintendent?"

Teresa turned around, startled. It was Chief Knauss, looking forlorn. She could guess what must be ruining his mood: the presence of the reinforcements Teresa had summoned from the city, casting even greater doubt on Knauss's role and authority.

"Why aren't you at your station?" she said, wanting to brush him off, and turning back around to watch the celebrations come to life.

"When you first arrived here, you said we could come to you with any problems, so I . . ."

"Well, what is it?" said Teresa, cutting him short.

The chief lowered his gaze to the tips of his shoes and stood with his hands on his hips, chewing a piece of gum without closing his mouth—a habit she detested.

"I was born on these mountains, as were most of my men," he began. "We know this place and its people better than anybody else. We're used to dealing with things by ourselves around here, we always have been. We're . . ."

"I'm sure you're all exemplary officers, Chief," said Teresa. "But this case is beyond your abilities."

Her words hit him with the force of a slap. He looked astonished, as if he couldn't believe anyone could be so brutally honest.

"Please do me a favor and return to your station, and stay there this time, at least for an hour or two," she went on. "And make sure your men do the same."

Knauss stopped chewing.

"I don't take orders from you," he said.

Teresa glared at him.

"That's true," she replied. "If you did, I would have wasted no time telling you, right here in front of everyone, exactly what I think of you for wasting my time—time that I would much rather spend saving the killer's next victim."

The chief went quiet.

Teresa gestured at something behind his back. Two of Knauss's men were trying, with little success, to disband an unauthorized stall that was collecting signatures for a petition against the construction of the new ski resort. Tempers were flaring.

"You say you know your people," Teresa goaded him. "Off you go, then, and see if you can solve whatever the problem is over there."

Knauss spat out his gum and walked away without another word.

Teresa looked at her watch. Not long to go before the start of the pageant. Presently, she noticed that someone else was walking up to her. This was going to be a long night.

"Jesus Christ, what is everyone's problem tonight?" she muttered.

The man was holding a piece of paper that Teresa immediately recognized. She'd drafted the document herself and arranged for the chief of police to sign it.

"Do we have you to thank for this, Superintendent?" the man growled at her.

"Good evening, Mayor."

He ignored the greeting and waved the sheet of paper in her face.

"What's this nonsense? We can't even turn the streetlights off, now?"

Teresa didn't even bother to look at him.

"A public safety measure, Mayor," she replied.

"How am I supposed to get the devotees down and the bon-fires going if the lights are still on?"

"I'm sure you'll manage to put on a good show regardless, and no one will mind too much. Now if you'll excuse me, I have work to do here."

Tearing the injunction up, the mayor retreated into the crowd. Teresa was relieved.

The radio at her hip croaked.

"Nothing to report here," said Parisi's voice. He was patrolling the churchyard, the kiosks, and the street vendors' stalls.

They still hadn't found Lucas Ebran. He had disappeared. His mother had told them it wasn't the first time it had happened; her son was sometimes gone for days, but she had no idea where he went. They hadn't found any fingerprints in the house other than the woman's own. If it hadn't been for the neighbors who said they'd seen him as recently as two weeks ago, spying on them through their windows, they might have thought Ebran didn't exist, that he was a figment of someone's imagination.

For now, all they had to go on was a grainy old photograph. It was all they had to help them spot him among hundreds of faces covered by hats and scarves.

Teresa saw Marini across the road. They nodded at each other as the church bell began to toll. Suddenly, at the eighth chime, the village lights went off, and a murmur of wonder—tinged with fear—rose from the crowd.

Teresa swore and radioed Parisi.

"Find out who did this!" she told him. "I don't care how you do it, just get those damn lights back on! *Now!*"

She put the radio away. In the shimmer of torches and candles, Travenì glistened, a stirring tableau in the heart of the Alps, irresistible for a killer on the lookout for fresh prey.

Teresa was joined by Marini.

"Now what?" he asked her.

"Now we wait." She didn't know what else to say. She kept

her eyes on the crowd—families, lovers, gangs of teenagers, and tour groups. The killer had to be there somewhere. He was probably watching them right now.

They saw a procession of nuns making its way through the crush. They each carried a taper, heads lowered so that only their chins were visible beneath their black veils. They wound their silent, orderly way into the church and out of sight.

"Where did they come from?" Teresa radioed.

"They're nuns from the convent in Rail," Knauss replied. "They've come to pray together and keep the demons at bay. Are you going to check them out, too?" he asked sarcastically.

"I'm thinking about it. Maybe I'll send you to do it."

The sound of a horn echoed through the valley.

"They're coming," said Marini.

A slice of starry darkness ensconced between two hills behind the cathedral lit up in a reddish haze, growing increasingly brighter until its source was finally revealed: a line of torches held aloft by dark, stooping figures. The column of demons advanced until it was clearly visible, and then broke up, with the devotees spreading out across the natural amphitheatre.

The hill was set ablaze with primitive bonfires rising and falling in a pagan dance. A line of flames kindled along the length of the horizon, separating the black clouds of smoke that rose to the sky from the compacted snow beneath. The demons were marching into the village, ash raining upon them as cameras flashed all around.

These were the *Krampus*. Teresa had heard that the word meant "claws." It seemed appropriate, somehow, considering the blood that had recently tainted the valley.

The masks were truly terrifying. Every detail was so realistic that you really did end up thinking you'd wandered into hell—a rural inferno of primordial allure. The goat-demons of Travenì wore thick wool trousers and tunics, with fur cloaks on top that reached all the way down to their feet. Bells tied to their waists announced their approach. They carried staffs and rods with which they lashed out at the audience. Their faces, crowned with sharp, curving horns, were fearsome, eyes glinting in the dark, fangs ready to tear into human flesh.

A few children started crying, and their mothers rushed to comfort them. But others clapped their hands in awe.

"They look real," Marini whispered. "It's amazing."

He was enchanted.

Teresa shrugged. "It's a residue of pagan fertility cults, a celebration of the winter solstice that survived the advent of Christianity," she said. "The legend says that on the night of Saint Nicholas, the *Krampus* would wander around in search of children who had misbehaved. They were the saint's own servants, acting on his command. I suppose that was their way of side-stepping the Inquisition."

Marini looked at her.

"You always manage to boil everything down to some logical cause. It's really quite extraordinary," he said.

She kept her eyes on the worshippers, whom she couldn't see as anything other than what she'd just described to Marini.

"I detect a note of sarcasm," she muttered.

"On the contrary. I'm genuinely impressed."

"Oh, shut up, Marini."

The demons began to mingle with the crowd, and the calm that had previously reigned made way for a hectic euphoria.

"What's Parisi doing?" Teresa barked. "Why aren't the lights back on yet?"

She was getting nervous. She kept thinking that the killer might be behind one of those masks, already stalking his next victim. Her team had vetted each devotee and had also checked them as they prepared for the ceremony, but now she felt as if she hadn't really seen any of them before.

The square was a whirlwind of activity threatening to submerge her at any moment. Faces, smells, sounds, lights . . . everything was moving too quickly, becoming a blur. Teresa closed her eyes.

She was afraid she wouldn't be able to complete the mission. She felt as if she'd aged years in the space of a few hours.

Calm down, she told herself. *Breathe.*

The suspect was out there somewhere, beyond the anxiety that clouded her vision. To find him, she had to push herself beyond her own limits. She tried to remember his features, studying the image in her mind. She focused on its every detail until she was familiar with them all.

When she felt ready, she opened her eyes once more. This time she didn't let the urgency to find him overwhelm her, but worked methodically, keeping her own gaze under a tight leash. Using landmarks to guide her, she checked the men milling about at the stalls and at the corners of the square, then looked over at those who were lingering outside the restaurants. Then, she divided the tide of moving people into streams and studied each one as it drifted past her.

Method, she thought. *All I need is method.*

That was how she found the one she was looking for out of the hundreds of faces around her.

Lucas Ebran was different from the photograph Teresa had found in his house. He did not possess any of the characteristics of the ectomorphic somatotype: he wasn't the tall, lanky figure she'd been expecting to see, moving awkwardly among the crowds. Time had dilated his flesh, though it had left his face unaltered; his body looked swollen, rather than overweight. It was a strange combination of youthfulness and decay. His dirty hair fell over smooth cheeks, and he had an almost translucent complexion. His tattered coat stretched tight over his abdomen and across his shoulders and seemed to be getting in his way.

Ebran was anxious. Teresa could tell from the lack of composure in his gestures, and the febrile glances he kept throwing at his surroundings. Something was undermining his self-control—perhaps the arousal produced by the presence of all those bodies around him, and the rising urge to kill once more.

He was pacing between the stalls in the square, tracing the same route over and over again—there was something systematic in his behavior, as if he were looking for something or someone.

Teresa was watching him from the steps that led down to the little square by the medieval clock tower. She could see him studying people's faces, scrutinizing their expressions.

"What is he doing?" said Marini next to her.

"He's choosing."

The parade of the *Krampus* reached its climax when the demons tried to catch and strike the bolder kids who came close enough to confront them. In the ensuing chaos and crush, it became harder to keep track of Ebran's movements.

"I'm going to move closer," said Teresa. "You stay here and make sure you don't lose sight of him."

She began tailing Ebran at a few yards' distance. She kept catching glimpses of his face in the crowd, but then he would momentarily vanish, only to emerge a few steps from where he'd been before. Teresa wondered how long this dance would last.

There was a sudden panic when a series of deafening bangs went off somewhere in the crowd. People started shoving and yelling at each other, trying to find a way out of the square.

Teresa was swallowed by the sudden chaos and found herself pushing against the tide.

"Someone's set off a bunch of firecrackers," De Carli reported through the radio.

Marini pushed his way into the crowd and tried to restore order, explaining the source of the noise, but it still took a few minutes for the panic to subside.

Meanwhile, Teresa had lost sight of the suspect.

"I can't see him," she radioed, with a curse or two thrown in.

"I think I can," Marini radioed back. "He's walking toward the church. He's leaving. I think he's stolen something. There's a bulge in his coat, he's got his arms wrapped around it."

Teresa stood on her toes to look in that direction, but there were too many people around her.

"Follow him! I'll get there as soon as I can," she yelled.

She called for reinforcements and sent out the order that no one was to leave the village. They'd prepared the roadblocks hours ago. She radioed Marini again.

"Have you caught up with him?" she asked.

"Almost. He's behind the church."

"Don't run. You might scare him off. I'm coming."

The crowds had begun to disperse, thanks to the efforts of Hugo Knauss and his men, and Teresa finally managed to catch up with Marini. Lucas Ebran was walking about ten yards ahead of them. His steps were quick; he was in a rush. He turned to look over his shoulder.

"He's seen us," said Teresa.

Ebran started running. Marini sprinted after him and was upon him in seconds, grabbing him by the collar of his coat. Ebran tripped and fell to his knees. He looked delirious. Teresa saw him glancing down at his own abdomen. He had hidden something in the folds of his too-tight coat.

"Superintendent!"

De Carli had arrived, out of breath.

"There's a child missing," he said. "He was taken from his stroller when the mother wasn't looking."

Teresa looked at Ebran and at the unnatural bulge in his belly. She undid his coat, and for a moment she just stood there, motionless.

"I just found them on the floor, I swear," said Ebran.

A camera and a purse, but no trace of the child.

53

Teresa woke up screaming and gasping for breath, her neck and the rest of her body stiff. Her diary lay open in front of her, squashed under her cheek. She lifted her head, her heart still drumming in her chest. The muscles in her back spasmed in pain. She'd fallen asleep on her chair. She swallowed with some difficulty, her throat burning, her lips dry. She was desperate for a glass of water.

She looked around in confusion, and it took her a while to figure out where she was; the meeting room of the police headquarters in Travenì was empty, and the lights had been turned down. She recognized Chief Knauss's hat on the coat rack and Marini's thick jacket on a hanger next to it.

She looked at her watch in alarm. It was a few minutes past 10 P.M. and she'd been asleep for almost half an hour. Someone had draped her coat over her shoulders.

She was furious with herself for showing such inexcusable weakness and felt deeply ashamed. What would her men think of her? Glancing at the open pages of her diary, she blushed; if anyone were to read it and work out her true physical and psychological state, the damage would be irreparable. She was relieved when she realized that the page it was open to held only a few hurried notes on the case.

She ran her hands over her face with a sigh, and noticed her cheeks were damp. She realized with a jolt that she'd been crying. Remembering the nightmare that had woken her up, she felt a wave of nausea and the onset of fresh tears.

"Oh God . . ." she murmured, exhausted.

Her hands moved to her belly, heeding that primal pull that had never really faded and still pleaded with her to remember.

And how could she forget?

In her dream, she had felt her baby's delicate movements inside her womb; he had responded to her touch and curled up against her warmth. It had been a tangible sensation, as if somebody had really been there. She would have given anything for it to be true.

But the dream had turned into a nightmare when she'd sensed someone wanted to take her baby away from her. That was when she'd woken up screaming.

Teresa stood up. The pain was still too raw to allow her to breathe properly. She dried her tears with the palm of her hand and took a couple of deep breaths to try and steady herself. This was not the time to allow her past, and the memory of the tragedy that cursed it, to overcome her.

She noticed then that there was some sort of commotion going on in the corridor outside—a tense exchange followed by the sound of someone crying—that swept away the last scraps of sleep from Teresa's eyes.

She knew whose voice it was, made hoarse by despair: the mother of the abducted child.

Teresa rested her forehead against the wall and closed her eyes. Every one of those wails tore into her heart and left her defenseless; they were exactly the same as the ones she had emitted in her nightmare.

Only then did she realize that there was a bandage around one of her hands. She looked at it in disbelief. She had no idea how she'd been injured, and that blindness made her blood run cold.

There was a knock. The door opened slowly, and Marini's head appeared. He seemed relieved when he saw that she was awake.

"The deputy public prosecutor is here, Superintendent."

54

"Lucas Ebran's profile is a perfect match for the killer's," said Deputy Prosecutor Gardini as he skimmed Teresa's report. He'd come down to Travenì as soon as he'd heard about the arrest and the kidnapped baby.

Teresa elected to say nothing for the time being, knowing that her own words in that report implied they had as good as solved the case.

Ebran knew how to set animal traps because his own father had taught him. He knew how to skin an animal and had been seen lurking around other people's homes, spying on little girls and their families. He was an outcast. He had probably always nursed a deep frustration, exacerbated by poverty and by a physical disfigurement that he was now desperately trying to hide by keeping his hands beneath the table. Teresa suspected he must suffer from some form of psychosis, but she would need a full psychiatric evaluation to know for sure.

The boys who'd crashed their car in the woods had said he could be the stranger who had assaulted their friend. But it wasn't a straightforward match: the stranger's face had been painted, the clothes he'd been wearing had concealed his physical build, and the teenagers' minds had been clouded by alcohol when they'd encountered him.

David Knauss hadn't been able to hide his uncertainty or his disappointment when they'd shown him Ebran's mug shot.

"These aren't his eyes," he'd said, though even he was aware that there was no way he could know for sure. He couldn't recall the details, couldn't clearly picture in his mind the moment he had—quite possibly—evaded death. But as Teresa had discovered when she'd spoken to him again, what really bothered him was something else: the realization that his attacker might not be the mythical warrior David had imagined him to be. She suspected the boy had developed a form of Stockholm syndrome. He was grateful to his assailant for having "brought him back to life" and felt indebted to him.

"Lucas Ebran's profile matches the killer's, but he is not the killer," Gardini murmured as he read through Teresa's concluding remarks, a look of dismay and consternation crossing his features.

"It's not him. It's clear. He's nothing more than a misfit," Teresa confirmed.

Ebran's hands were disfigured by scars caused by the fire he'd started in his school when he was a teenager. That was why they hadn't found his fingerprints in the house: he didn't have any. The skin on the tips of his fingers was smooth and swollen, hardened by time and wear.

They had wasted time, and there was still no trace of the child. No one had seen the person who'd picked him up from the stroller and taken him away, though they had found a clue on the baby's blanket: some white marks. The day had taken a turn for the worse when they'd heard the news that Abramo Viesel had died.

Teresa was looking at the millennial forest that surrounded the village.

"He doesn't use the roads," she noted. "So roadblocks are useless."

"We'll start searching the woods," Gardini assured her.

Teresa closed her eyes and let her thoughts run their course. She could see stretching before her thousands of acres of forest, traversed with gorges and crevasses. That was where he was, with the baby boy. Not inside a house, not in Travenì.

Now what do I do?

She felt the shiver of a private fear. The parents and brother of the abducted child were in the room next door. Teresa had put off meeting them in person until she'd read their statements. But their presence in the building was like having a white-hot branding iron almost touching the skin. Even from a distance, she could feel the burn, and she worried it might compromise her ability to think clearly. The only thing worse than hunting a killer was hunting a child abductor.

"Teresa, are you all right?" Gardini called out to her.

He's still alive, she told herself. She had to believe it, though she'd never in her life relied upon hope. She hardly noticed that her hand had come to rest on her stomach again, on the spot where she had, in her dream, felt life moving beneath her skin, and where her scar still stung sometimes. It wasn't possible, and yet the bond that had been severed before it could come to life, now refused to break, defying logic, time, the laws of the universe.

She looked at Gardini.

"I need more men," she said.

"You'll get them."

"And the army. We need to search the mountains."

Gardini nodded.

"I'll get right on it," he assured her. "Let me give Ambrosini a call. And we'll contact the district judge."

Once she was alone again, Teresa took a deep breath. The next few hours were crucial.

Marini walked in. "I've got the maps. They show every mountain shelter this side of the border."

He spread the papers across the table. Teresa didn't need

to look at them to know it would take the search parties several days to comb through the vast area they would have to cover.

They needed a clue that would steer the search in the right direction—otherwise it was like throwing a penny into the ocean and expecting to retrieve it with a fishing net.

"How many?" she asked.

"Just over a hundred."

"What about the vacant ones? Let's concentrate on those."

"That's most of them."

"We need drones. See what they say back at headquarters, when they can send them down."

"I'll give them a call."

They spoke as if all these questions were not quickly eroding their faith in what they had to do. But they both knew they had to set their misgivings aside. If even a single member of the team were to express any uncertainty about their chances of success, their doubt would spread like a disease and weaken the chain that was meant to stretch all the way across the valley and over the mountains, until it reached the child and brought him home. And Teresa needed every single link in that chain to hold.

She turned to Marini.

"We'll find him," she said.

He gave her a brisk, decisive nod. He understood.

Teresa picked up her diary. She had to keep taking notes, even though it felt like a hindrance sometimes—a waste of time, even. If she wanted to understand how her mind was deteriorating and at what rate, she had to be methodical about things, set herself rules and stick to them. It was only thanks to those notes that she'd managed to remember how she'd hurt her hand. But she refused to believe she could already be at the stage where she was forgetting her own life, and she desperately tried to convince herself that it was all down to how exhausted she was.

She held the notebook in her hands, her eyes scanning the last few things she'd written. They were little more than scribbles jotted down in the moments between wakefulness and sleep.

She couldn't remember them. She had no memory of those words. It felt strange to read them now, as if they belonged to someone else who lived inside of her. But that person was trying to help her.

"Is something wrong?" Marini asked her.

"Many things, but not what's in here," she replied, feeling a smile forming on her face. Her heart was beating faster. For the first time, she did not feel scared of what was happening to her.

"The children," she said. Those were the last words she'd written down before falling asleep.

"I don't understand."

She hadn't either, at the beginning, but now she felt like she could see what had finally clicked in her mind right before she had fallen asleep.

"Looks like I've been working a few things out in my sleep," she told him as she closed the diary. "The first victim is Diego Valent's father. The second is Lucia Kravina's mother. I imagine Diego and Lucia must be classmates."

"There can't be more than one class per grade, in Travenì. Do you think there's a link? But the kid who was attacked in the forest isn't connected."

"Abramo Viesel was the janitor of the school. Diego told us he was mean to his friend."

"The baby that's been kidnapped has an older brother. His name is Mathias. He's the same age as Diego and Lucia, too," said Marini.

"A coincidence, perhaps? It could be, in a town this small."

"On second thought, I suppose David Knauss also has a connection of sorts with the school. We saw him and those other boys outside the entrance; they almost ran some of the children over."

That was true, though Teresa didn't think it was the connection they were looking for.

"The attacker maimed the first, second, and fourth victim's sense organs," she noted. "Clearly his encounter with Knauss's son was an accident. It wasn't part of his vision."

She went to the window, opened the notebook, then closed it again. Her mind was working frenetically.

"A serial killer can lie dormant for years. But then one day, he might get fired from a job, or feel abandoned by someone, or suffer some sort of humiliation—any of these things can trigger his homicidal fury. It's never down to just a momentary loss of control," she mused. "It's always a process, but in this case it's difficult to see it because the motive is not one we are used to but has a psychopathological component."

"So maybe, in our killer's case, we should figure out what it was that triggered his homicidal spree," Marini reasoned.

Teresa turned to him, a surprised smile on her face.

"At long last you're talking like a cop, Inspector," she teased him. "Have you been studying?"

De Carli called out to them from the door.

"Superintendent, we have Lucia Kravina's father. He tried to cross the border. They're bringing him in now."

Dante Kravina was a mountain lad with all the bad habits of a city boy. In his interrogation, he told Teresa that he ran away because of his prior drug dealing convictions. "I didn't want to risk going to jail for a bit of dope," he said—as if the fact that he'd left his daughter behind wasn't a much more serious offense.

"Did you make Lucia clean the house to get rid of any traces of drugs?" she asked him.

"Yes."

"And you did the same yourself with your wife's car."

"Yes."

"Weren't you worried about her?"

He shrugged, his gaze empty.

"What could I have done?"

Plenty, thought Teresa. *You could have gone looking for her, saved her having to wander in the forest alone and in shock. You could have looked after your daughter, protected her.*

"Tell me about the man who came to your door that night," she said instead.

"I was high. I didn't really know what was going on. I saw that he was holding Melania's necklace. I thought she must have been in an accident and then I thought of how there was some dope in the house and in the car. I had to get rid of it."

"Do you think it could be someone you know? Someone with a score to settle, perhaps about some dope you haven't paid off?" Teresa asked, purely out of habit.

"No, it's got nothing to do with drugs. That man was . . . I don't know how to put it. He looked like he came from another world."

"Describe him."

"I told you, I wasn't myself. All I know is that he was pale, and he was staring at me with his eyes wide open. I've never seen a face like that; it had no expression at all. It was completely frozen, like the face of a dead person."

Those words sparked something inside Teresa.

"Like a ghost?" she asked him.

"Yes. He looked like a ghost."

Teresa thought back to all the people that populated this case. Their faces whirled in her mind now, paired to words that were slowly beginning to form an intelligible pattern. She replayed everything that had happened in the past few days, as if she were watching a film, and thought of the various characters involved, how, consciously or unwittingly, they were all interacting with each other in some way—and moving the story to its still unwritten epilogue.

The victims. The school. The community. The forest. The stranger with the painted face. And *them*. Teresa instructed De Carli to draw up the interrogation report and took Marini aside.

"His daughter Lucia is always talking about the ghost in the woods," she said.

"Do you think she knows him?"

Teresa thought it went a lot further than that. She had finally discovered the link between the killer and the victims. It had nothing to do with motive, nor with a psychopathology of any sort. It was something she hadn't come across before and could only describe, for now, as "pack behavior."

"I think I know what all the victims have in common," she said.

55

The child was crying. His wails were desperate and relentless, like those of a blackbird chick fallen from its nest. Featherless, wearing nothing more than his own skin, he kept his soft, pinkish beak wide open. Nothing could divert him from his mission. Though he was only a newborn, he instinctively knew that somewhere in the world his mother was doing exactly what he was doing—she was looking for him, and if he stopped crying, she would never find him. His tiny face was flushed with the effort and with the atavistic terror of being separated from that which had given him life.

The man was admiring the most remarkable battle for survival he had ever witnessed. He caressed the round, soft cheeks of the creature before him, touched the drops of water that fell from its eyes, and recognized something of himself in it. He removed his horned and bristled headdress and rubbed at his face until he'd scrubbed it clean of paint. The baby watched him, still sobbing, still inconsolable, but now with a spark of curiosity in its eyes.

He wrapped it in lambskin and held it against the warmth of his chest. Gently, he touched the baby's hand and saw it open in response. Its tiny fingers wrapped around one of his own. For a creature so small, it had a fierce grip.

The child started shrieking again, and when the man copied it, it opened its eyes wide and stared at him. They exchanged sounds for a while, both wanting to know who the other really was.

Slowly, the child's sobs subsided, and it was overcome by sleep. The man kept watch over it, listening to its breathing and to the little heart beating fast against his own.

For the first time in a long while, he was no longer alone.

56

Diego and Lucia were sitting side by side. Oliver was sitting to Diego's right. Mathias stood between them and the door.

He's the leader, Teresa thought. He was protecting them, putting himself between them and the unknown. He felt responsible for the whole group, even now that his little brother had been taken. He'd been crying, and perhaps he was ashamed of that, but he wasn't going to renounce his role. Nearly all of them had suffered some kind of horrific trauma over the past few days, yet now that they had gathered together, they looked like they would cope somehow; they were hurting, but they weren't lost.

Even this nighttime trip to the police station didn't seem to have alarmed them unduly. It was almost two o'clock in the morning, but there wasn't the slightest trace of sleepiness on their faces. Hugo Knauss had made them a cup of cocoa each and left a bowl of treats on the table. Almost half the sweets were already gone, which Teresa took as a good sign.

They responded timidly to her greeting. She sat on the table, ignoring the chairs, and dangled her legs over the side. With her eyes, she signalled at Marini to sit on the floor. He seemed surprised at first, but quickly obeyed, sitting cross-legged.

Teresa had thought for a long time about which words to choose, but in the end she'd decided that honesty was the only way she could earn their trust.

"I need your help," she told them. "I have to find the person who hurt your parents and took Mathias's little brother."

The children were watching her closely. They weren't used to seeing an adult needing their help.

"And you don't know what to do?" Lucia asked her.

"No, I have no idea."

"And that makes you scared?"

"Very."

The girl glanced at her friends. Teresa could tell what she was looking for: their reassurance that she could keep going.

"I used to be scared, too," she blurted out.

Mathias looked at her, and she went quiet. There wasn't anything aggressive about his glance, something that might discourage her—it was just a look, nothing more. But it was the look of a leader, and that was enough.

Teresa acted like she hadn't noticed.

"And now you're not anymore?" she asked the girl.

She shook her head, her eyes now fixed on a piece of candy in the palm of her hand, but she didn't reply. She was following an order after all.

"I want to find the person who did these horrible things," Teresa went on. "But most of all, Mathias, I want to find your brother."

He held her gaze without saying a word.

"Don't you want him to come home?" she asked.

The boy's lips were trembling now.

"Maybe he's better off out there," she heard him say.

Teresa noticed Marini's body stiffen and hoped that he, too, would heed the boy's unspoken command and remain quiet.

"Why would you think that?" she asked.

He was chewing on his fingernails now and seemed agitated. He didn't want to talk to Teresa about it.

"I know you want to protect him, but he's too little to be

away from his mother for so long," she explained. "And away from *you*. He needs *you*."

Teresa didn't mention their father. She had noticed the marks on the boy's neck that he kept touching without even realizing it; his shirt collar couldn't hide them. They were bruises, just like those his mother had on her arms.

But the boy was showing no signs of opening up, and Teresa could understand why: she was nothing but a stranger, and yet she somehow expected him to admit to his biggest, most painful secret. She felt selfish and tactless.

"There was once a person who hurt me," she began, without giving too much thought to Marini.

The children were all looking at her now.

"It was someone I loved very much," she continued. "Every time he did it, I would ask myself what I could have done to make him so angry."

"And what had you done?" Lucia asked. She was definitely the bravest of her friends.

"Nothing," Teresa answered. "There is nothing we can do—no matter how bad—that would justify someone hurting us. But it took me a while to figure that out."

"Then what did you do?" Oliver asked.

"I got rid of him."

"Did you kick him?"

Teresa laughed.

"I would have loved to do that," she admitted.

"I would have kicked him."

Teresa ruffled the boy's hair.

"It's not necessary that we stay away from those we love in order to protect them," she said, looking at Mathias. "But we do have to let people help us so that we can fend off those who want to harm us."

. . .

She waited in silence for the boy to react. Mathias was biting his lower lip, as if to hold his words in.

"Can Markus come home to just me and Mom?" he finally said, his eyes shining with tears. He was asking for her protection—for himself, for his brother, for his mother.

"Yes, I promise."

Mathias looked at his friends. Teresa could clearly sense the silent communication taking place among them; these kids were each other's family, and that was why they were guarding their secret. Loyalty was so important to children their age and so surprisingly fragile in adults. They had learned how to protect themselves without losing the enchantment of childhood. They had remained pure even when the world around them was anything but.

Amid that awesome landscape, those silent, fairy-tale peaks, the insides of people's homes in Travenì harbored unspeakable secrets. Teresa was disturbed by how many she'd already encountered. It was a startling disjunction.

Like looking for God and finding Satan and his horns, she thought.

But more than the sins themselves, what upset her most was the effort the community put into covering up for the sinners, leaving their victims at the mercy of their tormentors, and all for the sake of preserving the unity of the village against the outside world. She thought bitterly of the pamphlets strewn around town, calling for a popular uprising against the new ski slope. There was so much activism against the "invasion," yet nobody had lifted a finger to help these kids.

Lucia pulled at Teresa's trousers to draw her attention.

"We're not scared because we're together. We meet in the forest almost every day," she said, glad to be able to talk to her new friend. "You should try, too, if you're scared."

Teresa smiled.

"I should talk to a friend about it?"

"Yes."

"Like you all do?"

The girl nodded.

"We talk about bad things that scare us," said Oliver. "Then they become less scarible."

"That's not a real word," Lucia told him.

"Yes, it is!"

"Do you talk about bad things, too, Mathias?" Teresa asked the boy.

He nodded.

"But I'm not afraid for myself," he said.

"You only talk about your fears for your brother, don't you?"

"Yes."

"That's very noble of you," Teresa told him. "The strong must always look out for the weak."

He smiled, feeling gratified by her praise. He looked at Lucia and nodded.

"We have a secret spot, down in the gorge, just past the cave. It's near the waterfall," the girl revealed.

"Is it fun?" Teresa asked.

"R-really f-fun. We always h-have a n-nice t-time."

Diego, too, had decided to trust her.

"And is it just you, down there?"

The kids looked at each other.

"That man was spying on us," Mathias explained. "I noticed him."

"Me, too," said Oliver.

"Which man?" Teresa asked.

"The man who came to us when Lucia found her mom. We got scared and we screamed, but then we realized he just wanted to play."

"Play?"

"Yes, he had painted his face like a clown."

Lucia looked at Teresa.

"I told them he's a ghost, but they won't believe me," she said.

"It w-wasn't a gh-ghost!"

"What game did he want to play?" Teresa asked.

"He was walking on his knees, like he was a kid, too," Oliver explained. "But we had seen him before, moving around like an old person. He was outside the school, wearing a cape like a wizard in a fairy tale."

"Did he talk to you? Did he ask you to do anything?" she asked, feigning calm.

"No. He doesn't know how to talk. And we haven't seen him since," Mathias told her.

"I wasn't there when he came," said Lucia. "But he left this for me at home."

She unzipped her jacket and took out a rag doll with berries for eyes.

Teresa glanced at Marini. She had what she needed.

"Thank you," she told them. "I feel a lot better now. I'm not scared anymore."

"I told you it works!" said Lucia.

Teresa stroked the girl's hair.

"Go on, finish your cocoa and we'll take you home."

"Will you put the sirens on?" asked Oliver.

"For sure!"

Teresa took Marini aside. She tried to ignore his inquisitive look; he was wondering whether the story she'd told the kids was real or made up. He didn't yet have the perceptiveness, or perhaps the experience, to know that it wasn't possible to trick children. They had an infallible instinct for rooting out lies, and when they did, their trust was lost forever.

"He avenges the children," she whispered.

"He eavesdropped on their confessions."

"Yes. And he punished the grown-ups who hurt them. They each had someone in their life who was making them suffer. For Diego, an emasculating, emotionally distant father. For Lucia, a drug-addled, absent mother. For Oliver, a sadistic janitor." Teresa's gaze sought out the fourth child. "And finally, a violent parent for Mathias. The skinned animal left outside the girl's house wasn't a threat. It was a gift. We feed those we love."

"But he didn't punish Mathias's father, he kidnapped his brother," Marini objected.

Teresa didn't get a chance to respond.

"The man from the forest brought us gifts," Oliver interrupted. "Would you like to see them?"

57

The Sliva gorge was a black abyss between the village and the old train station, a trench that cut more than three hundred feet into the forest. That night, the path that threaded its way through the woods and down to the gorge was dotted with police flashlights, twinkling pinpricks bobbing in the dark like fireflies in winter, zigzagging their way to the bottom in single file.

The kids led the way, followed by Teresa and Marini, who were in turn followed by the rest of the squad and Hugo Knauss's men.

Lucia, Mathias, and Diego were skipping down the path like mountain goats, never losing their footing even on that precarious surface. But Oliver had chosen to grab hold of Teresa's hand, and would not let go. She stored up on the warmth and tenderness of that contact, such a stark contrast to the frigid landscape that surrounded them. The gorge was a steep fissure that led to a rocky riverbed, where the water had now almost stilled; it was so cold that even the stream had slowed down, and slabs of ice clung to the banks. Mist floated and curled over the water. Wind-carved stalactites hung from boulders and tree branches. It was like coming across the ruins of a world long gone. Teresa felt as if theirs were the only hearts beating down there. It was a disquieting, haunting sensation that made her understand, for the first time in her life, what claustrophobia might feel like.

The children led the way across rope bridges and down slippery steps. They moved with absolute confidence and no trace of fear. The night had no power over their minds; they were in communion with the wild landscape and had not yet become domesticated enough to fear it.

Teresa watched them face darkness and death, on that grimmest of nights, and saw a calm strength in them that was a testament to their spirit. She followed them trustingly, and though she kept watch over every step they took, she knew she was the one who needed to tread with caution, not them.

She thought of the worries that had besieged her in recent days, and all of a sudden they did not seem so insurmountable. It was up to her to decide how to live the rest of her life, and there were two ways to do it: by gradually fading away or standing up to it undeterred.

They crept through another gap in the rocks, and in that damp, musty blackness, Teresa saw her life suspended. Oliver's hand in hers squeezed harder.

"Don't be scared," she heard him say, his voice amplified in the tunnel.

"I won't be," she replied, and those words seemed to apply to so much more than what was happening in that moment.

At the other end of the passageway, they found Lucia, Mathias, and Diego waiting for them beneath a waterfall of ice. The children pointed to a crevice behind the frozen jets of water.

Teresa let go of Oliver's hand and approached the aperture with Marini. They pointed their flashlights at the moss. Ensconced in that natural pillow was a square-shaped object glinting in the light. Marini reached for it. It was a metal box. The design on its lid had begun to fade, but they could still make out a drawing of white rabbits riding bicycles.

"You can open it," said Lucia.

Marini lifted the lid and it was as if he had turned back time. He looked at Teresa, but even she wasn't sure how to react. Inside the box was another incongruous detail in a story that was about to take an entirely unexpected turn.

58

16 September 1993

Subject Alpha is active and conscious of his own existence. However, it is difficult to guess how he might perceive himself. I wonder if he is aware of the passage of time, and consequently of the concept of "future," by which I mean the image, the projection of himself onto a moment that has yet to come. I wonder if he is curious about who might be on the other side of the wall, handing him the provisions necessary for survival. As I have never revealed myself to him as anything other than a pair of gloved hands giving him food and clothing, I doubt he is cognizant of my presence. His whole world is inside that room. The Alpha has known no life other than the one I have given him, yet seems able to adapt painlessly to its considerable restrictions. I have asked myself time and again how a living being could possibly survive these conditions; the answer is that his inner world must be so rich and profound that it makes up for a lack of outside experience. His life force is entirely self-sufficient.

On the other hand, the Omega is wholly dependent upon the Alpha, the "Father." This subject is passive and would let himself starve to death. He spends all his time curled up in the corner he has chosen as his lair, and seems to exist exclusively as a function of the Alpha. I believe that in his mind, he is convinced he is no more than an extension of the "Father." He is alive because the Alpha is alive.

A few weeks ago, I introduced certain exercises aimed at

developing their language skills, in order to investigate whether or not these skills are innate, and whether the developmental delays they both exhibit are permanent or can be recouped. As expected, the Alpha has proven the more gifted of the two, and more predisposed to learning.

I am intrigued by the insights this particular angle might reveal, but considering the age of both subjects, I have begun to wonder whether it is appropriate to keep the experiment going, and if it is not, what might be the best way to terminate it.

59

The tin box lay on the table in the center of the room, its lid open and its contents visible to all those present. Nobody seemed able to look away from what was inside.

Teresa put on a pair of latex gloves and extracted the two objects. She placed the smaller one on the palm of her hand. It was a medal, gleaming beneath the neon lights. She turned it around: there was a carving on the back.

"W. Wallner," Teresa read out. It had a date, too: 01/09/1936.

No one inside the meeting room of the police station in Travenì seemed prepared to say anything more. Even Hugo Knauss had lost the congenial expression that was his trademark.

"Are they meant for some kind of Satanic ritual?" said Parisi, frowning and running his hands over his bearded chin. He always fiddled with his goatee when he was nervous.

Teresa let slip a smile.

"No. This is the seal of Hippocrates, combined with the Rod of Asclepius. It's the symbol of doctors," she explained, pointing out the snake wrapped around a staff.

"Wallner," Marini mused. "I feel like I've heard that name before."

"It's a fairly common surname in German-speaking countries," she said. "But I doubt that finding the original owner would be of much help."

Why give an object like this to the children? she wondered as she slipped the medal inside a plastic bag.

"What about the other one?" Parisi asked. "Is that a symbol, too?"

Teresa studied the second object. She wanted to believe it was completely innocuous, but could sense that that wasn't the case. She couldn't quite tell what it was for.

It was a simple white hood, a cone of cotton fabric with two holes for eyes covered by a thin mesh. It was dirty, and some of the stitches had come undone. It looked a little like the headgear that worshippers sometimes wore during Easter celebrations in certain villages in southern Italy. Or like the hoods of the Ku Klux Klan.

That particular association made the object seem all the more disturbing.

The elements that made up the killer's portrait were becoming increasingly hazy. Teresa had never come across a psychological profile so full of contradictions, not in any case study, nor in her own career. The level of sadistic aggression in his attacks didn't match his motivations for choosing his victims. He protected children, but at the same time he destroyed their families. It was likely that he felt some degree of guilt, which would explain why he had shown up at Lucia's house with something belonging to her mother, and why he had brought the little girl a gift. It was also the reason why he had arranged the first victim's body so carefully, let Melania Kravina go, and put Abramo Viesel's clothes back on as if to hide that he'd skinned him alive.

"Do you have any idea what these might be?" she asked Hugo Knauss, taking off the gloves.

"No, Superintendent."

"Are you sure? Someone in the valley with questionable hobbies, perhaps?"

"You mean with an interest in racist cults? Certainly not."

So he'd made that connection, too. Teresa had a feeling everyone in the room must have thought the same thing.

"Would you even tell me if there was?"

"What exactly are you suggesting?"

"I never *suggest*, Chief Knauss . . ."

"Superintendent?" said De Carli as he walked in, interrupting their exchange. When he saw what they were looking at, he stopped and stared, forgetting what he'd come in to say. "Is that what I think it is?" he said.

"Who can say?" Teresa answered. "If you have any dazzling insights on the subject, please do share."

"All I have for now is a report to hand in. It's the interview with Lucia's father."

He placed the file on the desk. Teresa leafed through it distractedly.

"I don't want that man going home any time soon," she said. "The girl can be placed in her grandparents' care for a few days."

"We have enough to charge him, Superintendent. Besides, he's already run away once, and he might do it again if we let him go."

"Let's hope the judge agrees with you."

She didn't mention that she'd already spoken to Judge Crespi herself and obtained his assurance that the man would not be allowed near his daughter for a while. He would need the support of the social care services first, to help him repair a bond he'd been on the verge of destroying—along with his own life.

Teresa looked at her watch and recalled how Roberto Valent's had been tied to the effigy's arm the wrong way around. She still hadn't figured out what that meant. There were only a few hours left now until dawn, when they could get started with the search. They just had to hope the weather worked in their favor. Meanwhile, no one had been able to rest: the thought of little Markus in the killer's hands made it impossible to catch even a moment's sleep.

She read through Dante Kravina's statement again, with her head in her hands and her back seizing up in pain.

"A lack of facial expressions," she muttered, reviewing the description of the killer Lucia's father had provided.

Marini approached her. "Are those his words?" he asked De Carli.

"More or less. Anyway, it was clear what he meant. He'd been pretty disturbed by it."

"Lack of facial expressions, imitative behavior, and difficulties with language," Marini summarized, reading through the report.

Teresa lifted her head up to look at him. He looked like he'd been gripped by a particularly interesting train of thought.

"Does that sound familiar?" she asked, not really expecting an answer in the affirmative.

He gave her a surprised look as if he were the first to doubt what he was about to say.

"The case of child number thirty-nine," he said.

Teresa didn't understand.

"Child number thirty-nine?" she repeated.

Marini sat down next to her and began typing something on the computer keyboard.

"I've been reading a psychology handbook," he said. "There's a lot of useless stuff in there, but this one really got to me because it's just . . . so improbable. To think that it actually happened—it's unbelievable. Here it is! Johann Albert Wallner," he said, reading out a newspaper headline.

Teresa felt dizzy. *Wallner*, she thought. Like the name inscribed on the Hippocratic seal.

"Who is he?" she asked.

"A psychiatrist who was struck off for an illegal experiment he conducted almost forty years ago," Marini replied. "Wallner," he muttered, looking at the Nazi-era artifact they'd found. "His father was Wolfgang Wallner, a medical officer in the SS. The medal must have something to do with his profession."

"Perhaps it's a graduation gift," Teresa suggested, counting the years in her head. She tried to remain calm and control her breathing, but it was proving difficult. How was it possible that she of all people—someone who had read everything there was to read when it came to psychology—had no recollection of this case? The article on the screen before her suggested that the case of child number 39 had made an enormous impact, enough to be included in the handbook Marini was reading.

Did I simply miss it, or has my mind already erased the memory?

"What experiment is this?" Knauss asked.

"A really quite twisted test on the effects of maternal deprivation, conducted just a few miles across the border," Marini explained. "Wallner got the idea from a study conducted by René Spitz. But he went much further."

"What did he do?" asked De Carli.

"He was the director of an institute that looked after orphans. He ordered the nursery staff who took care of the infants to withhold any kind of maternal care from their charges. The children weren't referred to by name, but only by the number attached to their cots. This was known as 'de-personalization.'"

"Is that even legal?" said Parisi.

"Definitely not," Marini replied. "But Wallner and his collaborators didn't mind. The nurses weren't allowed to speak to the children or even to make eye contact. They wore a hood with two holes for their eyes so their facial expressions wouldn't be visible."

Everyone held their breaths for a moment. All eyes were on the hood now.

"The infants were fed and washed regularly, but deprived of

any other form of care," Marini went on. "Soon they began to exhibit the first symptoms of this 'treatment': insomnia, rejection of physical contact, wasting away, delayed development of motor functions, and an absence of facial expressions. All except one: the child in cot number thirty-nine. This infant stayed alert and did not waste away. On the contrary, he continued to grow. Wallner thought he had found in him the 'Father' as theorized by Freud: a natural leader equipped with an extraordinary inner strength."

"What became of the children?" De Carli asked.

Marini scrolled down to the end of the webpage he was reading from.

"A nurse who had recently been hired told the authorities about Wallner, and the police stormed the institute. The children were rescued and within months their symptoms began to fade until they disappeared altogether. But Wallner managed to get away, and he took with him the child from cot number thirty-nine, his greatest discovery."

"What was the child's name? Does it say?" Teresa asked, trying to control the tremor in her voice.

"Andreas Hoffman. Wallner and the child were never found. Agnes Braun, Wallner's closest collaborator, was put on trial and sentenced to twenty years in prison. When the institute opened again, Magdalena Hoos, the young woman who had alerted the authorities, was hired to work there again. The police later learned that Wallner had been obsessed with Nazi theories of eugenics."

Andreas. Teresa finally felt she had a connection with him.

"Poor kid. I wonder what happened to him," said De Carli. Marini swore and Knauss looked down at his trousers, picking at them compulsively.

Teresa regained her composure and looked at them all incredulously.

"Don't you see?" she said. "It's him. The child who disappeared is our killer."

She got to her feet, her agitation making her forget her aches.

"He paints his face white because identification is the most primitive form of love, and all he saw every day were the white ceiling of his room and a white hood. At first the different ways he's interacted with people made me think he must suffer from some form of multiple personality disorder, but on the contrary—he has no personality to speak of, at least not in a clinical sense. He imitates the people he meets, in a sort of neonatal phase he's never overcome. It's his way of communicating."

Teresa finally understood why Andreas's psychological and behavioral profile had always seemed so incoherent: their basic assumptions had all been wrong.

"His case doesn't follow set patterns because on a psychological level, it's as if he'd never been born," she said. "So our usual tools of psychological analysis won't work on him."

"He's able to form relationships with children, though," Marini noted.

"Yes . . . But to understand how and why he does that, we need to find out how he survived," said Teresa. "Did he have a home? Someone to keep him company? What happened to his abductor?"

"Maybe Wallner ran away and left him behind. Or maybe . . . maybe he was here all along, hiding god knows where, for decades," said Parisi. "He may well be dead now, but the result of his experiment has survived. But what do you think triggered Andreas Hoffman's fury?"

Teresa thought of how the killer had stopped the teenagers in the forest, and the animals they had seen fleeing while they had been collecting evidence.

"His territory has been invaded, and that's thrown his world off balance," she said. "It has pushed him down the mountain, like the startled deer we saw the other day."

"What invasion?"

Teresa studied the map on the wall and pointed at the area where the new ski resort was being built.

"*This* invasion. The machinery and the construction workers. The clearing of trees. The inspections. We need to limit the search to this area, starting from the northern side, which is harder to reach and more thickly forested. We're looking for a shelter of some sort."

"There's only rocks to the north and north-west. I don't think we'll find him there. To the north-east you have the Osvan quarries. It's a barren landscape there, with no trees and no cover. Only loose boulders," said Knauss. "There's nothing there."

"What kind of quarries?"

"Rock, and lead and zinc mines. But it's like a desert now. The vegetation hasn't grown back yet."

"We'll use those markers as the perimeter for our search," said Teresa.

"There's just one thing I don't get," said Marini. "Why did he take the youngest of the Klavina kids, Markus, and leave his older brother at their father's mercy?"

Teresa had her own theory about that.

"Because Mathias never actually admitted to his friends that his father beats him. But he did voice his concern about what might happen to his little brother."

"But the killer could have just murdered the father and freed them both."

Teresa looked at the fading darkness outside the window. Just a little longer until she could go out to look for the child and a killer who now was, in her mind, the first entry in a long list of victims.

"He's changed his modus operandi drastically," she said. "The sight of the baby must have awakened something in him. Perhaps there are still traces of his peers from the institute somewhere in his subconscious. He can remember them crying. He can remember the nights they spent together, listening to each other's breathing."

Teresa took off her glasses and immediately stuck one of the temples in her mouth to tensely chew away at.

"He can remember his first life, now," she said. "And he wants it back."

20 September 1993

It is with great regret that I must conclude the time has come to terminate this experiment.

I believe this to be the case because in the current circumstances, I am no longer able to guarantee my own safety. I am referring, primarily, to the survival of the Alpha. My most extraordinary discovery is also the thing that might put my life at risk, a fact that fills me with great sorrow.

The subject has lived beyond my most optimistic predictions for his lifespan, and I now find myself in an increasingly difficult position with regards to managing his captivity.

I ask myself what would happen if he were to become fully aware of my presence and the conditions I raised him in. It is a question I do not wish to find out the answer to.

As for subject Omega, though he does not constitute a problem, he has now outlived his usefulness.

The solution lies in their next meal.

Day dawned over the valley, bringing a clear morning with it. Teresa sighed with relief as she saw light spreading through a clear sky; it bode well for their search. She'd managed to sleep in half hour snatches interleaved by bleak thoughts that made her shudder in the dark, her heart in her mouth. It had been difficult to stay put, to bide their time. It was even harder, now, to be forced to direct the search operations from the bottom of the valley. She wished she was up in the forest, doing the searching herself instead of having to rely on the artificial eye of a drone. The memory of how they'd chased down Lucas Ebran was exhilarating. She had felt alive, useful, her body and mind still working properly, performing their duties. That was no longer something she could take for granted, and yet she still felt the urge to throw her body forward in search of clues, to use every bit of energy she had left until she could stretch out her hand and reach for the child.

But which child? It occurred to her that there were two of them involved in this case.

Now that she knew how this story of abuse and death had begun, she could finally see the truth about who Andreas Hoffman was: a victim himself who had somehow survived and lived in this world despite everything he'd been through. Teresa had tried to imagine what his life might have been like to draw up a new profile for him, but neither statistics, nor research, nor her experience could come to her aid now, perhaps because no other creature like Andreas had ever existed in the world. No one had helped him learn the skills needed to adapt to life—yet somehow he had done it anyway, developing his own tools instead. She wondered what they might be. His mind was unborn, and yet it was active in its own way.

He had lived a life without love.

The air ambulance was waiting on the flat expanse next to the construction site for the new ski resort, ready to retrieve the baby as soon as it was found. Two more search and rescue helicopters were already circling the area. Hugo Knauss's men had set off at first light to clear the way. An army detachment had arrived and was preparing to comb through the wood-land that stretched halfway up the mountain. From that point onwards, expert mountaineers from various law enforcement agencies would have to take over the search. The Austrian police had also been alerted and the border was being closely monitored.

The search parties, with their sniffer dogs at the leash, were preparing to set off; the plan was for them to move forward in an arc, as if it were a hunting expedition. Teresa was becoming increasingly concerned about the weapons they were equipped with. Of course they wouldn't fire any shots until they were sure the child was safe—but what would happen after that?

Teresa saw Gardini and Ambrosini approaching. They were escorting a woman, the mother of the abducted child. She was holding a piece of cloth against her chest and made straight for Teresa as soon as she saw her. It was an encounter that could no longer be avoided.

Gloria Sanfilk's eyes, swollen from crying and full of misery, looked straight into Teresa's. Teresa was surprised by the strength she could discern beneath the surface of the woman's despair.

"He's alive," Teresa heard her say. It wasn't a question, but a warning to Teresa that she mustn't dare—not even for a moment—think otherwise and give up.

"I'm sure of it," the woman said.

Teresa looked for her husband but couldn't see him.

"He isn't here," said Gloria, reading Teresa's thoughts. "I won't take him back, I won't let him near us again, but you have to bring me my child back."

She handed the cloth she'd been carrying to Teresa. It was a baby's romper. Gloria placed it inside Teresa's hand, squeezed it between hers, and raised it to her own face to breathe in the scent of her baby, inviting Teresa to do the same. It wasn't for the dogs, she had brought it for Teresa; she wanted to make sure that the woman who held her son's fate in her hands would feel the child's smell on her as if it were her own baby.

Take my place, she was saying. *Take my place and bring him back to me.*

Teresa nodded. No words were necessary.

Ambrosini walked up to them and put his arm around Gloria's shoulders, gently leading her away.

Marini came over.

"It's impossible to predict how the killer might react," he said, eyeing the forest.

"You should call him by his name," Teresa murmured—more to herself than to her young colleague. "No one else has ever done that for him. He's never even done it himself."

Marini's expression shifted.

"I think I understand what you mean, now," he said. "I can't help but see him as a victim either."

He paused then, before uttering the question no one else had had the courage to ask her: "Do you think he's going to hurt the child?"

Teresa had spent all night thinking about that. She hoped

she'd found the right answer and not just the one that made her feel better.

"Not on purpose," she said. "He is the 'Father' who protects his people, the Alpha; the kids from the village are his tribe, though they don't even realize it. Still, we mustn't forget that the hands that are holding that baby now are the same hands that ripped Roberto Valent's eyes out."

Marini handed her the printout of an aerial photograph.

"The drones have come across an old derelict mountain shelter that doesn't appear on the map," he said. "It's surrounded by woodland, in the northern sector, just below the tree line and before the scree. It's the only one in the whole area. And there are signs of recent human activity in the clearing around it."

62

FOREST OF TRAVENÌ-ABERLINZ, 1993

The sun still shone brightly enough to warm the rocks and light up the fragrant pollens of late-blooming chamomile and wormwood, but the wind that blew from the north had grown colder in the last few days, heralding the start of the season of sleep. Plants and animals had already begun to prepare, the former shedding all that was no longer necessary, and the latter thickening their coats and filling their dens up with acorns and hay.

He, too, was getting ready to face the cold. He had noticed that after it rained now, the air was much cooler, and when it blew, it made minuscule flowers blossom on his skin. He had set a few more traps, the day before, knowing that there would not be such an abundance of prey for much longer. The flesh from his catch, sliced into thin strips and laid out to dry, would help him get through darker, colder days.

He crossed the stream, leaping from boulder to boulder, and climbed deftly up the cliff on the other side, emerging into a sun-drenched clearing. It was a spot favored by predators—foxes, badgers, and especially birds of prey—because any small animal that attempted to cross it was left exposed to attack.

One of the traps he'd laid out at the edge of the woods had caught something. It was a badger, and the more it struggled to break free, the more the noose tightened around it.

Upon reaching the beast, he realized that it wasn't as large as he'd initially thought: it was a female surrounded by her cubs, squirming and yowling helplessly at their mother's side.

There was enough meat on the creatures to keep him fed for days, possibly even weeks; but instead of proceeding to strangle the life out of them, he found himself paralyzed as he watched. Their cries had unleashed a storm inside him, like those dark clouds that sometimes rolled in from the east and ripped young saplings from the earth.

He let the mother go and watched them all scamper back to the forest. He had never seen a cub survive without its mother. And he had a pup of his own to think about.

He looked toward the edge of the bluff where his little one was hiding, waiting for him, and saw something that scared him: a black thread rising to the sky.

He broke into a run, darting through the trees. When he reached his lair, he saw smoke blowing through the gaps between the wooden beams. He ran to the back and lifted the plank he used as a door. The room was just as he'd left it, with one exception: in his absence, the hands that occasionally—and now so rarely—pushed food and clothing through a hole in one of the walls had left a plate of food on the floor.

His little one was in the corner from which he never moved and appeared to be sleeping, a half-empty bowl of food next to him.

He went to him and tried to wake him up, but his eyes wouldn't open. He had changed color, and his skin had gone cold. He rubbed at it repeatedly, but it refused to warm up. He called out in a howl, pinched his skin, but he was sleeping deeply. He thought, then, that it might be best not to wake him up at all, not even now that the smell of smoke was becoming stronger.

He curled up against his cub and held him in his arms where he would not be afraid and would soon wake up once more.

63

The only way to reach the abandoned mountain shelter was on foot. Teresa's muscles burned with the effort, and she was panting with fatigue. Marini was right next to her, steadying her every time her knees buckled, only for her to elbow him.

"You should have waited down in the valley," he'd said at one point, triggering a volley of insults in return.

Teresa could feel the weight of the baby's romper in her coat pocket, the burden of the responsibility she'd knowingly shouldered when she'd decided to concentrate the search in that particular area—and nowhere else. If she had made a mistake, there was a risk they would never find him again.

The search was advancing at a brisk pace. Everyone involved was fully aware that it had been almost twelve hours since the abduction, and that the child must be getting hungry. They were pushing as hard as they could, and their heavy breathing reverberated in the air. It was like a human net, stretching across hundreds of feet of undergrowth, inspecting every shadow and every nook as it ascended.

The snow that had fallen overnight had covered any traces of human passage, but Teresa relied on what the drone had spotted not far from where they currently stood. She wondered what kind of man could live up there, among eagles and foxes and not much else, in a place where even deer rarely ventured and mountain goats thrived instead, where the howling of the wind was the sound that dominated over all others.

"We're here," she heard someone announce from the group that was leading the way. The column came to a halt, and Teresa walked to the front.

A clearing came into view through the trees. There was a derelict structure standing in the middle, half-blackened by an ancient fire. The wooden planks that formed the walls of the shelter had been eroded by time, and its pitched roof rested on a base of simple stone. It was an abandoned barn, the kind where people used to store hay after the summer reaping of the highland meadows.

"Back in the old days our elders knew the best time of the year to harvest timber for building homes. It will go hard and it will blacken, but it won't burn," said Hugo Knauss as he observed the ruin.

The building was not vacant. Rusty, mismatched objects sprouting through the snow were strewn all around it next to other, newer arrivals. This, Teresa realized, was where anything stolen from Travenì ended up. Whoever it was that lived in the shelter must be a regular visitor to the village, returning here with treasures he then left outside, exposed to the elements.

She had instructed the helicopters to stay away from the area for the time being, to avoid scaring Andreas Hoffman into doing something he might not have intended. They had to do the same, make sure their presence went undetected for as long as possible.

Surrounding the shelter, interspersed among the scraps, were low totems made out of animal skulls. Bones hung suspended from the branches of nearby fir trees, chiming as they swayed in the wind, like rudimentary dream catchers.

Knauss spat on the ground.

"You're the expert, Superintendent. What the hell kind of killer is this?" he said.

"Would you call an animal who attacks because it feels under threat a 'killer'?" Teresa snapped, stepping away from him.

The team was waiting for the signal to storm the shed, with more men stationed in the forest to block off any escape routes. Though they'd done several exhaustive run-throughs of the plan, and of the special measures they would take to ensure the child wasn't harmed, Teresa was more afraid of this moment than she'd been of most things in her career. She had never been responsible for this young a life, and it surprised her to notice how the value of a creature's existence seemed to be inversely correlated to the time it had spent on earth. Her hand gripped the romper in her pocket, as if she were holding on to a thread that mustn't be allowed to break.

"Go," she radioed.

Moving in silence, the men at the edge of the forest closed in on the building until they'd surrounded it. Then, in a series of synchronized movements, they broke in.

Teresa counted the seconds and began to wonder why it was taking so long to secure such a small space. But she couldn't hear any gunshots or the sound of scuffling either. There must be something else in there that was giving the men pause. Teresa could only hope it wasn't a scene of death.

Parisi emerged to signal that the coast was clear, and Teresa sprinted to the shed.

Somehow the inside of the shed was even more chaotic than the outside. Objects of various shapes and functions had been stashed haphazardly inside the largest room; she envisioned the master of that place collecting them all without really understanding what any of them were for. Perhaps it was his way of feeling closer to the inhabitants of the village who looked so much like him but were otherwise so different, so distant. She remembered how Roberto Valent's watch had been strapped to the effigy's arm; at first she'd thought it must signify something, but perhaps Andreas had only put it on the wrong way around because he simply did not know any better. To him the watch was nothing but an ornament, something he had seen on the wrists of the people who lived in the valley.

A barn owl roused from its sleep flew from the mezzanine to the door and soared toward the forest beating its wings forcefully. De Carli looked down from the attic.

"There's nothing here apart from that bird and a rat. Just a bed of hay," he said.

"I don't think he lives here anymore," Teresa murmured. "Something has driven him away. Probably the deforestation of the area toward the valley."

Teresa knew that the people of the village would never understand the way she saw Andreas Hoffman. What they wanted was a monster they could abhor, a bogeyman they could set on fire to exorcise the evil that had descended upon them. And he was a perfect fit.

She thought of the effigy made out of the first victim's clothes, with berries for eyes. Teresa understood now why it had been facing the village: it had been an act of condemnation. Andreas saw Travenì as a threat. *It is you*, he was saying, *it is you who are invading my territory*.

The village was the catalyst for his murderous rage.

A small latched door led to a second room that was not much larger than a closet. Teresa kneeled to take a closer look. It was empty and windowless, with only a gap between the boards allowing a glimpse of the dark green of the woods. The walls were covered in markings etched into the wood, stylized depictions of animals, plants, and human figures. When she slid forward on her knees to study them properly, she noticed that one of the boards could be lifted. It was a passage to the outside world. She looked around. The untouched emptiness of that room seemed strange to her; Andreas hadn't let himself contaminate it with the mayhem that had encroached upon the rest of the shelter. There was something sacred about that emptiness.

She emerged from the alcove and continued with her search. In a corner of the main room, there was a table blackened by flames. The walls and the ceiling also bore the traces of a fire. There were a number of books: some had been devoured by the flames and reduced to little more than cinders; others had only burned partway, as if someone had arrived just in time to rescue them.

Teresa put on a pair of gloves and began leafing through them. She was surprised to find a notebook with some basic writing exercises. The marks in it—probably letters—had been traced by an unpracticed hand. But there were only a handful of pages like this, the rest of the notebook was untouched. Sifting through the other books, she realized they were basic literacy manuals.

A slim volume fell to the floor. Teresa picked it up and saw that it was a collection of poetry. A leaf from an oak tree slipped through the pages. It wasn't completely dry yet.

Had someone taught Andreas how to read and write? Had they spoken to him? Could it have been Wallner?

Teresa noticed Marini pausing at the threshold to another room and she could tell from his expression that whatever had caught the squad's attention was in there.

It took courage to take those last few steps. She forced her body to do it.

The sun was filtering through the gaps between the boards. A backlit figure sat on a chair at the end of the room.

Teresa could only make out its silhouette. Marini broke one of the boards with a kick, and light poured in.

Nobody moved a muscle. There was only a whorl of dust in the air, shimmering in the sun. Teresa sensed Knauss's presence beside her.

"God . . . It's a human corpse!" she heard him say.

They saw before them an ancient, time-worn skeleton. Its bones were covered in dust and had blackened in certain spots.

Upon it were the body parts that had been taken from each of the victims. At its feet were the leftovers of a recent meal.

"That's not quite accurate," said Teresa, wishing for once that she didn't have the kind of experience to know better. "It's the corpse of a child."

Another child.

Two children whose stories we don't know: one of them has grown up to be a killer, while the other has no name, only a skeleton. The third child has been taken from his mother and is somewhere in this forest right now, god knows where.

Children: they seem to be at the heart of this merry-go-round of death and hope. Children who survive, who fight back, who learn to love in spite of everything.

It is a celebration of life, a feeling that has spread through me since I first arrived in this valley.

A celebration of life and its ability to endure.

There is no force stronger than life, and we are at its service.

Antonio Parri was analyzing the skeleton and compiling a report on his findings. They had not yet moved the body from the position it had been found in.

Teresa stood to one side and watched the coroner at work. She knew that his inventory of the bones would be accompanied by detailed observations on the surrounding environment, a geographical and topographical analysis, and his conclusions on the nature of the remains. It would require him to spend hours studying the smallest parts of what had once been a human being.

But Teresa didn't have that kind of time. Parri knew that, so as soon as he could, he would provide her with any information he was able to glean from a preliminary morphological examination.

Teresa doubted it would be of any great help in finding the missing child, but there was not much else she could do at that stage other than hope. It had been almost fifteen hours since the abduction, and though they continued to search with every tool at their disposal, they had yet to find any trace of the child or of Andreas Hoffman.

At last Parri turned around and invited her to come closer. Teresa did so, though she stopped at a good distance from the remains. She tried to picture the child they had belonged to. It was a painful exercise, but not one she wished to avoid, she needed that pain to keep her going, to continue the search.

"It is possible that the body was repositioned over time," the coroner explained. "I doubt it was ever interred. The spinal cavity is clean. The longer bones present traces of animal bites that date to a time after the corpse was reduced to a skeleton."

Teresa nodded. Perhaps the body had never been buried because Andreas was not acquainted with the idea of religion, not even in a primitive sense. Or perhaps he still considered it a living being. A meal had recently been left at the skeleton's feet: a piece of charred meat, pink on the inside, and some walnuts still in their shells.

"You will have noticed that someone has pierced holes into the bones and tied them together with fishing line," said Parri.

"He was trying to piece it back together, to keep it intact for as long as possible," said Teresa softly.

She did not feel any revulsion, but only a deep sorrow for the person who had done this, who had tried desperately to put those remains back together and bring them back to life. Someone whose understanding of life and death differed from theirs. Someone who, in his own way, and despite everything he had been made to suffer, had loved that child, and continued to love what was left of it in the world.

Teresa didn't see anything morbid in this act, but interpreted it instead as a sign of devotion, the poignant expression of a need to keep the object of his enduring affections close. Where they saw only bones and broken remains, Andreas could still glimpse the spark of a fierce bond.

"Do you think he knew him well?" Parri asked.

Teresa looked at the coroner.

"He loved him. I'm certain he's not the one who killed him. He tried to bring him back to life."

"If it is true, as I believe it is, that the remains have always been left exposed to air and to moisture, the corpse must have decomposed much faster than it would have had it been buried," the coroner resumed. "Bearing this in mind, and noting the absence of corpse wax and of desiccated fleshy tissue, I would estimate the passing to have taken place twenty to thirty years ago. But I won't be able to provide you with a more exact time-frame until after the lab tests and x-rays."

It had happened a long time ago, Teresa thought, perhaps too long to hope they might ever find out whose body it was.

"Can you tell me age and sex?" she asked.

"The forehead is flat, the pelvic cavity and the pubic angle are narrow. I'd say a Caucasian male. A young one."

Teresa kept her eyes on the corpse.

"How young?"

"The second molars weren't yet fully grown."

She felt a wave of nausea rise to her throat. This confirmed what she'd been thinking the moment she'd set eyes on those bones. She had measured them in the time it had taken her to blink and had immediately realized the truth, her stomach cramping at the knowledge.

"No older than twelve," the coroner continued, "though

based on an initial measurement of the bones, I'd say ten or eleven. I haven't detected any signs of trauma."

Neither of them spoke for several moments.

"I've already extracted a few samples to test for biological anomalies," Parri resumed, handing a box with the samples to an assistant. "I'll have them sent to the lab immediately so we can get some answers quickly. We'll need a few more hours here before we can move everything."

"Is there any way we can run a toxicology test now? I want to understand how he died."

"I could remove the skull right away to get going on that, and it would also allow us to test the tissue he took from the victims."

"Thank you, Antonio."

Marini called out to her from the blackened table.

"Superintendent, you might want to come and see this."

65

Marini had found something among the burned objects that were impossible to identify and the remnants of the partially scorched books: a handwritten notebook, with each entry dated at the top. The last entry was marked 20 September 1993.

It was in German. Teresa's understanding of the language was limited to what she had learned at school, and those ancient memories were of no use to her now.

"Do you speak German?" she asked Marini.

"I know a few words here and there."

"Chief Knauss!" she called.

The chief approached them.

"I know you're all bilingual here. Translate this for me," she said, pointing at the diary.

"Now?"

Teresa stared at him, wondering how it was possible that he would always find something to say—even a single, insignificant word—that was bound to irritate her.

"You tell me. Would you rather take it home and settle down with it by the fireplace?" she replied.

It took Knauss a while to realize she was joking. He fished for his reading glasses in the pocket of his jacket and sighed as he put them on, leaning with his face close to the notebook.

"It looks like a diary."

"Yes, we surmised as much from the dates."

Teresa watched with increasing impatience as Knauss read a few lines and tried to figure out what he was looking at. She saw him turn a few pages, go back, then stop to think before he resumed his reading.

"What's wrong?" she asked him.

"I don't understand," he muttered.

"Ask one of your men to help. There must be someone else here who can read it."

Knauss lifted his gaze from the notebook.

"I can read it myself, Superintendent."

"Then what's the problem?"

"It's what they've written in here. It sounds like an experiment."

Teresa was no longer in the mood to make jokes.

"Read it to me," she commanded.

Knauss ran his finger down one of the pages.

"Subject Alpha attempts to interact with Subject Omega, but the latter appears indifferent, and to have fallen into a passive state. The delay in his motor skills is now evident. He is almost always lying supine and makes no attempt to . . . wait, this part is unclear . . . makes no attempt to reach for his food ration." Knauss stopped speaking and looked at Teresa. "Is this about animals?"

"They're children," Teresa declared. She saw Knauss hesitate. "Keep going," she ordered.

"What is most surprising is that Alpha does not claim Omega's ration as his own, but instead tries to push it toward him. I believe he is beginning to consider him a companion."

Silence had fallen over the shelter, all activity put on hold.

Everybody was listening to Knauss, who kept on reading. Teresa raised her eyes for a brief moment and saw denial and disgust on the faces around her. She was sure they had a different perspective, now, on the skeleton sitting just a few feet from them all, eternally waiting.

You can stop waiting now, Teresa thought. *Someone's finally come to save you—but it's too late.*

"I doubt the child has any conscious perception of its imprisonment. He knows no other life but this one," Knauss resumed, "but his subconscious does, and it abandons itself to death."

Teresa exhaled tensely. She could imagine the epilogue, picture it in her mind, but something—perhaps the tremors that rippled through her arms every time she leaned over to touch those pages—told her that the horrors contained in those entries were not yet over.

"Go to the last day," she told Knauss.

He obeyed. Teresa saw his eyes running over the words, widening, then seeking out her own before turning quickly away. When he read out the details of Wallner's final plan, Teresa couldn't take it anymore. She had to leave the shed, get some fresh air in her lungs, and wait for her heart to slow down, letting the wind dry her tears before they could fall.

66

As soon as she'd stepped outside the shelter, Teresa breathed more easily. Marini followed her; he could never seem to tell when it was best to just leave her alone.

She didn't give him time to ask any questions.

"Parri confirms that the remains belong to a boy," she said. "About eleven years old. It could have been a death by natural causes; there's no guarantee Wallner actually put his plan into practice," she said, though she was conscious she'd only added that last remark as a way of consoling herself.

"How could anyone do that? They were just children."

"It seems Wallner practiced the same beliefs as his father. He did not possess a conscience in the way we understand it. We should look for his body, too, around here. His might have been interred. He lived in this area long enough to raise two children, though we still have to figure out how."

Marini looked around.

"What kind of life would it have been?" he wondered aloud.

"A difficult one, without question, but still preferable to a trial and to prison," Teresa replied. "He must have made the occasional trip to the village, though. To stock up, to get a hold of medicines . . . Wallner was bilingual, and he perfected his experiments here. Go and find out whether anyone remembers him, even vaguely. If anyone ever saw him. We need to find out whose skeleton that is in there. He's three or four years younger than Andreas Hoffman. He can't have come from the orphanage."

"We've discovered some photographs of Wallner, but they're all quite blurry."

"It's not the photos I'm worried about, but how the people of this valley understand the concept of cooperation."

"Why would they care about protecting a criminal who might have made a few trips to the valley some thirty years ago?"

"That's not it; they're protecting themselves, the community, the group, its collective stability. Individuals don't matter."

"I'll be back as soon as I've found out more."

Teresa glanced at the sun; it had already begun to set. Parri's assistant emerged from the building, carrying a metal box that held the skull they had just extracted.

From a distant point in the forest, on a slope that faced the clearing with the mountain shelter, several flocks of birds took flight in unison as if startled by the sound of a bullet, though none had been fired. The sky above the treetops briefly turned black.

Teresa couldn't move. A familiar sensation held her rooted to the ground where she stood, her eyes fixed on that distant spot. She could feel that she was being watched, and she knew he was the one watching. Andreas was hiding up there and observing them all. Why was he still lingering there, where he risked getting caught?

The answer to her question was being carried out past her, sealed inside a small steel coffin.

She finally understood what Andreas was protecting from the advance of the outside world: not his lair, but the only human relationship he'd ever known. He had somehow sensed what was being taken away from him.

"He became violent because he felt threatened by the expansion of the construction site," she said. "He was afraid they would take away his companion. That's what drove him to kill."

"But that little boy's been dead for decades," Marini protested.

Teresa looked at the spot on the mountain where the birds had flown from. That was where the baby was.

"I don't think he truly understands what it means to die," she said in a soft voice. "Sure, he knows about life and death, but only in terms of cause and effect—he's learned that by observing nature. But as for what happens next, the question of whether it is possible to come back from a kind of sleep that consumes the flesh . . . That's something he can only imagine, just as we do, just as humans have done for millennia. He was simply trying to wake his companion up. But now he's not alone anymore. He's found himself a cub."

67

The search party was now concentrating its efforts on the stretch of sloping ground that Teresa had indicated. The men worked relentlessly, refusing to take any kind of break as they climbed toward the peak in ever tighter formation. Not a grain of sand could have slipped by them without their noticing.

The orders were to halt their advance as soon as they sighted the target and wait for Teresa to reach them—she was worried about how Andreas might react to feeling surrounded, and she needed to figure out a way to communicate with him. She had moved from her earlier station at the bottom of the valley to a helipad that had been set up on some flat land further up the mountain.

The temperature was rising and the sky remained clear. All she could think of was the child. He'd been wearing heavy winter clothes when he'd been abducted, with a Babygro to shield him from the chill. But while he might not suffer the cold, he must certainly be hungry and thirsty by now. How would Andreas cope with its incessant crying?

She kept going back to Wallner's diary. It had stopped in September 1993, and Teresa couldn't bring herself to imagine what had happened next. There was only one thing she was sure of: child Omega had died, while child Alpha had survived and had continued to live in what he considered his lair, near the source of the only human contact he'd ever experienced in his life, and which time had reduced into nothing more than a skeleton.

Her mobile vibrated in her pocket. It was Marini calling from the Travenì police station.

"Any news?" she asked.

"Nothing. I've had the archives searched in full. No children have gone missing in the valley in the last thirty years. There's no sign of any missing person's report. I also called headquarters in the city and ran a search at the public library. There's nothing in the newspaper clippings from that period, either."

Teresa feared that the mystery of Omega's identity might never be solved. But perhaps there was one more path they could try, running beneath the surface of those seemingly flawless, immaculate lives.

"I think I know someone who can help us," she said. "Wait for me."

She hung up. The helicopter's blades were already in motion; she signalled at the pilot to wait for her. The aircraft took flight with Teresa on board, and from the air she could see the true face of the forest: an ocean of green and white, of towering waves and fathomless depths. Andreas and the child were down there somewhere, both equally terrified, and both in need of help.

68

The whole village seemed to have gathered at the cathedral, as if Travenì itself were kneeling at the altar. Gloria Sanfilk and Mathias were in the front row, praying for Markus's safe return home. The church was ablaze with votive candles, the air heavy with hundreds of breaths, incense smoke, and the musty odor of age-old friezes.

"Why do you want to talk to him?" whispered Marini.

Teresa hadn't yet shared her thoughts with Marini. She had spent the past half hour on the phone with Parisi, who was updating her on the search party's progress.

"You stay put," she said. "He'll be more at ease if I go alone."

She let her eyes roam over the downturned heads until she spotted the man she was looking for and walked up to him. He was sitting with his elbows on his knees and his forehead resting against his clasped hands; his eyes were closed and his feathered felt hat lay on the bench next to him.

"Doctor Ian?" she called out softly.

He looked up at her in surprise.

"Can we talk?"

"Of course."

Ian crossed himself, quickly kneeled, and followed her out to the churchyard.

"Any news? Have you found him?" he asked.

Teresa went straight to the point.

"No, no sightings yet," she replied.

Ian closed his eyes for a moment and let out a worried sigh. He seemed tired and suddenly older.

"We found this in an abandoned mountain shelter," said Teresa.

She showed him Wallner's diary, preserved in a transparent sleeve.

Ian looked at it.

"What is this?" he asked, putting on his reading glasses.

"It's a log," Teresa explained. "It relates to an experiment conducted on two children who were kidnapped and held captive on these mountains."

Teresa watched the blood drain from his face.

"Here? In Travenì? That's not possible."

"We know the identity of one of the two children: he is the killer and the kidnapper we're looking for. But we have no information on the other child. I hoped you might be able to help us with that."

"Me?"

"Has any local woman ever asked you to perform an abortion on her? It would have been around thirty years ago, but I know this is not the kind of thing one tends to forget."

"I've never done anything of the sort. I would have never agreed to it!"

"I don't doubt that, Doctor, which is why I believe that the woman—assuming there was such a woman—must have borne the child and found some other way to get rid of it."

"How?"

"By handing it over to someone who could guarantee no one would ever find out what had happened. Do you remember any foreigners passing through the village around that time? A German speaker, perhaps?"

Ian looked grave.

"Everyone here speaks two languages, Superintendent, often three. We're half-bloods, we're proud of our identity, and though

I know we can seem brusque in our dealings with outsiders, I can assure you no one would ever have given their child away, especially not to a stranger. We don't have that kind of monster in Travenì. As you can see, we're all God's children here."

"That's not what you said at the pub the other night," Teresa pointed out. "You told me people would abandon their children sometimes. And sometimes they wouldn't even give birth to them."

"Those were starving, desperate people. They cannot be blamed. Anyway, that was all a very long time ago. A distant and harrowing past."

"Perhaps the echoes of that past have lasted longer than you thought?"

"No, I don't think so, Superintendent," the doctor replied, looking grim. "You must do everything you can to find that child, to bring some kind of justice—earthly or divine—to bear on the monster who took him away from his mother. But you are wasting your time down here. You won't find your man, or the key to bringing Markus back home, among these people and their stories." He gestured toward the church. "Now, will you join us in prayer?"

Teresa looked up at the golden crucifix that shone from the top of the slate roof.

"I pray by doing my job, Doctor," she replied, putting the diary back inside her shoulder bag. "I must return to the search now."

"God be with you," Ian said in farewell, touching his hat.

Teresa watched him walk away, his shoulders looking more stooped than she remembered.

Marini walked up to her.

"Did you get the answers you were hoping for?" he asked.

"Not yet."

"So what now?"

"Now we dig deeper."

69

The darkness was like a wet void absorbing the rhythm of their heartbeats. It had been a long time since he had last heard the sound of another breath near his own.

The air down there smelled of soil. The rock walls oozed water, a constant dripping that complemented the baby's wails. He had brought the child to a safe place, a place where the hunters who were following their trail would never be able to find them. He knew that the dark could be scary, and he held the child pressed against his chest, so that it could feel his warmth and be reassured by his presence.

In time he would teach him that there was nothing to fear about the night, about small spaces, tall peaks, and secret nooks—but first he must learn how to silence the child's cries. He had seen the women in the village do it and tried to imitate the way they would rock their arms back and forth, their gentle cooing—though the noises that issued from his own lips sounded more like gruff howls.

He dipped a piece of cloth in water and brought it to the child's mouth. The boy sucked on it greedily. Though he couldn't see his face, the child had learned by now to recognize his voice and would stop crying when he spoke.

Those tears stirred something in him, inside his chest, where the muscle that pumped life through his limbs beat faster and faster. It was a new sensation, something that urged him to cradle the baby in his arms and shield it from anything that might frighten it. He knew that every creature on earth had been a cub once—and that included him. He wondered who had soothed his tears when he was little, who had chased away his fears, whose face had leaned over his bed at night and watched over him as he slept.

He couldn't remember, and he felt alone again.

70

What if we never find this child, or what if the forest gives us back nothing more than his lifeless form? What will become of me then?

I'm afraid, so afraid that all my other fears have disappeared. I can cope with anything, but I can't cope with losing another child.

The search had continued until sunset, but had yielded no results. It had been twenty-four hours since the abduction. Teresa did not see how it was possible for Andreas to come as close to them as he had—close enough to watch them at work—only to seemingly vanish, leaving no trace, not even a trail that the dogs could follow. How could he move around so often and so fast when he had the child to carry? Teresa was almost sure he wouldn't have left the baby behind, hidden in some secret recess; Andreas knew the perils of the forest better than anyone, and he wouldn't put the young life he was taking care of at risk.

But what if I'm wrong? What if I'm romanticizing the actions of a killer?

It was a possibility Teresa couldn't allow herself to dwell on. Now more than ever she had to believe in herself, in spite of the exhaustion and confusion that periodically assailed her. She had to fight back. The face of the forest was shifting again as it became shrouded in shadows. Now was not the time to give in to doubt and fear.

"We're all here, Superintendent," Parisi informed her.

Teresa joined the team that had assembled in the meeting room of the police headquarters in Travenì. The heads of the search and rescue agencies, the mountain rescue teams, and a Rifles regiment had all gathered there, as well as her and Chief Knauss's men. Maps and geographical surveys of the local area were spread across the table.

The fifteen-square mile area they had been searching had been divided into quadrants and combed through from dawn to dusk in shifts, eighty men at a time. The men had only stopped when night had fallen—and if it had been up to them, they would have carried on. But the public prosecutor and the district judge had agreed that putting lives at risk to save another life was out of the question. Teresa wasn't sure whether, given the choice, she would have adhered to the same principle.

"Where's Marini?" she asked De Carli.

"I haven't seen him in a while, Superintendent."

"Then call him, for Christ's sake."

"Right away."

The meeting began, chaired by prosecutor Ambrosini. It was torture for Teresa to have to listen to a summary of what had been a day of fruitless searching, but worse than that was the knowledge that she couldn't go straight back out to the forest to keep looking. A long night awaited her, twelve hours of darkness and enforced paralysis.

It was too long to wait, too long for her and the child both.

Soon, Ambrosini began running out of things to say, his words evaporating on the fire of Teresa's impatience. She turned toward the window and looked out at the village. Travenì was not asleep; a column of flames snaked through its ancient, gloomy streets. The procession had started at dusk, when the inhabitants had assembled at the foot of the medieval clock tower in the main square, lighting hundreds of candles to carry with them.

While the people out there were busy praying for the child, those inside this room were actually looking for a way to bring him home. Seeing those lights, the bowed heads moving forward in single file, Teresa felt furious. Travenì had missed another chance to redeem itself in her eyes: no one from the village had volunteered to help with their search. They had elected instead to gather together spontaneously and look for the child far from the areas Teresa had identified as potential hideouts.

She had hoped they might be right, that one of them might come back cradling the baby, but that hadn't been the case. Things had taken an almost farcical turn when a group of villagers had become trapped on a rock face, and a search helicopter had to be sent over to rescue them.

The serpentine procession fell out of sight as it reached the end of the street, and the sound of subdued chanting faded, as if the line of people had been engulfed into a black sea that was slowly submerging them all.

To Teresa it seemed a fitting metaphor for the hidden dynamics of this case. It was like the village had for many years been infected by a dark, tainted humor that had slipped beneath its surface and festered there, out of sight.

She studied the map on the wall again. The small patch of green before her was in reality a wide expanse that covered an area stretching from the valley itself all the way to the impregnable peaks that marked the Austrian border. It was a vast and in parts impenetrable surface, dotted with insidious crevasses. And there were cracks in the earth that led to underground alcoves, concealed beneath thick layers of vegetation.

Teresa stood up, suddenly animated.

An impenetrable surface. We're only searching the surface, and that's why it looks as if he's disappeared.

"We need to change our strategy," she said, interrupting the prosecutor. Ambrosini looked startled.

"What we're doing now isn't working," Teresa went on, "and we can't afford to waste any more time."

"We're doing all we can," said the district judge.

Teresa turned to look at him.

"But we're going about it the wrong way." She pointed at the map. "This is his world, not ours. We're kidding ourselves into thinking we can beat him on his own turf, but really we can't take two steps without tripping."

"I think you're being unfair, Superintendent. The men are more than prepared for this."

"But that's exactly it: they're only *men*."

The judge looked bemused.

"Isn't he a man, too?"

Teresa shook her head.

"Not in his own mind. We have to start thinking like he does, alter our perspective on things, or else we'll never find him in time."

"You're making it sound like we're hunting an animal," said Ambrosini.

"He has very sharp instincts, and yes, there is an animalistic side to him that determines his actions," Teresa replied. "That's how he's survived."

"So what would you suggest we do, Superintendent?" asked the district judge.

Teresa studied the map.

"He won't go back to the shelter. We breached its borders so he no longer considers it safe. But he won't stray too far." She gestured at the area they had surrounded. "This is his territory."

"Don't you think we should start looking elsewhere?"

"No! He's still here. He would never abandon the thing he values most."

"You mean those bones?"

"I'm referring to his *friend*, Judge. The only companion he's ever had. Hoffman's plan is for the baby to take its place, but it's still too early. The transition isn't yet complete."

"How can you be so sure?"

Teresa didn't reply. On another day, in another time, she would have been the first to doubt her own words. *But not today.*

"I'd like to call in a team of cavers," she said instead. "I think he's hiding underground."

"In a cave? Like a bear?"

Teresa didn't take the judge's bait.

"Yes, exactly like a bear," she replied. "But he won't have picked any old hole in the rock. He knows it would be too easy to track him there. What I'm thinking of is something larger, like an underground cave system."

The silence that followed her words was effectively a vote count of those who were prepared to follow her in this new mission—and those who thought she had finally gone insane.

"I think that's an inspired suggestion," said Ambrosini. "We must look into it."

"I'm not fully acquainted with the geology of the area," said Knauss. "But I think the mountain rescue team know some people who could help us."

"Yes, we've done joint search and rescue drills with the speleologists in Burnberg, over in the next valley," the head of the mountain rescue team confirmed.

"Call them," said Teresa. "We're not going to spend another night here doing nothing."

71

There were no caves in the forest of Travenì. The only natural feature that fit with Teresa's hunch was a cleft between two rock slopes that clung to the side of the mountain. The fissure, which reached all the way to the surface, was a forty-foot black hole emitting putrid vapors. Over time, it had been covered by creepers and filled with loose soil that now formed a steep, almost vertical path down. At its base was a more spacious chamber, embedded among limestone boulders and tree roots.

"Could he really have climbed into that with a baby in tow?" said Parisi.

Standing on the edge of that silent hole, Teresa had felt a sense of vertigo and had doubted her own conviction. But then the flashlights had illuminated the snow beneath a scattering of pine needles: there were footprints there that could be a match for those they had previously measured, and a number of branches in the leafy undergrowth had snapped. Someone had clearly been there recently.

"I guess we'll have to go in and find out," she replied, more for her own benefit than Parisi's.

It hadn't been easy to decide who should be the first to descend. They couldn't rely on guns for this operation, and it was possible that there was a killer waiting at the bottom, ready to attack anyone who got too close. The only person Teresa would have no qualms sending down there was

herself, but the limitations of her body made that impossible.

Until then, her focus had been on finding Andreas, but
once she'd managed that, she would have another problem to
contend with: how to communicate with him. The usual nego-
tiation techniques would be useless. His mind was different, its
architecture in many ways alien.

She glanced at Parisi. One of the cavers was strapping a harness onto him. The equipment would help him negotiate the
sheer path that led into the cave and would catch his fall in
case he slipped. All the preparations had been conducted in the
light of a single flashlight, so as not to draw attention to their
presence. Parisi would have to climb down slowly, looking out
for signs of Andreas's presence at every step of the way. Physically, he was the strongest in the team and the best trained.

Once again, Teresa found herself wondering where Marini
had gone, now feeling less annoyed at his disappearance and
more and more concerned. He hadn't been seen since the half
hour break they'd all taken for dinner, and his phone seemed
to be off. She hadn't gotten to know him properly yet, but she
could tell that this unexplained absence was out of character.

"We're ready," said the speleologist. A mini-cam designed
for this kind of expedition had been affixed to Parisi's helmet.

"Find him," said Teresa, "then come right back up."

He smiled.

"Sure, I'll be in and out before you know it."

She squeezed his arm, wishing she didn't have to send him
down.

"Don't do anything stupid, Parisi. Heroes usually come to
a sticky end."

"Thanks, Superintendent, that makes me feel *so* much
better!"

Now, Teresa was smiling, too.

"Go," she said, releasing her grip on him. All she wanted was a sight of what lay at the bottom of the passageway. She needed to know where Andreas was hiding, where the baby was, and how to get to it without precipitating the wrath of the "Father."

But wasn't it too quiet inside that black tunnel? Teresa tried not to notice the unexpected absence of the sound of a baby crying, tried not to think of it as a bad omen.

Meanwhile, Parisi had begun his descent. He hadn't gone more than a few feet before the mini-cam began transmitting images of animal bones hanging from the exposed tree roots that wound into the tunnel. There was no doubt these were man-made artifacts, just like the small totems they'd found around the mountain shelter and the dream catchers on the edge of the forest. This was someone's lair.

A blur of black and white camera footage followed. Nobody breathed.

Then, Teresa's phone vibrated with an incoming call. It was Parri. He hadn't stopped working either. Teresa moved a few feet away to pick up, her eyes fixed on the entrance to the tunnel.

"Yes, Antonio?"

"I have the results of the toxicology report you'd asked me for. I thought you'd want to know straight away."

"I do."

"There are traces of cyanide in the bone tissue. The child was poisoned."

Teresa said nothing. Wallner must have put his plan into action after all.

"Teresa?"

"I'm here."

"There's more."

As the coroner spoke, Teresa saw Parisi emerging from

the tunnel. From his calmness, and his colleagues' unhurried manner as they helped him out of the harness, Teresa deduced the cave must have been empty.

This had been Andreas's refuge once, but it wasn't anymore. He had smelled danger and found himself another den, in the same way animals did, moving their cubs from one safe place to another.

"Could you repeat that?" she asked Parri.

"Blende and galena," he repeated. "I hope that helps."

It did.

"Now I know where to look for him."

72

"I'm sorry, Inspector. The walls here are thick, and there's no signal."

Massimo looked up from his mobile phone screen to find a woman observing him. Considering the position she held, she was younger than he'd expected; her face, devoid of makeup, showed the traces of interrupted sleep, but her black, sparkling eyes were alert and curious, and only a little bit cautious.

He recognized her from the Saint Nicholas's Day celebrations. He held out his hand, and she shook it with a delicate but resolute grip.

"I must apologize for the late hour," said Massimo.

The abbess bowed her head slightly.

"I was informed that the matter was urgent," she replied.

"It is. There's something we need to check."

"I see. What is it?"

Massimo's eyes darted to a room near the main entrance. It was closed off by an imposing door, reinforced with studs, and sealed by a handmade wrought-iron latch, the metal thick and coarsely molded. Everything inside the convent of Rail was ancient—except for the lives of the women who inhabited it.

"I've come to enquire about the foundling wheel," Massimo said. "I need to find out how long it was in use, and how the babies who were left there were looked after."

Sister Agata looked astonished.

"The wheel hasn't been in use for a long time, Inspector."

"I know. But the case that brings me here has its roots in the past."

"And you think you'll find the answers you're looking for here?"

"I hope so."

She smiled.

"I hope so, too," she said, "but I'm afraid it's unlikely. This is a place of prayer and not much else."

"If you don't mind, I'd still like to try."

"Of course."

"We have found some human remains in the forest of Travenì, around eighteen miles from here."

The nun frowned.

"I know that village," she said. "Whose remains are they?"

"They belong to a young boy, not yet a teenager. We know nothing about his identity."

Sister Agata crossed herself.

"That's awful," she whispered.

"The date of birth is likely to be 1982," said Marini. That was the year when child Omega had made his first appearance in Wallner's diary, though no other details had been included in the entry.

"How can I help?"

"I need to know what became of the children who were left in the foundling wheel."

The woman glanced at the door behind Massimo.

"I understand," she said. "But the wheel has been closed for much longer than that. Follow me, I'll show you."

She led him through the corridor, the hem of her long black habit sweeping the stone floor. A double lancet window gave out onto the inner cloister and garden, illuminated by tall lamps. A sculpture of an angel with outstretched wings and a melancholy expression on its face gleamed among skeletal fruit trees.

Sister Agata unfastened the latch and opened the door. Massimo looked inside.

"We've preserved everything as it was, in memory of our late sisters' good deeds," the abbess explained. "You can go in, if you want."

Massimo stepped into the room. It smelled of dried lavender, and looked pristine, as if someone cleaned it every day. There was a bed against the wall on the right hand side, made with plain cotton sheets and a rough wool blanket. A ceramic chamber pot peeked out from beneath the bedstead. On the opposite wall, beneath a wooden crucifix, were a table and a chair with a straw seat. An open book rested on the table.

"That's the wheel," said Sister Agata, pointing at the wall opposite them. The wheel was a revolving metal hatch with room for a tiny bed. Massimo noticed the fine linen bedspread, painstakingly embroidered. It was touching to witness the care those nuns had shown for the babies that had been left there. The cot stood in marked contrast to the frugal bed reserved for the nun whose turn it was to spend the night inside that room.

"You could open the hatch from outside the building, and put the baby inside," Sister Agata explained. "Then you would turn the hatch, and no one would see you or know who you were. But people would usually leave something tucked inside the child's blankets, so that it could be identified in case they changed their minds and repented."

Marini was surprised to notice the sadness that had engulfed him since he'd entered that room.

"This particular wheel dates back to the second half of the eighteenth century," Sister Agata continued. "It was always in use, except during the Fascist era, when it was banned. It was opened again in the fifties."

"Were there many abandoned children?"

"Not as many as they had in the big cities, where the effects of industrialization forced many working women to give up their babies. Then again, I suppose that up in these mountains, that same unfortunate role was played by poverty and famine."

"When was the wheel closed?"

The abbess pointed at the book on the table.

"That's the most recent register, and it will record the last date."

Massimo read the entry out loud.

"18 October 1972. Female."

"They named her Clara. She was the last foundling to ever come to this abbey."

Massimo looked at her.

"What became of the children?"

"They would live in the abbey for two weeks. A wet nurse would be brought in from the village to feed them, and the sisters would handle everything else. During those two weeks, they would pray for the mother to change her mind and take the child back, but if that didn't happen, the baby would be handed over to the care of the State and placed in an institute for children born out of wedlock."

"It's a sad story," said Massimo.

"I wouldn't say that. Those children were spared a far more terrible fate. But as you can see, Inspector, the child you are looking for cannot have been left in this convent—and even if it had been, it would not have crossed the confines of these four walls except to continue its life in an orphanage."

Massimo exited the convent in Rail weighed down by a sense of oppression. Before walking away, he stopped to study the wheel. A devil's head was carved into the stone over the mouth of the revolving hatch, its wicked gaze following Massimo no matter where he stood. It had a pair of twisting horns, a pointed chin, and gaping jaws, the tips of its fangs touching its lower lip. It was a gruesome sight, a last attempt to deter those who came there to abandon their child.

He thought of how the Church was always so strict with others, yet so quick to forgive itself.

The sense of unease that had fallen upon him refused to go away; it was a subtle but persistent sense of nausea that made his stomach churn. The thought of all those abandoned infants had shaken him deeply—even more shocking was the knowledge that it had still been happening until not too long ago.

From the moment he'd set foot in that valley, Massimo had been struck by the splendor of the natural landscape in which it was immersed. It gave the place the appearance of an unspoiled paradise, but he knew now that there were sins in its past—perhaps even in its present—that could not be forgotten. If it was indeed an Eden, it was already lost, tainted—much like the rest of the world—by what Massimo thought of as the "human stain." But the people of Travenì weren't ready to admit that, not even to themselves. There would have been no shame in facing up to the truth, in accepting that they lived in a flawed yet redeemable reality. Instead they'd chosen to surround themselves with an invisible wall that kept out anybody who dared doubt the righteousness of the community, and Massimo felt an urge to shout at them, tell them that by acting in this way, they were becoming accomplices to the crime. There were only a few exceptions, and they usually took pains not to voice their thoughts in public.

Except, perhaps, for one person.

He recalled Lucas Ebran's mother, the anguish and disdain with which she'd defended her son against their questioning, and against the people of the valley.

She'd called them hypocrites. She'd spoken of all their

bastard children. She'd challenged the criminal reticence that was ubiquitous among the inhabitants of the valley.

Massimo looked again at the demonic face. It appeared to be laughing at him.

No, he thought, *it's not laughing* at *me*, *it's laughing* with *me*.

He tried calling Superintendent Battaglia, but her phone couldn't be reached. An idea had begun to dawn in his mind. Ebran's mother had talked about secrets. Now, Massimo was ready to hear them.

73

Parri had found traces of blende and galena—zinc and lead sulphides—on the bones and tissue that Andreas had taken from his victims. The same traces had also been detected on the food he had recently left at the skeleton's feet. It had to be residue from Andreas's hands.

The Osvan quarry was a lunar landscape three thousand feet above sea level, just beyond the line of the Alpine border.

Once they'd passed the forest, the police cars had followed a road that wound through stacks of pale scree jutting through the snow, and across the exposed underbelly of the mountain. Ancient riverbeds were dotted with rusting, abandoned machinery and stacks of timber that looked like fossils in the moonlight.

Below the surface of the quarry lay zinc and lead mines. A number of mining shafts had been dug at various depths, alternating with water drainage tunnels that surfaced across the border. According to Chief Knauss, those tunnels had been used to transport supplies and military equipment during the two world wars.

After a cave-in decades ago had compromised its structural stability, the quarry had been shut down, and the whole site abandoned due to rising extraction costs and falling demand. The administrative offices and the workshops where the ore had been refined were enormous, drab constructions typical of the Fascist period, their straight lines, smooth surfaces, and confined spaces indicating a fixation with grandeur manifesting itself—in the midst of that natural landscape—as a blight on the face of the earth.

The entrance to the mine was blocked off by a wire fence. The chain that had once fastened it to a set of hooks embedded in the rock had fallen to the ground, corroded by rust. A line of footprints in the snow led into the darkness beyond.

Teresa ordered the fence pushed aside and peered into the gloom. She shone her flashlight into the tunnel, illuminating a set of railway tracks inside.

"The temperature in there is constant throughout the year, around nine degrees, with humidity levels at ninety-eight percent," Knauss informed her.

De Carli and Parisi arrived.

"Have you brought what I asked for?" she said.

"Yes, Superintendent."

Teresa checked that she'd turned her phone off, before putting on her fluorescent yellow vest and a hard hat mounted with a headlamp. This time, she would be the one to take the lead.

"What if it's another red herring?" said Knauss.

Teresa had been asking herself that same question ever since she'd decided to concentrate all their efforts here, but she kept thinking they had nothing left to lose—there were no other leads to follow.

She stared into the darkness again, at those footprints leading into the belly of the earth. Perhaps they were old. Perhaps they belonged to someone else. And still, the only sound they could hear from the depths of the tunnel was the monotonous dripping of water.

"I told you," said Knauss, spitting on the ground. "He wouldn't have made it all the way here."

"Make him shut up," Teresa whispered to De Carli.

"We're wasting our time, I . . ."

Teresa—who was shorter than him, weaker than him, and yet determined to emerge victorious from this new confrontation—grabbed him by the lapels of his coat.

"You didn't tell me about the protesters, you didn't tell me about Ebran, and you didn't tell me about these tunnels," she said, her voice quiet but shaking with rage. "You're lucky, Chief Knauss, that I don't have time to deal with your incompetence right now. But rest assured, that moment will come. I truly hope we find what we are looking for when I walk in there, because that would mean three things: one, that we've rescued the child; two, that we've caught the killer; and three, that we've shown once more to those who need to know how utterly superfluous you are to the police force."

She let go of him in disgust.

A sudden wail broke the silence that followed her outburst. Teresa heard it over the ringing in her ears and the sound of her own furious breathing. She turned to face the quarry again, and heard it once more: it was coming from inside the black tunnel.

"That's the sound of crying," said Parisi.

It was the sobbing of a tired, hungry child. Teresa quickly zipped up her vest and prepared to go in.

"You have your answer now," she told Knauss.

De Carli handed her the sheets she'd asked him to print out. She folded them carefully and put them in her pocket, ignoring the tremor in her hands.

"Superintendent!"

A woman was running toward them, illuminated by the light towers. She'd arrived just in time.

"Who told her?" asked Knauss.

Teresa motioned at De Carli to pass her another vest.

"I did," she answered.

74

"Superintendent, I hate to agree with Knauss, but the last thing we need right now is a frantic and terrified mother to deal with," Parisi said softly. "What if things get out of hand? What do we do then?"

Gloria Sanfilk came up to them, her hair—wet with the snow that had just begun to fall—sticking to her sunken cheeks. The expression on her face was not what Teresa had expected to see: it was neither distraught, nor exhausted, but burning with a heat that could have easily melted the glaciers that had laced those mountains for thousands of years.

"Is my son in there?" she asked.

"Yes," Teresa replied.

"Are you going to get him?"

"We're going together. Would you be up for that?"

Gloria nodded without a moment's hesitation.

"No. Absolutely not," said Parisi. He was worried, but Teresa was sure there was no other way. All of them—Teresa included—had to be ready to sacrifice something, to risk all that they held dear, if they were to succeed.

"I will go to my baby!" said the mother, as if to make clear to all those present that the matter was not up for discussion.

"It's about safety, Gloria," Knauss intervened. "Yours and Markus's."

They heard another wail coming from the tunnel. Gloria flinched, then took a step toward the blackness.

"My son is calling for me," she said. "Don't you see? He's calling for *me*."

"Gloria . . ." said Knauss in a murmur.

The woman turned around and sought Teresa's eyes with her own.

"I can feel him, right here," she whispered, bringing her hand to her chest, "and I know he can feel me, too."

Teresa didn't doubt it. She knew the nature of that bond—ineffable, arcane, primal—better than anyone else. It was an enigma as old as mankind, perhaps older still. And from the moment she'd arrived on the scene, the scar that marked her abdomen had begun to burn, the force of that connection suddenly resurfacing through her body.

Teresa nodded. "Give her a vest and helmet," she ordered.

"But, Superintendent . . ."

Teresa silenced Parisi by placing a hand on his arm.

"I'm relying on you to keep everyone in check," she told him, with an eye on the clearing outside the entrance to the mine. It was crowded with police, army, and search and rescue vehicles, all lit up by light towers. Two ambulances had also just pulled up.

"When we come out, nobody shoots. Understood?"

Teresa summoned De Carli to her side and squeezed his arm as well.

"Don't forget he's a victim, too," she reminded them.

"I won't forget," De Carli replied, "but if he hurts you, I . . ."

"No one's going to get hurt, so long as you lot don't make a mess of things."

Parisi laughed, but he was visibly nervous.

Teresa let them go.

"Are you ready?" she called out to Gloria, who was shivering. Gloria nodded.

"Stay a couple of steps behind me, and if I tell you to do something, do it immediately."

"All right."

Teresa looked into her eyes.

"Even if I tell you to run away," she said. "Got it?"

"Yes."

Hugo Knauss pulled her aside, and for a moment, Teresa couldn't help but admire the courage it must have taken him to do that.

"She's a civilian," he objected. "Do you realize the risk you're taking? She's not trained for any of this."

"Is anyone here, really?" Teresa retorted.

"Superintendent . . ."

"She won't come to any harm."

"How can you be so sure?"

"Because I'll be in the way."

Teresa returned to Gloria's side. Together, they entered the tunnel.

The damp, persistent sound of dripping water echoed across the rarefied air inside the tunnel, an eerie accompaniment to their footsteps. The walls, shored up to prevent further cave-ins, were lined with rivulets of water that ended in puddles on the ground. Beneath the soles of their feet, the gallery stretched for more than half a mile onward and was connected to other galleries by passages and cavities called drifts. At one time, they had been employed to transport ore between tunnels, but now they were traps that could open up and swallow them whole at any given moment.

Teresa listened to the sound of her own breathing and of her forceful heartbeats beneath the safety vest. But all she really wanted to hear now was that wailing from before, which had since gone quiet.

The cone of light from their flashlights shimmered before them, bringing the shadows to life. And just as Teresa was beginning to wonder how much further they would have to descend into that inferno of rock and water, the wailing picked up once more, as if to answer her question. It was close. Behind Teresa, Gloria let out a soft moan, an instinctive response to her baby's call.

The tunnel started to curve and slope downwards. Teresa hadn't brought a gun, as she didn't want to run the risk, in case they were attacked, of losing her cool and harming the child by mistake. But without it she felt helpless.

They heard a sullen grunt issuing from somewhere in the darkness, and stopped walking. It was a half-human, half-animal sound, and for a moment, it made their blood freeze. It was impossible to describe. It filled them with terror and seemed to turn their bodies into dead weight.

Slowly, Teresa turned around. The sound had come from a small tunnel to her right. The light from her headlamp shone upon a figure crouching a few yards from where they stood, facing away from them. It was Andreas Hoffman, holding a bundle in his arms. He was trying to put something in the child's mouth. When he saw the gleam of the torch, he turned around.

The shaft of light hit him square on the face, and at last Teresa could see his eyes. They really were as blue as David Knauss had described them. But they were green, too. Andreas's eyes were heterochromatic.

She put her hands in the air and hoped that Gloria, standing behind her, would do the same. He growled, like a wild animal. As far as Teresa knew, he could speak a few words and was able to copy other people's speech when necessary. But it was obvious that in that moment his instincts had already taken over.

Very slowly, Teresa removed her helmet with the headlamp and put it on the floor so that the light wouldn't bother him but would continue to illuminate the alcove he was hiding in.

The baby let out another cry, and Andreas attempted once again to feed him what looked, to Teresa, like a thin slice of meat. He seemed to have forgotten about their presence, as if he had suddenly found something more important to do that required his full attention. Teresa could tell that he was scared, but what Andreas feared most wasn't their presence: it was the fact that the baby wouldn't eat.

"No," she told him softly.

He looked at her again. He had high cheekbones and regular features, framed by a beard and long hair. He looked younger than he was, though life outdoors had roughened his skin. He was tall, and even though he was wrapped in a mutton coat, Teresa could tell that he was physically fit.

With measured gestures, and alert to his reactions, Teresa brought out the pieces of paper she had been carrying in her pocket. Slowly, she bent down until she was kneeling, and spread them out in front of him.

She knew that Andreas had learned the basics of language. But while he might be capable of understanding some of her words, she doubted they would be sufficient to explain. Andreas's world was not like hers; it was made of silences, the howling of the wind, the calls of wild animals. She had been obsessed with the problem of how to communicate with this creature, how to connect with a mind that was so unique, and finally she had understood—or so she hoped—what she had to do. Everything he knew he had learned by observing the natural world, which had been his home until that day—*that* was the language Teresa had to use to connect with him.

Andreas studied the pictures that had been placed at his feet. They showed females of different animal species suckling their young: a vixen, a doe, a wild sow, and a woman.

Teresa saw him look at her and at Gloria, then back at the bundle he held in his hands.

"Take a step forward and unzip your vest," she whispered to Gloria. Gloria did so, showing no trace of fear. Her breasts, swollen with milk, stretched at the fabric of her sweater. Their message was clear.

He noticed them, and spent a moment studying them. His eyes showed no hint of emotion, but Teresa could sense the deep sorrow that a sudden realization was causing him: he could not keep the child he had chosen as his own. She could feel his pain, his loss, his fear of being alone once more.

She stretched her arms toward him, ready to receive the child.

She remained in that position, praying he wouldn't interpret it as a threat. Parisi and the others were hiding in the shadows behind them, watching the scene, ready to act.

She closed her eyes, her hands shaking, her mind straying to the past. She wondered what it was like to be a mother. Throughout their lives, neither she nor Andreas would ever be able to touch that sacred, inviolable mystery. She felt a profound empathy for him—a killer, a victim, a man, a child—all at once. Alone, like she was. Accustomed, like she was, to being self-sufficient. Until one day some part of him had dared to want something else, something more. Now that he had found it, would he be prepared to part with it?

It was in that moment that she felt a soft weight on her arms. She opened her eyes and saw the child there, wrapped in lamb fleece. She moved her hands to steady her grip on it, and for a long moment, her fingers brushed against Andreas's. Teresa sensed a kind of wordless communication pass between them, a feeling of compassion and shared hurt that only grew when she cradled the child against her chest and realized just how difficult it must have been for him to let go. She, too, would have wanted the child to be hers; she, too, would have wanted to clutch it to her heart and fall asleep beside it every night.

She barely registered the tears that were trickling down her face as she handed the baby over to its mother.

"Feed him," she told her.

Gloria obeyed, her face marked with tears and relief. The child suckled greedily at her breast.

Teresa looked at Andreas. She understood that he wasn't

going to hurt them, because he knew, now, that the child was where it was meant to be.

"Let's go," she told Gloria.

She made Gloria back away first, and didn't move at all until she was reasonably sure Gloria had made it out of the gallery safely. Those minutes seemed to last for an eternity, and Andreas's eyes never once stopped staring into hers.

It was difficult to walk away from him, to interrupt that moment. Teresa retreated and disappeared into the black tunnel.

"Don't shoot. Don't shoot," she muttered as she hurried past the armed officers who were hiding in the shadows, pressed against the rock walls. She was afraid. For the first time in her career, she feared for a killer.

When she emerged into the open air, she saw Gloria and Mathias embracing little Markus. Teresa looked around at all those who had gathered and couldn't see the children's father. So Gloria had been strong; she had kept her promise. Teresa had done the same for Mathias; she had retrieved for him a brother's love, but she had also gifted him a renewed family. The boy looked up and saw her. Teresa would remember for the rest of her life the fond memory of that shared glance.

She turned her face to the sky and savored the gentle, soothing weight of snowflakes on her skin.

All of a sudden, she felt quite empty. Her body went limp and crumpled onto the snow. Her mind remained alert for a few moments more, long enough for her to become aware that she was lying on the ground, surrounded by the cold that had been her constant companion for the past few days, both within her, and outside. Then, there was darkness.

It was the middle of the night, yet Lucas Ebran's mother answered the doorbell at the first ring. She looked uncomprehendingly at Massimo, then remembered the context in which she had first met him and slammed the door in his face.

"Please!" he said, trying to stop her. "It's important."

The windows of the house were completely black, but he knew she was still there. He looked around: the road was deserted. The man Massimo had brought with him was standing a few feet away, with his back against the wall and his head bowed almost down to his chest. He hadn't spoken a single word since Massimo had forced him to follow him.

He knocked again.

"I've come to hear you out. To find out the secrets of the valley," he said, raising his voice.

A few moments later, the lock clicked, and a pair of hostile eyes peered at him from around the edge of the door.

"What do you want?" she asked him.

"What I said: I want to know who the sinners are, and how they have sinned. Have I come to the right place?"

"Maybe," she snapped, "but I don't talk to people like you."

"Aren't we talking now?" he asked her with a half-smile.

She made as if to close the door, but Massimo was quick to block it.

"Go away!"

She flung the door open once more, but this time she was brandishing a hatchet.

Massimo immediately let go of the door.

"Hold on, hold on! I have a gift for you," he blurted out.

The woman stared at him, more intrigued now than angry.

Massimo turned toward the man he'd brought with him, who had kept his eyes fixed on the cobblestones as if there were nothing else in the world. The woman followed Massimo's gaze.

"Lucas!"

As soon as she'd caught sight of her son, her voice had turned sweet.

Viola was a fragile being trapped inside a gargantuan form. As she made them coffee in the kitchenette her thighs kept bumping against the furniture, knocking her off balance.

"My legs don't work anymore, and my back's about to give up on me, too," she told him, noticing his expression. "This body won't carry me for much longer."

Massimo didn't know what to say to that, so he decided to change the subject.

"I was surprised to find you awake at this hour," he said as she opened a pack of cookies and placed some on a saucer between their two coffee cups. She poured the coffee and handed Massimo another cup, which served as a sugar bowl.

He thanked her.

"I was waiting for Lucas," she said, sitting down with some difficulty. "I hadn't seen him since he was released. He likes to disappear, to get away from the world. And from me. Everything is difficult with him."

Massimo became conscious that he was struggling to hold her gaze. He'd watched her cuddle her son for a long time, whispering words into his ear that only the two of them could hear. He'd waited patiently for her to take him to the bathroom and wash him. He'd listened to her singing tender songs to him. Viola had taken care of the child that Lucas Ebran still partly was. She had only come back downstairs once she'd tucked him safely into bed.

"I'm sorry," was all Massimo could muster. "I'm sure it'll all work out for the best."

The look she gave him seemed to say that there was no point in lying: she no longer believed in anything good, anything that didn't cause her pain.

"My son hasn't been well since the day he had to clean up his father's blood from this floor, Inspector. He's sick right here," she said, tapping her forehead, "but he's no monster. But you treated him like one, waving your guns about when you came here looking for him."

"It was our duty to investigate . . ."

She made a face at him that suggested she didn't think it mattered anymore. Massimo suspected that what had upset her most was to have suffered yet another blow to her dignity.

"I've come to talk about something you said yesterday about the inhabitants of this valley," he said.

"Yes, I remember. I tend to start shouting when I'm afraid. It's a weakness."

"I apologize if I scared you."

She left his apology unanswered.

"You said you came here for the secrets."

"Yes. I was surprised to hear you talk about illegitimate children. You're all pious people in this valley, aren't you?"

She flicked her hand in a gesture of irritation, sending all the preachers, the saints, and their ilk to hell.

"The more they show their face in church, the more they sin," she said.

"I visited the convent in Rail," Massimo told her. "I saw the wheel. A troubling story."

The woman nodded.

"It's not the worst thing about this place, you know. Our little valley has plenty of sins to hide," she said. "They like to think people have forgotten by now, but I can't help but laugh when I come across them on the street."

"Come across whom?"

"The nuns."

Massimo leaned forward.

"The nuns have a secret to hide?" he said, wanting to be sure he'd understood her.

She gave him a sly grin, the smile of someone who knew a lot more than they let on. She picked up a cookie from the plate and began to chew on it.

"Clandestine liaisons," she said. "That's what we're talking about."

Massimo's excitement vanished. He wasn't interested in this particular piece of information. He picked up a biscuit too, and bit into it.

Viola's smile widened.

"Do you want to hear the story or not?" she said.

"What story?"

"The story of a child born between the walls of the convent, and who never crossed beyond those walls either. Maybe it's just village gossip—maybe, yes—but my husband did say to me that he heard that newborn soul's first cries loud and clear and the screams of the woman who bore it."

77

Teresa opened her eyes and wondered for a moment whether it was daytime. The snow was so white that it was painful to look at. She had to blink several times before she managed to focus on her surroundings, and at that point she realized that the whiteness actually belonged to a neon-lit ceiling and a set of laminated furniture. She was lying on a bed in what appeared to be a medical clinic. There was a photograph on a desk, next to a computer, of a man she knew. Looking younger, and lean, the person in the image watched her from the summit of a mountain, his hair ruffled by the wind.

Teresa tried to sit up, but her muscles refused to cooperate. She fell wearily back onto the pillow.

"I believe you've had a hyperglycemic seizure," someone announced.

Teresa turned her head. Doctor Ian was watching her from the door, smiling.

"Will I die?" she asked him gravely.

He laughed and moved closer. He held her wrist and counted her heartbeats.

"Not today," he replied. "Your colleagues told me you are diabetic. I imagine you must have forgotten your insulin."

Teresa closed her eyes once more. She couldn't remember. She couldn't even remember the last time she'd injected herself.

"Perhaps," she said.

"Don't worry. I sorted it out. Your blood sugar levels were rather worrying. But please, lie down now. You've only been here fifteen minutes. I've sent your colleagues away. You need to rest for at least two hours."

Teresa felt confused, but mostly foolish.

"Thank you," she said sheepishly. "Doctor Ian?"

"Yes?"

"Did they catch him?"

She was afraid of the response but couldn't bear not knowing. He nodded.

"Yes. He's unharmed," he replied.

Teresa sighed with relief.

"And the child?"

"He's been taken to the hospital in the city as a precaution, but he's fine. You're the only one who actually needed an ambulance. I'll be back in a minute."

Teresa stared at the ceiling. In his own way, Andreas had taken care of his child. She wondered what he must be feeling like now, surrounded by strangers, and far from his forest.

Scared. Disoriented. Desperate.

She had to go to him. She pulled the cover aside and sat upright. She didn't have her coat and didn't even know where her bag and her gun were. Her colleagues had probably taken her weapon for safekeeping. She got up, but a light spell of dizziness forced her to lean on the bed. Her clothes were wrinkled, and she tried to smooth them as best she could with her hands. She did the same to her hair but doubted she'd managed to make herself look presentable. She looked for a napkin in her pocket and only found a paper tissue. It was as wrinkled as she was and covered in scribbles. Teresa was shocked to realize it was her own handwriting. It was something she had noted down in those last, hectic hours and hadn't had a chance to transcribe into her diary yet.

It bore that day's date, and though she couldn't recall writing it, what worried her most in that moment was not the advance of her illness, but the note she had addressed to herself on that scrap of paper.

78

The nuns' dormitories were located in the cellars of the convent of Rail. The cells predated the first blueprints of the building and had been carved into the limestone back in Roman times. The Celts had repurposed them as crypts, and now they housed the nuns from sunset until just before dawn.

Massimo descended the steps that led to those ancient catacombs, preparing to finally solve the mystery of child Omega.

The abbess had agreed to escort him there only after much insistence on his part. When he'd shown up at the convent again, Massimo had uttered just two words, and those two words had been enough to frighten Sister Agata, and wipe away the smile with which she'd greeted him. Like an incantation, they had granted Massimo passage.

Lucas Ebran's mother had told him a story that, thirty years ago, had been the whispered talk of Rail: the story of a nun too pretty and too young to go unnoticed. The villagers had followed her every movement, and watched her belly grow larger and larger beneath her Benedictine habit.

Earlier, Sister Agata had denied there had ever been any kind of scandal connected to the convent. But she'd also said that she hadn't been around for that long. Massimo had pounced on that small detail—perhaps her attempt at distancing herself from some kind of past crime—and persevered until she'd agreed to help him.

She had finally capitulated when he'd reminded her that

he'd come for the soul of a nameless child, twenty-five years after his death. Perhaps they owed it to him to reveal the truth of what had happened.

Massimo followed Sister Agata through to the end of a long tunnel carved into stone and lined on one side with cells. The doors that led to each room were low; the occupants of the cells would have had to stoop down to go through. Each door had a peephole, covered in thick mesh, through which one could look inside. All the cells were dark, except for the last one.

The abbess gestured toward the illuminated square.

"She's expecting you," she told him. "I'll wait for you back at the entrance."

"Thank you."

Slowly, Massimo walked toward the door. Something about that place demanded respect and silence, but he knew that what he was about to say would bring turmoil to the convent, uncovering a secret that its inhabitants had long believed forgotten.

A nun was looking at him from behind the grille. Her name was Marja Restochova: the two words that had so disturbed the abbess.

When he'd discovered that she was still in the convent, Massimo had been left speechless. He couldn't see the nun's features clearly, but her face still held the visible traces of a past beauty. Her skin, almost transparent, looked like velvet, and gleamed in the quivering candlelight.

Massimo wasn't sure what words to start with, but she was the one to break the silence first.

"So you know my name," she said.

"I know your name, Sister, and a story that I hope you might be able to confirm."

"Ah, yes. That story. It happened so long ago, and yet there are still those who claim to know the truth of it."

"Tell me your side, then."

"They were all lies, Inspector. Now please leave me alone."

Massimo heard something shake in her voice. At first, he assumed it was frustration, but then he recognized it for what it really was: fear.

"I'm here to find out about a child," he explained. "A child who was born inside these walls, and then disappeared."

Marja did not respond.

"What are you afraid of, after all this time?" he asked her. "People's judgment? Shame?"

"It was a lie!"

"Your lie, perhaps. And you felt so guilty that you decided all those years ago to renounce the world and take a vow of enclosure!"

"You should leave. You will not get the answers you're looking for here."

"Maybe you're right, but there are other ways. DNA testing, for example."

She hesitated, then, and suddenly seemed more wary.

"What do you mean?"

Massimo leaned toward the grille.

"We've found the remains of a child who died twenty-five years ago. I think it's your son."

The woman opened her mouth as if to speak, but no words came out.

"You gave birth to him, and then you abandoned him. I need to know who helped you."

"How did he die?" she asked, her voice breaking.

"He was killed by the person who raised him."

Marja lowered her head and closed her eyes. Tears began to fall from between her lashes. Massimo realized that up until that moment, she had convinced herself her son had been living a full and happy life far from her.

"I was scared," she confessed. "But I didn't do anything wrong. I left him in better hands than mine, someone who could give him a family that would love him."

"Was he sent to an orphanage?"

"No."

"Who was it, then?"

"The same person who helped him into the world."

Massimo grabbed hold of the grille, bringing his face close to hers, unmoved by her silent weeping.

"I need a name," he said.

Marja sighed and whispered the name into his ear, as if she were still afraid, after all that time, to say it out loud.

Massimo looked at her, horrified. He knew that man. But the discovery led him to make one final connection: that man had the same blue eyes—only older now—as the man in the blurry photo Massimo had found in the file of an old unsolved case from across the border.

Teresa couldn't recall assigning Marini that task. She couldn't remember a single thing about their conversation on the subject, and yet it seemed that a few hours ago, she had ordered him to visit the convent in Rail. The only clue she had was a hurried scribble on a piece of tissue paper she hadn't yet transcribed to her diary. At the end of the note, she'd written the following words: "refer to diary."

She did remember writing something down about the foundling wheel after her conversation with Doctor Ian at the pub. That must be what those words meant.

Her coat and her bag were inside a cabinet by the bed. She took out her diary and began to leaf through it, but though she was sure she'd written that entry, she couldn't find it. She checked again, but the page where she'd recounted her conversation with the doctor was missing. Yet her memory of it was clear, unsullied by her spells of confusion.

"I had advised you to lie down," said Ian, entering the room. "How are you feeling?"

Teresa had been asking herself the very same question. It was as if a stranger were coming in every now and then to take over her life for a while, leaving nothing more than hints about her visits—which, though always brief, had the power to turn everything on its head.

"Has anyone had access to my belongings?" she asked.

Ian looked at her in surprise.

"Not that I know of. They've been in the cupboard all along. Your colleagues put them there. Is there a problem?"

Teresa looked at her diary again.

Are you really sure someone's opened it?

"There's a page missing from my notes," she told him.

Ian approached her and peered at the notebook in her hands.

"Are you sure?"

"Yes."

"But how can you be sure the page wasn't already missing? Or even that it's missing at all? It's a spiral-bound notebook."

Teresa looked at him and didn't know what to say. The truth was that she couldn't be absolutely sure, because she could no longer trust her own mind.

She went to the window. It was so dark outside that it was impossible to actually see the landscape—which was a little like what was happening to her with her own thoughts. Perhaps she'd convinced herself she'd done something when in fact she'd only thought about doing it.

"Teresa, are you all right?"

"I . . . yes."

"You're pale. Please lie down."

"No . . . I have to fight back."

Ian moved closer and placed a hand on her elbow, as if to support her.

"Fight back against what?" he asked.

"I'm not exactly sure." It was the truth. She twisted away from his grip and took a few steps as if to test her balance, physical and otherwise.

"You seem confused. Is this a regular occurrence? Memory loss, fainting, panic attacks . . ."

Teresa felt a bitter taste in her mouth.

So this was how it all began. She had expected it to take

longer, but there she was, sinking, spiralling so fast she'd already lost her bearings.

But she had that note: "refer to diary." And she had a memory, however disjointed. She couldn't deny she was ill, but she had to believe in herself, she had to keep going at least until this case was closed.

She tried to figure out who might have wanted to destroy that entry, that handful of words indicating a possible lead— one of many that had emerged, and probably not even a particularly promising one.

But that was precisely what made the missing diary page such a crucial clue: whoever had torn it out had done so out of fear, knowing that those words might lead to a much bigger secret. But they'd come too late: she'd already sent Marini there.

But the person responsible for this had made a serious mistake: they had ripped the page out knowing that she might not even remember writing it or that it would be easy to make her doubt she'd ever written it.

They knew that Alzheimer's disease had already begun consuming her memories. But she hadn't told anyone about her illness. She hadn't even had the courage to write it down in the pages of her diary.

Teresa glanced at the computer on the desk. The screen showed a page with her medical records. The program that collated them was connected to the network of the national health system, which held information on every medical test she'd ever undergone.

"Superintendent?"

Teresa felt a surge of vertigo and clung to the bed to stop herself from falling. She looked at Ian.

"Are you unwell?" he asked her.

She remembered that he'd given her an injection.

"What . . . What did you inject me with?" she asked him, her voice hoarse.

He laughed in surprise.

"Insulin, obviously. Don't you remember?"

Teresa felt weak, but she couldn't tell if it was from lack of sleep, insufficient food, or some kind of poison running through her veins. Perhaps it was only fear.

"You know my secret, don't you, Doctor Ian?" she asked him, gasping for breath.

Inside the cabinet behind the doctor, Teresa's phone rang. She didn't move.

Ian's expression shifted. It became remote and vaguely hostile.

"Aren't you going to pick up, Superintendent?" he asked her.

"Why don't *you* answer it, Doctor Wallner?"

He closed his pale, ice-cold eyes. He didn't much resemble the photograph from when he'd been a young man running an orphanage. Life had altered his features, and more importantly, he had cloaked his true nature with smiles and an affectionate manner; but inside, he was the same person he had always been, and Teresa could finally see him, his true nature reflected in those eyes that lacked any trace of remorse. She thought of how much strength would be required to live your whole life wearing such a heavy mask. Or perhaps it wasn't about strength, perhaps it was some warped sense of vocation.

Teresa thought of the moment she'd shown him her diary. He'd looked at it as if he'd genuinely never seen it before. His self-control was astonishing.

"I always thought there was a monster in this case. But it's not Andreas Hoffman," she said. "It's not subject thirty-nine. The true monster is the person who stole Andreas's life from him and killed his only companion: it's you."

Wallner's lips stretched into a sickening smile.

"I am a scientist, Teresa. Scientific research requires certain sacrifices to be made."

"You killed that child, but you wanted to get rid of them both, didn't you? Why didn't you go back to the shelter to make sure you'd achieved your aim?"

"Oh, but I did, Superintendent. It's just that I only found one body. I knew what the Alpha was capable of, so I fled. He was fifteen years old and possessed the physical strength of an adult. He would have killed me."

"So you set fire to the shelter and ran away."

"That was the only mistake I made: I assumed that the fire would destroy all traces of my presence. As I was fleeing, I stumbled, lost my balance and fell from a cliff. I dragged myself to the village with my leg broken in three places, and I was bedridden for months. I was forced to give up mountaineering. I never got the chance to go up there again and behold my creation."

"You're a criminal, just like your father before you, and all those like him."

"It has been seventy years since the end of that war, and still people like you won't stop complaining about it."

"Why don't you tell that to a jury?"

Wallner burst out laughing.

"Why do you think I didn't run away?" he asked her. "I could have left as soon as you started getting too close to the truth. But I'm seventy-five, and I have a serious cardiovascular condition. Starting a new life under a false name isn't as easy as it was forty years ago. The truth is that I will never go to prison. It'll take years for them to sentence me, and then there is always the court of appeals. Whatever happens, I've already won, Superintendent Battaglia."

Teresa saw Parisi and the rest of the squad lined up behind the doctor's back.

"I will make it my mission to prove you wrong, Doctor Wallner," she replied.

He followed her gaze, and realized they were no longer alone. His expression changed completely; all his bravado disappeared. Parisi took his arm and led him away, but just as he was walking out, Wallner turned around to look at Teresa.

"There was only insulin in that needle," he told her. "You're not going to die, Superintendent. At least not today."

Teresa was worried she might faint again, so she sat back down on the bed. Her knees were shaking and her breath was short. She needed a minute to recover.

"Is everything okay, Superintendent?"

She raised her head and saw De Carli.

"It's over," she said, as if those two words answered his question.

He nodded and smiled.

"What are you doing here?" she asked him.

"Marini sent us. He told us about Wallner. He's on the line, he wants to talk to you."

He handed her a mobile phone. Teresa hesitated briefly, searching for the right words to say, then took the phone.

"I got there first," she said.

He started laughing.

"What makes you think that?"

"Statistics. You always come in second."

She heard him laugh again.

"How are you feeling?" he asked.

Teresa thought about it.

"I'm fine," she replied, and it was true.

In spite of everything, and against all expectations, Teresa felt alive in a way she hadn't experienced in a very long time. She was still, and would still be, the maker of her own destiny.

She looked at her reflection in the windowpane.

She saw a woman with wrinkles, dishevelled, her face tired, her eyes moist.

That face belonged to her. It was the face of a fighter.

80

EPILOGUE

A light mist was forming in the Sliva gorge. It was no icy winter fog, but an unexpected breath of spring blowing over the water. It brought the scent of fresh shoots about to pierce the soil and reach toward the sun. The stream, which had been nearly still until a few weeks ago, now burbled and swirled and leapt across boulders. The ice was withdrawing from the banks and the undergrowth, like a vanquished army in retreat.

The forest was waking up a little more every day, stretching its limbs, filling with the first songs of the birds returning from the plains.

To Mathias it seemed that his and Lucia's and Diego's and Oliver's lives were also starting from scratch, like the nature around them. They had learned in school about the cycle of seasons, and now he could observe its effects on the gorge, the place where it had all started, and where the first buds had now begun to blossom.

That was how Mathias pictured himself and his friends. They were no longer standing still, stuck in some awful moment from their past; they had moved on, like clouds racing in the sky, like water streaming over the pebbles, and wind moving between blades of grass. They were like plants that had been hungry for light and had finally found it.

He ran down the path, his lungs filling up with new and vibrant smells. He reached the riverbank and took the familiar route up ladders and across rope bridges. Freed from the winter frost, the wood along the path sounded different beneath his feet; it made the rounded, supple noise Mathias associated with warm weather. The water had changed color, too, resplendent now in deep green and glittering turquoise.

Down there, in that ravine that carved its way past the village, he didn't feel alone anymore. He stopped with his face tilted up at the light blue sky, conscious of the hundreds of minuscule hearts hiding among the tree branches around him, beating in time with his own.

In that moment, the sun reached its highest point in the sky, and a ray of light lit up the gorge, unleashing a kaleidoscope of colors.

Mathias laughed elatedly and let out a yell that echoed through boulders and crevasses, and his friends responded like a pack of young wolves.

He ran toward them, past the cave and all the way to the waterfall, now thawed and free to rush onward in a cascade of rainbow-colored jets.

Lucia, Diego, and Oliver were waiting for him with their backpacks on their shoulders and a map of the mountain paths between them, ready to set out on a new adventure.

Mathias took a step toward them, then turned to glance at the forest behind him. Among all the new sounds and calls that animated the forest, there was one missing. He paused for a moment, secretly hoping to hear that presence again, to spot it somewhere among the trees, but there were no shadows left in the woods.

81

The old asylums for the criminally insane had been replaced by institutions commonly known as psychiatric rehabilitation centers.

Teresa hoped that the change was not purely a matter of semantics. She had to believe that the man who was waiting for her behind that door would have, at long last, an opportunity to learn how to live, rather than just to survive. Perhaps this was naive of her, but now more than ever before in her life, she needed something to hope for.

"Ready?" said Marini beside her.

Teresa nodded, and a warden opened the door.

There was Andreas Hoffman, sitting before her not with the air of a convicted killer, but of a king in exile. His throne had been usurped, his reign handed over to bulldozers and diggers that would tear it to pieces. Yet he took up all the space in the room with the majesty of a conqueror.

He was sitting on a chair, staring ahead at the bare wall with his back straight and his head held high, and with his hands—restrained by flexible handcuffs—resting on his lap. They had cut his hair and shaved his beard. He had a strikingly beautiful face that looked as if it had been carved out of some golden, luminous wood. Studying his face, Teresa understood that nothing would ever corrupt his soul, not even the blood he had shed.

Andreas existed on a different plane from theirs: a primordial place stripped clean of all hypocrisy and human iniquities. Not even death seemed to have tainted him.

Teresa was awed by the power he radiated: it wasn't just a question of physical vigor, but of a vital energy that seemed almost tangible, and that she could feel pressing against her, even at a distance. It was that animal magnetism that Wallner had described in his diary.

But, she reminded herself, it was also a lot more than that: it was the force of leaders and kings, the charisma of commanders; it was *mana*, a spiritual energy that few were blessed with, and which could be used to rouse another's conscience or indeed to crush it.

Teresa wasn't sure whether she was imagining it all, or if the creature in front of her truly was special.

Stay calm and think clearly, she told herself as she sat across from him.

The expressionless stillness of his face was unnerving, but more impressive than that was the sway he seemed to hold on his surroundings. Wallner was insane, and a criminal, but Teresa found herself thinking that perhaps his theories on child number 39 might have been more than just the ramblings of a madman.

She'd thought long and hard about how to establish a rapport with Andreas. She didn't think words were worth much to a creature who'd grown up immersed in the silent world of the forest and solitude. He understood words, and he could even utter a few himself, but they certainly weren't his natural language.

Andreas communicated through the senses, just as a deer or an eagle would have done back in the world he came from. He understood the world through nature. So Teresa had followed her instincts and decided to reach out to him through the place his mind still lived.

It was time to show him the gifts they'd brought.

They put a photograph of a woman breastfeeding her baby on the table. Teresa had downloaded it from the Internet, but she was sure it would make no difference to Andreas: he would regard that child as his own, as little Markus, the heir he'd picked out for himself. Teresa was trying to tell him that Markus was all right.

Andreas had been staring at the wall since they'd arrived, but that photograph immediately caught his attention. He picked it up and inhaled deeply, filling his lungs with its scent. Before coming to the rehabilitation center, Teresa had placed the photograph next to the child. She was astonished to see that Andreas could tell.

The second gift was a sprig of mountain pine that they had picked near the mountain shelter that had been his home. Teresa watched his expression as she offered it to him: the change was minimal, a barely perceptible dilation of the pupils. The smell of that evergreen plant was the smell of his world. Andreas closed his eyes for a moment, and Teresa could see that he was there again, back on his mountain.

The third gift belonged to the nameless child. It was a scrap of fabric they had found on his remains. Teresa had had to fight to obtain permission to bring it to Andreas, but she had stood her ground until the "no" had turned into a "yes."

Andreas recognized it. He would have recognized it among thousands of scraps. He picked it up and Teresa saw his hands shake for the first time since his life had been transformed. He ran the cloth over his face, his lips, and down to his chest, where he let it rest against his heart. His eyes closed and he mouthed a series of low sounds that Teresa couldn't understand.

What she did know was that Andreas was rocking the baby. That's his flower, she thought. The most beautiful flower among all those that stopped him from looking into the inferno.

Afternoon had turned into evening. A last, scattered light still gleamed on the horizon. The distant mountains in the background reminded Teresa of where this incredible tale had begun. The air outside the rehabilitation center was effervescent and carried the early traces of a premature spring. She thought she caught a whiff of dormant buds and took that as a message of hope.

Teresa had always been a little allergic to hope, but then again, she supposed she had to believe in something. So why not believe in something good?

Marini was walking by her side across the car park. It was hard to know what he was thinking. He had seemed upset, perhaps even moved, during their meeting with Andreas, and that had affected Teresa. Somewhere inside him, in that chest of his that was always bursting with a pride she delighted in needling, was a soft heart.

They reached their respective cars and looked at each other, standing face to face without saying a word, like a pair of gunslingers too exhausted to shoot. The same thing seemed to happen at the end of every shift they shared.

She noticed that his face was lined with fatigue. He was probably thinking exactly the same about her.

She wondered if she hadn't perhaps been unfair on her young colleague recently, burdening him with too many tasks. But perhaps she'd been unfair on herself, too; she was always with him after all, encouraging him, in her own way, to keep going and do the best he could.

Teresa put her hand in her pocket. There was a rustle of candy wrappers.

He looked at her askance, and she thought of what an unlikely pair they made. He had this terrible habit of reproaching her with silence, without even giving her the satisfaction of saying a few choice words to put him in his place.

Teresa opened her mouth to speak, but quickly closed it again. She placed the temples of her glasses between her lips and chewed on them nervously. The streetlights came on. The wind blew a little colder.

"Right," she said, walking toward her car. "See you tomorrow."

He waved at her.

"Till tomorrow."

Teresa opened the car door, then changed her mind, turned around, and threw a sweet at him. He caught it.

"I'm meeting the boys at the pub for a beer," she said. "If you're not busy with that librarian tonight . . ."

"I'll see you there."

She nodded with a scowl that might have been a smile, biting her tongue to stop herself from pointing out how ridiculous he looked with that smug expression plastered all over his face.

She got into her car. She could see him in her rearview mirror, still standing there and watching her.

What the hell is his name?

She shrugged, turned the key, and drove off.

AUTHOR'S NOTE

This novel has its roots in the landscapes of my homeland. In that sense, none of it is made up. Travenì, with its millennial forest, the gorge, the quarries, the alpine lakes, and its vertiginous peaks, really does exist, if by another name. The mountains, the seasons, the smells, the colors of nature have been part of my life since I was a child, and it was inevitable that they should become the backdrop to this story—and even play an integral part in it, like a separate character.

The land I come from is generous, but it can also be demanding. Its sons and daughters have been shaped by the toil of an agrarian past, and the violence of an earthquake that has erased countless homes and families, but has not dented their determination. Everything has been rebuilt exactly as it was before, where possible, by anastylosis, with the fallen bricks already tagged and numbered while the dead were still being counted. We moved on, but we did not forget, and the earthquake became a part of our DNA.

This novel is dedicated to my homeland, too.

The study of the devastating effects of emotional deprivation on infants, to which I allude in the novel, was conducted by René Spitz, an Austrian psychoanalyst who was later naturalized as an American. Between 1945 and 1946, Spitz observed the behavior of ninety-one children housed in an orphanage. Bereft of the most basic manifestations of love, the children found their growth stunted, suffered delays in the development of their cognitive and motor skills, exhibited an absence of facial expressions, and an overall weakening of their immune defenses. After a few months, they fell into a state of lethargy. Spitz termed their condition "anaclitic depression."

Nearly 40 percent of the infants under observation died before they reached two years of age.

The study, which was in its time considered to be pioneering, would today raise serious ethical questions, but it did establish irrefutably that in order to survive, a child needs more than just the fulfillment of its material needs. To develop properly, including in its physical features, it must form strong and lasting emotional bonds.

The exposure to emotional stimuli enables the formation of a physiological correlation between aggression and libido—intended as the vital force that perpetuates life and ensures survival. In the absence of any form of tenderness, the children whose development Spitz observed released their aggression on their own bodies, which were the only outlets at their disposal. Thus, despite being adequately fed, they allowed themselves to die.

Being caressed, kissed, and shown physical affection was as important as being properly nourished.

And finally, Teresa Battaglia.

Teresa was born two years ago. I was searching for a story to tell, and she appeared in my mind, this slightly tetchy but compassionate woman, no longer young, struggling with being overweight and with illness. I pictured her hunching over and writing things down in the light of a desk lamp. Those notes would become her memories in paper form.

Teresa is part of my life now, her investigations whirl in my mind, demanding to be written. She entertains me with her barbed wit, and she moves me with her wonderful maternal and protective instincts, though she has never been a mother herself.

Teresa is a rational being, but she knows when to let her instincts guide her. She bedevils the young officers who work with her, but she is also drawn to their energy, and she fosters it. She's tenacious, as I hope I will know how to be in my life. She possesses an integrity I admire and the strength to maintain it.

I watch her suffer and fight her own private battles between these lines, and page after page, I feel as if I am growing with her.

This novel is also dedicated to the many Teresa Battaglias of this world, those who wake up more tired every passing day, and who battle solitude and illnesses of the kind that target both the body and the mind. May they never cease to love themselves.

ACKNOWLEDGMENTS

Dreams are born and quietly nurtured in private, but in order to come true, they need other people to believe in them and contribute to their realization. I have had the privilege and good fortune to meet those people:

Stefano Mauri, my publisher.

Fabrizio Cocco, my editor (four words that thrill me). Indispensable. An exemplary professional and an extraordinary person. Thank you for having loved this story.

Giuseppe Strazzeri, the editorial director of Longanesi. Thank you for your faith and for having grasped the beauty of those flowers over the inferno.

Viviana Vuscovich, thank you for helping Teresa travel across borders!

All the staff at Longanesi, who have helped me feel at ease even in the face of what felt like an epic endeavor. Thank you for your enthusiasm.

Thank you to Federico Andornino and my W&N, Orion and Hachette family for bringing my novel to English-language readers in the UK and around the world. A special mention to the incredible team at Hachette Australia and New Zealand for their hard work. It's been a privilege getting to know you all.

Ekin Oklap, my English translator: thank you for taking such care with my words—and with Teresa, too.

Michele, my most eager reader. Sometimes friendship can blossom even without a meeting.

Mom, Fedora, and Franco, for all your help, without which I would have been lost these past few months. Dad, who would have been proud.

The most important thanks: to Jasmine and Paolo, for being part of my life.

When a dream comes true, the time comes to set it free on its journey: thank you to the readers who will, I hope, come to the end of this tale and love Teresa as much as I do.

Continue reading for a preview from the next
Teresa Battaglia novel

THE SLEEPING NYMPH

THE BEGINNING

The sanguine chalk glides across the paper, shaping arabesques into familiar curves, drawing valleys that blossom into open lips. It traces tender arcs and soft, smudged lines. A delicate profile. Long dark hair. The paper, like her skin, a luminous white.

The redness overflows and seeps into the fibers of the sheet until color and paper are one. Fingers press and spread the hue out, soak and color the paper, desperate to capture the image before its beauty vanishes.

The fingers tremble, they smooth and caress. The eyes weep, and their tears mix with the redness, dilute it, reveal unexpected crimson hues.

The heart of the world suspends its beat. The fronds and the birdsong fall silent. The pale petals of wild anemones cease to thrum with the breeze and the stars seem too abashed to show themselves in the twilight. The whole mountain is leaning in to watch the miracle unfolding in the valley, on a bend in the gravelly river where the water comes to a quiet rest.

The Sleeping Nymph takes shape beneath the painter's hands. She is brought into the world, as red as passion and love.

The sun cut sideways into Massimo Marini's face, drawing out a blaze of color as it filtered through his brown eyelashes. He was walking with nervous steps down a street flanked by hidden gardens, kept out of sight by thick walls. Petals from the taller branches of the trees behind the walls had fallen onto the street. It was like treading on something that was still alive, a carpet of dying creatures.

It was a drowsy, placid spring afternoon, but the roiling black mass at the edge of his line of sight announced an upheaval. The air crackled with electricity, a contagious force that made the inspector restless.

The entrance to the La Cella art gallery was marked by a brass plaque on the coarse plaster exterior of a building from the 1600s. Reflected on the metal, Massimo's eyes looked as twisted as his mood. He rolled down his shirtsleeves and put on his jacket before ringing the doorbell. The lock clicked open. He pushed the studded knocker and entered.

The day's warmth reached no farther than the threshold. The moment he stepped through the door a wet weight seemed to settle on him. The floor was checkered black and white, and a stairway of veined marble curved upwards toward the second floor. Light filtered through some of the high windows onto a chandelier made of Murano glass, launching emerald shimmers into the semi-darkness of the ground floor. There was a smell of lilies in the air. It reminded Massimo of incense, the inside of a gloomy church, endless litanies, and the stern look on his father's face whenever Massimo—then still a child—dared show any sign of boredom.

His head began to pound.

His cell phone vibrated with an incoming call, and in the silence of that solemn place the sound seemed to belong to another universe.

He took out his phone from his breast pocket. It writhed in his palm like a cold, flat artificial heart, but Massimo knew that on the other end of the line was a real heart in which love wrestled with rage, and disappointment with pain. His phone had been ringing with that number for weeks now, often several times a day, relentless.

He ignored the call, his mouth pasty with a sickening mixture of remorse and guilt. He let the call ring out and switched his phone off. Circumventing the marble stairway, he descended a set of wrought-iron steps that spiraled, ivy-like, into the basement. Muffled voices floated through the semi-darkness. A hallway dimly lit by lamps set into the floor, a door made of pebbled glass, and beyond, the gallery.

La Cella, finally. The vaulted ceiling of coarse tiles stood above a smooth slate floor. Along the walls, most of the plaster had been scraped off to reveal the original stonework beneath. Each splash of light fell precisely onto each of the pieces on display, drawing them out like jewels from the shadows. Bronze sculptures, glass vases, and dazzlingly colorful abstract paintings were the characters on that spare underground stage.

The inspector followed the murmur of voices to a cluster of people standing in the most spacious room in the gallery.

Two uniformed policemen stood guard along the edges. Past them were two officers Marini recognized, Parisi and De Carli, both in plainclothes. Olive-skinned, muscular Parisi was talking quietly on the phone, while De Carli—as skinny and ungainly as a teenager—watched and occasionally intervened. They had become Marini's team ever since he had requested a transfer from the city to this small local precinct. He had thought—or at least hoped—that this change in trajectory might be a way to find solace and perhaps start over. He had ended up finding a whole lot more than he'd expected, but solace remained a fire-breathing chimera that burned him every time he reached out to grasp it.

He walked up to his team.

"What's going on?" he asked De Carli.

De Carli pulled up his jeans, which had slid down his thighs.

"God knows. They haven't told us a thing yet. It's all a big mystery."

"Then why did you tell me it was urgent?"

Parisi covered the phone with his hand and tilted his chin toward the opposite side of the room.

"Because she needs us. And you."

Marini's eyes searched for the person who had made every minute of his life hell over the past few months, but in doing so, had brought him back to life.

At first, he only saw her feet, glimpsed between the legs of two officers. She was wearing wedge sneakers and kept shifting her weight from one leg to the other; every now and then she stood on the balls of her feet to give her legs a rest.

She's tired, he thought. And although he had no idea why the team had been dispatched to the Cella, he knew she would be the last person to leave that day.

Then the two officers moved and he could finally see the rest of her, standing between a bronze sculpture of a half-liquefied heart and an installation of Perspex wings hanging from the ceiling. Heart and soul, just like her.

And determination, a vitality that sometimes threatened to crush those closest to her, but which always managed, at the very last moment, to pick them up and push them beyond what they thought possible.

It so happened that she was also a bit of a bitch.

There was a raggedness in her appearance which had less to do with her age (sixty) than with some inner torment that Massimo could not yet name, and which only seemed to find release in the notebook she kept permanently clasped in her hands, filling it with frenzied notes at every opportunity.

He walked up to her and noticed the single blink with which she registered his arrival. She didn't even turn around. She was holding one of the temples of her reading glasses between her lips and chewing nervously on a sweet.

"I do hope it's sugar-free," he said.

She finally looked at him, though for barely a second.

"And that is your business because . . . ?"

Her voice was hoarse and dry, and leavened with a note of amusement.

"You're diabetic, Superintendent. And supposedly a lady, too," he muttered, ignoring the curse that followed. It was a familiar game they played, one he almost never won.

She stopped gnawing at her glasses.

"Isn't this supposed to be your day off, Inspector?" she asked, boring into him with those terrible eyes of hers, so adept at seeing well below the surface.

Massimo gave her a half-smile.

"And haven't you just finished your shift?"

"All this diligence will not compensate for your recent lapses, Marini."

Massimo decided to avoid the minefield of a possible response. Already she appeared to have lost interest in him. He watched her closely, this woman whose head didn't even reach his chest, but who habitually rolled over his ego like a tank. She was almost twice his age, but frequently left him behind, exhausted, well before her own energies were spent. Her manner was often brutal, and her hair, styled in a bob that framed her face, was dyed such an artificial shade of red that it was almost embarrassing. Or at least, it would have been on anyone but her.

Teresa Battaglia could bark, and there were some who swore they had seen her bite, too—quite literally.

"So? Why are we here? What's with all the mysteries?" he asked, in a bid to draw her back to the hunt—that territory she could navigate better and faster than anyone else.

Teresa Battaglia was staring straight ahead, as if she were looking at someone, her eyes narrowed, black thoughts lodged in her furrowed brow.

"Singular, Inspector, not plural. There is only ever one mystery."

Superintendent Battaglia wiped the lenses on her reading glasses, as she did every time she was thinking. She was putting her thoughts in order.

"Why else would we be here, if not to solve the mystery of death?"

Other Titles in the Soho Crime Series

STEPHANIE BARRON
(Jane Austen's England)
Jane and the Twelve Days
    of Christmas
Jane and the Waterloo Map

F.H. BATACAN
(Philippines)
Smaller and Smaller Circles

JAMES R. BENN
(World War II Europe)
Billy Boyle
The First Wave
Blood Alone
Evil for Evil
Rag & Bone
A Mortal Terror
Death's Door
A Blind Goddess
The Rest Is Silence
The White Ghost
Blue Madonna
The Devouring
Solemn Graves
When Hell Struck Twelve

CARA BLACK
(Paris, France)
Murder in the Marais
Murder in Belleville
Murder in the Sentier
Murder in the Bastille
Murder in Clichy
Murder in Montmartre
Murder on the Ile Saint-Louis
Murder in the Rue de Paradis
Murder in the Latin Quarter
Murder in the Palais Royal
Murder in Passy
Murder at the Lanterne Rouge
Murder Below Montparnasse
Murder in Pigalle
Murder on the Champ de Mars
Murder on the Quai
Murder in Saint-Germain
Murder on the Left Bank
Murder in Bel-Air

LISA BRACKMANN
(China)
Rock Paper Tiger
Hour of the Rat
Dragon Day
Getaway
Go-Between

HENRY CHANG
(Chinatown)
Chinatown Beat
Year of the Dog
Red Jade
Death Money
Lucky

BARBARA CLEVERLY
(England)
The Last Kashmiri Rose
Strange Images of Death
The Blood Royal
Not My Blood
A Spider in the Cup
Enter Pale Death
Diana's Altar

Fall of Angels
Invitation to Die

COLIN COTTERILL
(Laos)
The Coroner's Lunch
Thirty-Three Teeth
Disco for the Departed
Anarchy and Old Dogs
Curse of the Pogo Stick
The Merry Misogynist
Love Songs from a Shallow Grave
Slash and Burn
The Woman Who Wouldn't Die
Six and a Half Deadly Sins
I Shot the Buddha
The Rat Catchers' Olympics
Don't Eat Me
The Second Biggest Nothing
The Delightful Life of
    a Suicide Pilot

GARRY DISHER
(Australia)
The Dragon Man
Kittyhawk Down
Snapshot
Chain of Evidence
Blood Moon
Whispering Death
Signal Loss

Wyatt
Port Vila Blues
Fallout

Bitter Wash Road
Under the Cold Bright Lights

TERESA DOVALPAGE
(Cuba)
Death Comes in through
    the Kitchen
Queen of Bones

Death of a Telenovela Star
    (A Novella)

DAVID DOWNING
(World War II Germany)
Zoo Station
Silesian Station
Stettin Station
Potsdam Station
Lehrter Station
Masaryk Station

(World War I)
Jack of Spies
One Man's Flag
Lenin's Roller Coaster
The Dark Clouds Shining

Diary of a Dead Man on Leave

AGNETE FRIIS
(Denmark)
What My Body Remembers
The Summer of Ellen

MICHAEL GENELIN
(Slovakia)
Siren of the Waters